D1093133

ELEVEN STORIES
&
A BEGINNING

THE WORKS OF HOWARD SPRING
(1889–1965)

Novels
SHABBY TIGER 1934
RACHEL ROSING 1935
MY SON, MY SON 1938
(originally published as O ABSALOM)
FAME IS THE SPUR 1940
HARD FACTS 1944
DUNKERLEYS 1946
THERE IS NO ARMOUR 1948
THE HOUSES IN BETWEEN 1951
A SUNSET TOUCH 1953
THESE LOVERS FLED AWAY 1955
TIME AND THE HOUR 1957
ALL THE DAY LONG 1959
I MET A LADY 1961
WINDS OF THE DAY 1964

For Children
DARKIE & CO. (O.U.P.) 1932
SAMPSON'S CIRCUS (Faber & Faber) 1936
TUMBLEDOWN DICK (Faber & Faber) 1939

Autobiography
HEAVEN LIES ABOUT US 1939
IN THE MEANTIME 1942
AND ANOTHER THING . . . 1946
THE AUTOBIOGRAPHY OF HOWARD SPRING 1972
(containing the above three volumes)

Plays
THREE PLAYS 1953
Jinny Morgan
The Gentle Assassin
St George at the Dragon

Criticism
BOOK PARADE 1938

HOWARD SPRING

ELEVEN STORIES

&

A BEGINNING

With an Introduction by
Marion Howard Spring

COLLINS
St James's Place, London
1973

First published 1973

ISBN 0 00 221214 5

© Marion Howard Spring

Set in Monotype Baskerville

Made and printed in Great Britain by
William Collins Sons & Co Ltd Glasgow

CONTENTS

INTRODUCTION

Since my husband, Howard Spring, died in 1965 I have had hundreds of letters from his readers all over the world, telling me how they loved him through his books, and how sad they were that there were no more of his books to look forward to. These letters have been a great comfort to me in my loneliness, but I wondered if I could do anything about it.

Then four things happened in one week which made me, so to speak, roll up my sleeves and get to work.

First, on Monday, I had a letter from an Irish Catholic priest, a Dominican friar, the Superior of his Priory. He said: 'Here in this Priory we have several of your wonderful husband's wonderful novels. His language is a real help to me in my preaching . . . I tell the community to read Howard Spring if they want to preach from the heart.' Then again in a later letter he told me: 'I have just finished *Fame is the Spur* and *Time and the Hour* within the past few weeks. Actually I am a late starter as a reader of novels (I'm 47). I had always thought them a waste of time – being simply fiction – which to me had always meant "concoction". Actually I think I had always been searching for someone like Howard to tell me what a novel could be – what "creation" was as opposed to "concoction".'

To go back to the miraculous week . . . On the Tuesday came a letter from a man who belonged to the third generation of a theatrical family, and who, apart from his service in the army, had toured in music-halls since he was fourteen years old. He was now an agent for seven different night clubs. He first discovered Howard when on service in India, reading *Rachel Rosing*, *Shabby Tiger* and *Fame is the Spur*. When he got back into show business he adopted Hamer

Shawcross's slogan – 'to scorn delights and live laborious days' – as his own. 'Everything I read of Howard Spring's is tremendous. Normally, when I read I skip parts all the time. I read every word of his books and when I have finished them all I shall begin all over again.'

Then on the Thursday came a letter from a Brigadier of the Salvation Army. She was born in a public house in Ancoats and lived there for the first twenty years of her life. She discovered Howard when she had left Manchester, and she wrote to me, saying: 'I was wondering if I dare ask if there is any possibility of your writing an Anthology of extracts from your husband's writings? I say this because your husband had such a gift for descriptive writing and conveying beauty – all the sights, sounds and atmosphere of nature, and his mastery of words was such that again and again they amount to sheer poetry. Denied, as I was as a child, of anything in the way of natural beauty – I was surrounded by England's "dark Satanic mills" – I find myself soaking up all these passages that equal, and in many cases surpass, anything I have read. They should not be "lost" in the novels. I know one can read these, as I do repeatedly, but to have a book of selections that one could pick up when the mind is too tired for lengthy reading, would be inspiring. I am sure that his fans who mourned that there would never be another one of his books, would be overjoyed.'

On Friday, Osborne, my gardener, knocked at the door and said that there was a young man who would very much like to see me, but was reluctant to disturb me. I went into the garden and there he was, holding a little boy by the hand. He was a young writer and he introduced me to his son whom he and his wife had called Howard after my husband. He was a great admirer of Howard's works, and asked me if there was not *anything* new, even book reviews or journalistic articles, which could be published to satisfy a hungry public.

And so I decided to put together some of his short stories that had appeared in magazines; and the beginning of the novel on which he was working when he died.

Howard, who was the soul of neatness, had made this work very easy for me. I found the magazines with his short stories in a book-case in his study; and I had the manuscript of his unfinished book – *The Little Victims Play* – another four-word title which had become for him a kind of mascot.

He was not superstitious, but 'just for fun' he always touched his finished works on the upturned trunk of a Copenhagen stoneware elephant before sending them off to Collins, his publishers.

When I began to write at the age of seventy-four, I followed suit, and *Memories and Gardens, Howard* and *Frontispiece* all paid homage to the elephant before going on their journey.

If I live to finish this book – I am now in my eighty-first year – I shall once more ask the elephant to bless my work.

GHOSTS

My House of Love is thronged with ghosts.
    Pale fingers touch me on the stair;
Pale sunlight shines through children's limbs
    And firelight falls on silken hair.

Row upon row, old volumes stand
    In candleshine that lets me see
Grave elfin children hand in hand
    Or struggling to a mother's knee.

Sometimes, when I am half in dreams,
    Melodious laughter drifts from room
To empty room in vagrant streams
    Like laughing water in the gloom

Of solemn forests. Then perchance
    Towards a half-closed door I steal
At sound of voices telling low
    Secrets that I would fain unseal.

Upon the shining table oak,
    Four points of yellow light are thrown
From four tall silver candlesticks;
    Four heads are clustered, curled and brown . . .

But nothing's here save the drab room,
    The spluttering gas, the paper flowers,
The dusty furniture, the gloom . . .
    I must have been asleep for hours.

Howard Spring

EDITOR'S NOTE

I'm afraid the first two short stories are, by to-day's standards, rather sentimental and even dare to have a happy ending. They were written in 1926 and at that time magazines *wanted* sentimental stories. Howard and I had two little boys, aged five and two and a half years, for whom nothing was good enough but the best, and we needed to supplement the meagre *Manchester Guardian* salary. The £15 or so paid for a story at that time meant much more to us than the large sums paid by American magazines after the publication of *My Son, My Son!*

Howard and I used to go to the Manchester music-halls on Monday evenings, and Harry Weldon often appeared on the stage, and sang 'a little sentimental song' about roses round the door making him love Mother more, and so on. After hearing this same song for the umpteenth time, Howard ventured to write to Harry suggesting that it would not be a bad idea to introduce a new song into his act. Harry wrote back: 'My dear Chap: I am all with you, but my public *won't have* a new song! Yours ever, Harry.'

Nowadays there is nothing like those old magazines – the *Windsor*, the *Strand*, *Pearson's*, *Harper's*, *Munsey's*, etc. When I look at them it is like turning back a few pages in my life. There is an interview with a young and beautiful Beverley Nichols, who had just written *Down the Garden Path*, an article by Suzanne Lenglen on Tennis, contributions by Sheila Kaye-Smith, E. F. Benson, Barry Pain, G. B. Stern, S. P. B. Mais, Horace Annesley Vachell, etc. The stories and articles are profusely illustrated, both in colour and black-and-white, and these monthly magazines must have kept many artists working very hard. I hope they were well paid!

After the first year of the Second World War there were no more of Howard's short stories. He never felt really happy with them, and his time was much more joyfully used on the wide canvas of his long novels.

M.H.S.

SWEET-SCENTED
MANUSCRIPT

'Amity, you're just a little fool. A little feather-brained fool.
Do you hear me?'

Miss Priscilla Raw, Amity's aunt, did not turn as she made
this pronouncement. Her back was to the drawing-room;
in each hand she held a heavy velvet curtain – held them
slightly apart, and gazed down upon the gleaming wetness
of a London square, whose traffic was little and noiseless.
Perhaps it was a sense of contrast that made Miss Raw bitter.
She looked at the splashes of lamplight shining in the wet
road and at the motor cars which occasionally slid by with a
soft, contented purring, as though the noise were expressing
the feelings of the well-dined, well-dressed folk within, and
she thought of the two small rooms, with a poky kitchen
thrown in, that she and Amity shared on the second floor
of a house plagued day and night with the racking clamour
of commercial traffic.

At last she dropped the curtains with a sigh, turned, and
faced the even greater contrast of Mr James Tremlett's
drawing-room. No cabined confinement about it; you could
take with ease ten or a dozen swinging paces. The furnishing
was sparse but exquisite, from the dark gleaming of the
grand piano in which the ruddy fireshine came and went to
the tiniest of the few ornaments. Amity, in a *bergère* chair by
the fire, pointed a pretty toe to the blaze. And from the
pretty toe to the dark hair close-cropped on her shapely
neck, she looked quite at home in her surroundings, as Miss
Raw did not. That fact struck Miss Raw with force, and she
burst out again: 'A young fool! Can't you see it's all yours

for the taking? Can't you see he's head over ears in love
with you?'

Amity turned a slow, indifferent glance upon her dead
mother's sister. 'And is that all that is necessary?' she asked.

'It would have been quite enough for me, at any rate,
when I was your age,' said Miss Raw a little hotly.

Amity smiled annoyingly. 'Of course, Aunt, I like him,
I always have done; and I know he likes me.'

'Likes you! You don't overstate the case, anyway! Here's
a man worth – well, look at the house! And he invites you –
his three-pounds-a-week typist – to dinner with him. And
I've got eyes in my head. I can see the way he looks at you,
waits on you. Why, you could hook him with your little
finger! I don't know what nonsense you've got in your head.
You're likely to have another chance like it, aren't you!'

'Probably not,' said Amity quietly. 'But you see, Aunt,
there's one objection. There's my side of the matter to be
considered as well as his, and I happen to love someone else.'

Miss Raw dropped into a chair on the other side of the
fireplace as though she had been shot. 'Someone else?' she
gasped. 'Who, in the name of fortune? I've heard nothing
of this, and I'm responsible for you, aren't I?'

The lazy smile continued to play round Amity's red lips.
'Yes, I suppose up to a point you are. But I'm afraid this is
something you wouldn't understand, Aunt.'

Miss Raw's thin arms folded grimly across her sunken
chest. 'Oh, a mystery, is it? Well, I think I have a right to
know what you are up to, Amity. After all, I am your
guardian, and if Mr Tremlett speaks to me, I shall want to
know where I am.'

'Pardon me, Miss Raw, it will evidently not be necessary
to speak to you.'

Both the women started to their feet and swung round,
Priscilla Raw agitated and confused, Amity outwardly self-
possessed, but betraying by a rising colour the feelings that

James Tremlett's words had caused. Her employer seemed as undisturbed as when he sat in his office in Mincing Lane and dictated to her letters about his dealing in tea. The impeccable front of his dress shirt, the sit of the dinner-jacket on his broad athletic shoulders, the close-cropped grey hair surmounting the strong face of a successful man of business – all contributed to a picture of strength and unconcern that seemed in no way shaken by what he had heard.

'I'm sorry, Miss Armstrong,' he said, addressing Amity; 'you and Miss Raw were so deeply in conversation that I'm afraid you didn't hear my approach, and I came in just in time to hear something that wasn't intended for my ears.'

He took a chair between the two women, and the firelight fell upon his face. Forty-five years had graven themselves upon it and left no doubt of their passing, but they had left nothing unkindly, nothing bitter, nothing that a square-dealing man need be ashamed to show. But, still, he was reflecting, forty-five years were not thirty – not twenty-five. Twenty-five, he would guess, was Amity's age. And she loved someone else. Well, he was not surprised. He eyed her askance – the head well held up, the rounded arms lying straight down the body, the toe still pointing at the fire. A delicate ebb and flow of colour was still playing in her face.

Miss Raw was taken fairly between wind and water. She simply sat still and awaited developments. Amity, feeling the crisis was none of her making, a little resentful at the situation she had been forced into, did not feel called upon to speak first. Mr Tremlett handed her his cigarette-case, took a cigarette himself, and having lit it, blew a cloud of smoke into the air.

'Miss Raw,' he said then, 'it is evident that I must speak plainly about something I had no intention of mentioning just yet. I wanted you and Miss Armstrong to take this opportunity of knowing me a little better than is possible in a business way. There would perhaps have been other opportunities. But – er – so to speak – we have – missed some stages. It was certainly my intention to ask Miss Armstrong to marry me if I observed in her anything to encourage me to make an offer, because – I – I – for a long time I have – Miss Armstrong has been with me now for three years – and I – I – have taken an affection for her which is not a boy's fancy. It goes rather deep . . .'

He paused as if finding some difficulty in proceeding, and threw his unsmoked cigarette into the fire before going on. He now addressed Amity. 'I'm not a young man, Miss Armstrong – far from it. Perhaps I was rather presumptuous in thinking you might. But still, we needn't discuss that. I've had your answer without asking for it. And perhaps that was the best way. Believe me, the matter is closed.'

He stood up and offered her his hand. She stood up, too, and took it, trying hard to be calm. Then suddenly her head bent over the hand that was gripping hers, and hot tears fell upon it.

'Really, Mr Tremlett,' she sobbed. 'I wouldn't for worlds. I . . . Oh dear, dear!'

Miss Raw rose with the intention of being a comforter. But as soon as she placed her hand on Amity's shoulder, she felt the girl shrink nearer to Mr Tremlett. It was a movement of sheer instinct, the movement of a hurt thing to someone it feels can comfort and protect; and Miss Raw, being no fool, did not interfere further. It was not till she and Amity were in a taxi which Mr Tremlett had called that she once more turned her tongue upon the girl, and when they were undressing in their bleak little bedroom, fireless, shabby, cold, her mind was filled with vicarious images of fire-warmed rooms, downy beds, bright lampshades that one dimmed with a click when snugly between the sheets. With a sigh she blew out the candle and groped her way to the bed, where Amity already lay, sobbing quietly. After all, it was not for herself that Miss Raw wanted these things. She would be left to lie alone in the cold bed if Amity went. Let us say what we can for her, and put it to her credit that she crept close to Amity, put her thin arms about the girl's warm young body, and tried to comfort her.

No, it was not for herself that Priscilla Raw was concerned; and, truth to tell, it was hardly for Amity. It was for a memory – for the memory of her dead sister, Amity's mother. Prudence Raw, like Priscilla, had been a somewhat grim and calculating woman, and no one could understand how she came to fall in love with that attractive scapegrace, that incurable romantic, Jimmy Armstrong. They had not been happy. Anyone prepared to take chances and laugh at disaster would have been happy with Jimmy. Prudence wasn't. Now they were both long since gone; and what alarmed Priscilla Raw was the perception, forced upon her more clearly day by day, that Amity – who but Jimmy could have given the girl so attractive and absurd a name! – was her father over again. None of the Raw caution; a leap-before-you-look romanticism was what made Aunt Priscilla tremble for Amity's future.

How impulsive that romanticism was, Mr Tremlett was to learn. On the Monday following the Saturday evening dinner, Amity sat in her chair opposite his, a wide table between them. She had finished taking the day's letters, and Mr Tremlett ended up with the words he had used day after day for the three years she had been with him: 'And – er – let me see – yes – that's all, Miss Armstrong.'

He turned dismissively to the work before him as Amity rose, but, instead of going, she stood holding the table before her with both hands and said: 'How long notice will you require, sir? I've decided I can't stay.'

Mr Tremlett dropped his papers. 'I thought I made it clear on Saturday that we had heard the last of this?' he said.

'I want to make quite sure that it will be the last,' Amity answered. 'I have thought it over carefully and have come to the conclusion that I must go. It wouldn't be fair to you, sir, if I were to stay. Oh, I can't stay now – I can't! Surely you see that?'

James Tremlett, realising more than the girl before him what it cost him, agreed. 'You are right, Miss Armstrong. I'm sorry. I've placed you in an impossible situation.'

Amity interrupted him. 'No, no, sir; it's not your fault at all. You are not responsible. But it's happened that way, and there it is.'

'Yes, there it is,' Tremlett echoed; and there indeed it was, clearly enough before him – the wreckage of a dream cherished in secret for hard upon a year, a dream shattered as soon as he had sought to touch it with the cold finger of reality.

'Well – Amity,' he brought out after a pause, 'I've never said it before in so many words, but I love you with all my heart. I must say that, just once, and now no more of that for ever. But because of it, I think you will forgive me if I ask you who it is you love? You know, I couldn't help over-hearing what you said on Saturday.'

Amity crimsoned to her ears. 'Oh, sir, you'll think me very ridiculous. I'm ashamed to tell you.'

'Don't be ashamed at the idea of loving too high, if that's the trouble,' said Mr Tremlett. 'I don't care if the man's the Lord High Chancellor, I'll tell him he's not good enough.'

'It's not that. Oh, it's something you'll never understand! You'll never understand how a woman can refuse you for a shadow. And it's just that – a shadow! I don't know him. I've never seen him. But I love him all the same. Do you think I'm mad?'

Tremlett paused, nonplussed. 'Miss Armstrong, will you sit down?' he said then. And once more he faced her across the table. 'Miss Raw hinted during the dinner the other night that you had inherited the instincts of a father who was what she called a romantic. It appears to be so. Frankly, I am out of my depth. Can you put some dry land under my feet?'

Amity hung her head as she answered: 'Oh, call me a fool if you like, as my aunt does; but the fact is I've fallen in love with this.'

From her bag she produced a reproduction of a photograph, and handed it across the table to Mr Tremlett. He took it and studied his rival carefully, with eyes that needed no spectacles. The picture had evidently been torn from a book. It was of a young man. His age would be about twenty-five. Abundant hair crowned a pleasing, wistful face, notable for the sorrow of the eyes.

Mr Tremlett studied the picture long, his face averted from the girl. At last he handed it back. 'Yes, I know the face. It's Hilary Martindale. I, too, have been reading *Sweet-Scented Manuscript*. This was the frontispiece. You tore it out?'

'Yes.'

'And you seriously . . .'

'Oh, Mr Tremlett, please don't let this upset you. I know how you feel at the thought that I should give up all that you can offer me for the sake of a wraith – a nothing. I've never met him – I probably never shall. But even if his picture had not been there, I should have loved him just the same. It's a glorious book. You say you've read it. Perhaps you don't see it as I do, but there's something in every word of it that makes me love the man who wrote it. Oh, how he understands! It seems as if he understands *me* – yes, me myself. He must be good – good through and through. And then there's the picture. Look at those eyes – so sad and beautiful. He looks as if he's dying for love.'

'Miss Armstrong, your aunt was unquestionably right. You are indeed a romantic.'

'Now you're laughing at me.'

'I'm not, I assure you.'

'Oh, you are. And you'll laugh more when I say that somehow I seem to know those eyes. They haunt me. Somewhere, some time, I've seen them, and I shall just go on till I see them again. Sometimes these author-people come round lecturing,' she ended practically.

'Ah, Miss Armstrong, the poetry of the arts is evidently more than the realism of the tea-trade can contend with. Well, one thing I can tell you. If you meet Hilary Martindale, you'll be meeting a wealthy man.'

Mr Tremlett was right. Hilary Martindale had suddenly sprung upon the public with a conquering pounce. Perhaps nothing like his success had ever before been achieved with a first novel. Unknown a year before this interview between Mr Tremlett and Miss Armstrong took place, his name was now in everybody's mouth. The success of *Sweet-Scented Manuscript* had ravaged England like a fire, nothing staying its advance; and, passing to America, it had swept from Atlantic to Pacific. Even now, a famous English actor was adapting it to the stage and Los Angeles had turned its best resources upon a film version. Hard-up authors enviously calculated what Hilary Martindale had made by his one venture. The highest estimate was £100,000; the lowest was £50,000; and the truth was somewhere in between. Martindale was not to be rushed. Though twelve months had passed since *Sweet-Scented Manuscript* had appeared, his publisher had not yet announced a second novel. And that was unusual with a best-seller.

It was no wonder if Mr Tremlett felt that this quixotic passion of Amity, unfortunate as it was for him, was no less doomed to be fruitless for herself. He brought the interview to a close rather wearily. 'Well, Miss Armstrong, I shan't worry you with any limit on your notice either way. Go as soon as you have something fixed up, and if I can help you to another place, I will.'

The keen-faced visitor had been in Mr Tremlett's room for an hour; their conversation had been earnest and helped out with excellent cigars. 'Well,' said the visitor at last, 'let's have a look at her.'

James Tremlett touched his bell and Amity came in, note-book in hand.

'Miss Armstrong,' said Tremlett, 'I want to introduce my friend Mr Harry Jardine. He is news editor of the *Morning Witness*.'

Jardine shook hands with Amity, looking her keenly up and down. 'Mr Tremlett and I have been having a talk about you, Miss Armstrong,' he said when they were all three seated. 'I understand from him that you are tired of the tea-trade and have a romantic affection for the arts.'

'Well, sir,' Amity answered, 'certainly circumstances have made it necessary for me to change my place.'

'We won't go into those circumstances,' said Mr Jardine. 'All I need say is that Mr Tremlett has been interesting me on your behalf. He and I have been friends for many years, and it's because of what he has told me about you that I'm going to make you an offer – if you have not something already in view?'

Amity had nothing in view and said so.

'Well, now,' Mr Jardine went on, 'the *Witness* wants a woman reporter. It's a beginner's job and a beginner's pay. I understand you write shorthand well, and Mr Tremlett has stood bail for your general sense and alertness. What do you say?'

There was little indeed to say, and a fortnight later Amity reported at the *Witness* office and began her new career. It was all very strange and exciting. In place of the ordered, regular life she had been accustomed to, she found herself a straw blown this way and that in the current of events. She did not know to-day where she would be to-morrow or what she would be doing – it might be watching a princess open a baby show; it might be attending the trial of a felon. Miss Raw was not happy about it. To have to go to bed alone and to be aware of Amity coming in at one or two o'clock in the morning seemed to her outrageous, another and more reprehensible example of the Armstrong quixotry.

For a month or two Fleet Street held Amity in thrall. She had a natural aptitude for her work; she made friends; she travelled to distant parts of the land and became very self-possessed and assured. But the first thrill had worn away by the time the spring was advancing to summer; and one day she had an experience she was to remember to the end of her life. She had been down into a Sussex village where exploration was going on among some prehistoric earthworks. She had written her story and telegraphed it to the *Witness*, and she stayed for the night at an old inn, intending to return to London early in the morning. She was awakened at dawn by something stirring the curtain at her open window, and jumping out of bed she was just in time to see a kingfisher drinking at a rain-filled saucer on the window-sill. He flashed away like a blue jewel at her approach.

Flinging a wrap about her shoulders, Amity leaned from the casement. A few birds were drowsily cheeping in the hedges and a distant brook kept up a musical monotone. Apart from these small sounds, the whole world seemed holding its breath. The roses were still sleeping, and they and all the flowers were giving up their fragrance as they slept. The east was flushed and throbbing. As Amity watched, one solitary dove tumbled from a dovecot to the lawn, and, as though his noiseless descent were a signal, a thrush began suddenly to sing with all his heart. Then two larks went up singing to the tremulous sky, and all at once it seemed as though the world were full of roses and singing birds.

Amity felt her throat tighten at the beauty of it all; and she thought of the men who built so long ago the earthworks she had looked at but yesterday. 'They, too, knew the morning and birdsong and roses,' she murmured; and the burden of the fleeting generations came upon her heart and with it a great longing for love. 'Oh, I am only half alive,' she cried.

Back in her room, she took up the portrait of Hilary Martindale and gazed at it long and earnestly. 'Oh, what a fool I am!' she said. 'And yet I love him – I do – I do.'

How Martindale would have understood her at that moment! The very title of his book – *Sweet-Scented Manuscript* – was at the heart of the matter. She murmured the lines to herself:

> *'Alas! that Spring should vanish with the rose!*
> *That youth's sweet-scented manuscript should close!*
> *The nightingale that in the branches sang,*
> *Ah, whence? – and whither flown again?*
> *Who knows?'*

She propped up the photograph on the dressing-table by the window and took out her copy of Omar Khayyam, to read again the whole of the poem that had been so much in her mind of late.

> *'One thing is certain and the rest is Lies:*
> *The Flower that once has blown for ever dies.'*

'I'll find him out! I'll meet him somehow,' she reflected as she dressed slowly.

But a woman is a paradoxical thing, and when Amity was back in town and the lunch-hour came, the vague restlessness of her heart turned her steps to a restaurant where she knew it was James Tremlett's habit to lunch every day. Three months had passed since she had seen him, and his familiar, comforting face, she felt, would do her good. It is true he had not been much in her thoughts, for, faithful to his promise, he had allowed the affair to end absolutely. But somehow to-day she thought how good the days had been when she would find on her desk in Mincing Lane a book, well suited to her tastes, or a few choice flowers on a winter day. All that seemed far away in the harsh competition of her present existence. There was no one in the *Witness* office to whom she might speak of the thoughts that were troubling her; instinctively she felt that Mr Tremlett would understand. Her mind was strangely complicated about it all. Just as she felt that Martindale would comprehend her mood, so she felt that Mr Tremlett would understand how she felt about that need for comprehension by the man she had never met but had learned to love. Not that she meant to open her heart to Mr Tremlett, but just to be with him would ease her.

But he did not lunch at the accustomed restaurant that day. All Amity got for her pains was the stares of a few impertinent young men. It happened, too, that for the first time Mr Jardine found fault with her work that afternoon. He was kind, but firm, and Aunt Priscilla had a crying Amity to comfort that night.

The next day Amity went again to the restaurant. She went earlier and stayed later, and again she was disappointed. The same staring young men were there, and she left at last with heart bursting with rage and frustration.

For two days after that she was working out of town, and she wondered why she felt resentful at being sent away, when formerly she had regarded it as so desirable an adventure. She hurried to the restaurant on her return; and still there was no sign of the man she was now most unreasonably anxious to meet. She summoned up courage to speak to the waiter about it. Yes, said the man, he certainly did know Mr Tremlett.

'I've served his table, miss, for ten years without missing

a day except holidays. And now he's gone – told me about a month ago that he was giving up business and leaving London altogether. A good sort, he was.'

Amity cloaked her disappointment, but made small head-way with her meal. It was evident, she reflected, that she must set about finding Hilary Martindale for herself. She still persuaded herself that all she wanted was someone to talk to about Martindale – someone who would understand that passion for a shadow, and perhaps help her to make the shadow a reality.

Then came the astonishing adventure, and Mr Tremlett was put clean out of her head. It happened that very after-noon in the *Witness* office. Mr Jardine sent for her and began in his casual way: 'Miss Armstrong, I suppose you've heard of a person called Hilary Martindale?'

Amity looked at him sharply. Had he somehow heard of her romantic infatuation? But Jardine was sharp and business-like as usual. Without waiting for her to answer, he went on: 'Of course you have. Everybody has heard of him. But nobody knows anything about him. His photograph has been published, and that is all the public has been allowed to know of the most amazingly successful young man living. You can imagine that a great many newspapers have been after him, but they can't find him, and that makes them all the keener. You are always keen on the thing you can't find, Miss Armstrong.'

He gave Amity one of his piercing looks, and scarcely knowing why, she blushed violently.

'Yes,' he went on quickly, 'Martindale's publishers have not given him away. All they say is that he doesn't want publicity and they won't part with his address. Astonishing youth! I should have thought that there was no young writer, or old one for that matter, who would not die to get a column puff in the *Witness*. Here's an exception. He's got to have it against his will. You've got to get it.'

Amity could scarcely speak for the furious beating of her heart. 'I?' she managed to exclaim at last.

'You, Miss Armstrong. I happen to know a partner in the firm that published *Sweet-Scented Manuscript*. I was in his office this morning, and in the letter-basket I happened to see a letter addressed to "Hilary Martindale, Esq., The Croft, St Arbuthnot-in-Roseland." Dishonest? Well . . . Make a note of the address. Roseland, you know, is in the south of Cornwall – Falmouth way. Pack your bag, and don't dare show your face in Fleet Street again until you've got a column in your pocket about Martindale – what he's writing now – what he eats for breakfast – whether he shoots or fishes – whether he is married – any children – what he's made out of *Sweet-Scented Manuscript*. See the sort of stuff? Nothing literary.'

Jardine rose dismissively, and the next moment, a frayed bundle of nerves, Amity found herself outside the door.

When the G.W.R. *Riviera Express* pulled out of Paddington the next morning, there was no one aboard in a more upside-down state of mind that Amity Armstrong. She did not know whether she was happy or terribly mortified. She was at last – she hoped so, at least – to meet Hilary Martindale. That was to the good. But in what a guise! As an unwanted spy into his secrets, as a person intruding across the line which he had made taboo. Would he refuse altogether to see her? Would he see her only to say in what contempt he held her, and then have her turned from the door? Insoluble puzzlements! And all the time the swift train was hurrying her to the inescapable test. Mixed with it all, too, was professional pride, and a determination to make good. Mr Jardine's recent reproof must be wiped out. With her mind she was thinking of Hilary Martindale as someone quite impersonal, while in her heart he was a sore disturbance.

She rested in Falmouth that night, and in the morning

crossed the harbour in a small steamer to St Arbuthnot-in-Roseland. It was a small village, inhabited chiefly by fisherfolk. The Croft she found to be a cool-looking house, long and low, overgrown with roses, and set above the red roofs of the village over which it looked to the dreaming blue of the sea. The garden was a riot of flowers; white garden furniture stood before the house front.

It was a tremulous hand that pulled the bell, and Amity's heart thumped as the clang sounded in the quiet interior. A neat maid came to the door, and Amity had to moisten her lips before she could ask whether Mr Martindale could be seen. Mr Martindale was busy; could the visitor's business be stated?

Then Amity plunged. She asked if she might write a note; she was set at a little table in a window-bay overlooking the sea, and frankly she told of her mission, trusting to Mr Martindale's generosity not to make her journey fruitless. She waited with a palpitating heart, and presently the maid returned with the answer: Mr Martindale would be pleased if Miss Armstrong would dine with him at seven.

How she got through that day she scarcely knew. She spent most of it in a little cove reading *Sweet-Scented Manuscript* again from cover to cover and marvelling afresh at the understanding of the man who had written it. Now and then she came out to look up at the house, hoping to catch a glimpse of someone in the garden who would answer her mind's vision of Mr Martindale. But no one moved there; only the flowers burned on in the noon-day heat. Green sunblinds were drawn before the windows. In a little hotel she ate her lunch and tea and finally tidied herself for the call.

The quiet, cool interior of the Croft was welcome after the heat of the day, and was somehow comforting, reassuring. She had been taken straight into the dining-room and was waiting for him. The sunblinds were up now and the sloping rays of the sun stretched across the harbour with its ships, rosily touched the red roofs just below the lawn of the Croft, and filled the room with a gentle light. The glass and silver shone mildly on the white table, set, Amity noted with a quickening pulse, for two.

She was standing at the window with her back to the room, when she heard the door open and a voice say: 'Miss Armstrong?'

She turned sharply, as James Tremlett softly closed the door behind him and advanced holding out his hand.

Amity could not take it. Overwhelmed with surprise, she could only stand and stare, clutching with both hands a small table behind her. Tremlett stood still, too, until she had recovered sufficiently to stammer: 'But wh-where is Mr Martindale?'

'Here,' Tremlett answered, lightly touching his shirt-front. 'Shall we be seated now and let the interview proceed?'

The meal was almost a silent one, and the interview made small progress. But when dinner was over, Tremlett brought a wrap from somewhere and put it over the girl's shoulders and took her out to one of the garden-seats before the house. Coffee was brought to them there, and they sat for a long time looking at the glowing mast-head lights . . . And Amity felt her heart suffused with a strange peace and reassurance, as though this after-glow were the answer to that dawn in Sussex not long before.

At last Tremlett said quietly: 'Well, I suppose you've guessed. I was in love when I wrote the book. It was in my last year at Oxford. I was not much more than twenty. Twenty-five years ago. The photograph, you know, is an old one, taken at the time the book was written. Do you remember saying that somehow you felt you knew the eyes?'

'Yes,' Amity answered very quietly.

'I hope the eyes have not changed. I like to think that it was the eyes you fell in love with . . . Well, she didn't want me. No money, you know, and no prospects; and perhaps, anyhow, she didn't love me. It seems a terribly long time ago, and she's been dead ten years. I thought, of course, that it was the end of life. I wrote the novel then. "Alas, that youth's sweet-scented manuscript should close." I thought it was closed for me. We do, Amity, when we're twenty. All that boy's passion went into it, and that's what has made the world go mad over it, because there's no passion more terrible and poignant than a boy's – or usually, more transient. And I suppose I managed to get all that into it. It was written for her – to break her heart. It was sent then to only one publisher. He refused it – not the first publisher to turn down a gold-mine – and I was in that mood of utter morbidity and wretchedness that I threw the thing into a drawer, intending never to look at it again. I fled my fate, taking a job on a tea plantation in the East, and there I put on fat and prospered and became more or less the inartistic hulk you see. I came home and founded the firm you worked for, and prospered even more. And then this awful avalanche of fame came suddenly upon me. I had been reading of how a famous writer sent a manuscript to dozens of publishers, how it was rejected time after time, and how at last, being accepted, it had a mighty success. Mind you, I had almost forgotten that I had written a novel, but the thing had followed me about the world; and it happened that, that very night, turning out some old trunks, I came upon it. In a spirit of sport I thought I'd try my luck. I had the thing typed and sent away, and you know the rest. A grave business man, of course, can't father a thing like that, so I put a fancy name to it and suggested to the publishers the deceit of the old photograph. But now that the name has become famous, I've taken it by Letters Patent. I shall stick to it and try to write some more. I think I can.'

'You can, you can,' Amity said earnestly. And when they had been quiet for a while, she said: 'I don't think a rose is

the best symbol of love, a rose that only comes in June and
lasts a little time. I think love is like this great harbour, and
ships may come into it in the morning or at noon or in the
evening. It is big enough and deep enough for them all.'

He took her hands. 'It was the eyes?'

'My beautiful one,' she answered, 'it was the eyes and all
the lovely things behind them.'

INSTITUTIONAL ANN

Thirty-five, Ann Bennison reflected, was a rotten age to be if you were unmarried. Her sister Kate, it is true, was thirty-nine; but then Kate was married. Her sister Jane, like herself, was unmarried; but then Jane was only thirty. It was that irritating combination of being thirty-five and unmarried that made Ann so thoughtful as she stood at the french window and watched the spring sunlight on the cherry blossom in the garden. There was one dreadful moment in her meditation when she remembered the saying that the years of man's life are three-score years and ten. Half the allotted span! Good gracious! Before the cherry blossom had whitened the lawn Ann would be over the peak and following her shadow downhill; for, though she was not prepared to admit the awful truth, it was a fact that Ann was thirty-five years plus three hundred and sixty days.

It was not that she didn't want to marry. She was quite clear in her mind that she wanted to marry Robin Elder.

Robin Elder sat on a stool at the end of the garden. An easel was before him, and he was engaged in putting the cherry trees upon his canvas. He was smoking a pipe as he worked. His hat was off, and his tight-curled fair hair, his tanned face, blue eyes, boyish mouth, made him, Ann thought, most desirable. He didn't look his age. He was thirty. So was Jane who stood behind him. And Ann was thirty-five. A rotten age! Poor Ann!

'Old Ann.' For how long had she been that? It seemed impossible to remember a time when she wasn't 'old Ann' – so well beloved, so indispensable; but still, old Ann. Even her senior, Kate, had fallen into the family habit. If anything went wrong, 'We'd better see old Ann about it,' was the first thing to be said. And the confidence was rarely misplaced. It had begun in doll days in the nursery; it had lasted through that momentous time when Kate came into her sister's bed one night, and with her arms about old Ann's neck had talked to her about Tony Sinclair, and old Ann had approved him and given her blessing; it had lasted right up to date, when everybody in the vicarage was looking to old Ann to make Robin Elder's visit a success. You could hardly expect the Rev. Robert Bennison to do it. It was only last Sunday that he had posted his sermon and tried to preach from a letter which he produced from his pocket in the pulpit; he was that kind of man. For a long time there had been no Mrs Bennison to look after jobs of this sort; and Jane was too busy helping Robin to enjoy himself to be of much use in seeing to the mere domestic details of his bed and board. So to old Ann, once more, all looked for the successful oiling of domestic wheels and hinges.

She realised her position quite clearly as she stood at the window. She realised that she was highly regarded and that everybody would be shocked at the thought that injustice was being done her. But she realised, too, that she was an institution, and that if anything happened to alter her status there would be as much consternation as if the Bank of England suddenly began to do unaccustomed tricks. Institutions are not expected to vary; they are just expected to function – normally, calmly, unchangeably.

Now something in the spring morning, some enchanting breath blowing through that quiet vicarage garden of St Arbuthnot-in-Roseland, made her profoundly dissatisfied with being an institution, with being respected by everybody in general and loved by nobody in particular. The daffodils that trembled in the grass under the cherry trees were like little flames; and Ann felt that she would rather be a little flame burning brightly for a brief season and then passing away for ever than an institution that grew steadily more and more venerable and respected and sterile and austere.

It was very disturbing. Such ideas had never worried her before Robin Elder came. She was turning from the window when Jane's voice called. 'Oh, Ann, Ann! Come and give us a hand in with the things.'

Ann went in her grave, almost matronly way on to the lawn where Robin and Jane were assembling cushions and easels, palettes and stools.

'Thanks, Ann, thanks so much,' Jane said when, in the house, Ann deposited an armful of cushions, a couple of stools and sundry other impedimenta on the floor. Jane carefully put down the canvas, her sole burden.

'Ann, Ann!'

It was the Rev. Robert Bennison's voice calling from his study. Ann found him, watch in hand, at his table.

'We're rather late with lunch, dear, aren't we? I'm afraid Jenny's all behind. D'you mind giving her a hand. You know, Robin and Jane have some scheme for going up the river this afternoon. They'll want to go as soon as possible because the evenings fall pretty quickly still. And we want them to have as much time as they can manage – eh, Ann?'

And if such a thing were believable, Ann would have sworn that her reverend father nearly achieved a knowing wink. She hurried from the room to help Jenny in the kitchen, and on the stairs ran into her brother John.

'Hallo, Ann! Seen my pipe?'

'Yes, John. It's on the dining-room mantelpiece. I found it in the hammock.'

Finding and replacing lost things and mending broken ones were also part of the functions belonging to the well-established institution that was Ann.

Ann carried the cushions down to the boat after lunch, and saw Robin and Jane embark. She pushed them out with the boathook. With his sleeves rolled back, Robin hauled strongly on the oars. Ann watched the play of his muscles as the boat moved towards the spot where the harbour narrowed down to the tidal river that wandered away among the hills. She watched his lithe body bending backwards and forwards with the swing of his strokes till the river took him out of her sight.

She returned slowly up the hill to the vicarage. John was fiddling with his motor bike in front of the house.

'Give us a push off, Ann. I'm running over to Truro.'

Ann gave John a push off, and he honked and exploded away into the quiet afternoon. Then the sound of him ceased, and there was nothing to be heard save the steady stertoration of the Rev. Robert Bennison, taking his afternoon nap on the drawing-room sofa.

Ann sat on a seat on the lawn, and looked over the blue harbour, pondering. She had helped them both away, and now she was left alone with the old sleeping man. It seemed to be her fate to be always giving folk a push off – shoving out the boat, pushing off the bike – and then finding herself left behind.

She hadn't minded till now. But the idea that she would be left behind once more when Robin Elder went to Nigeria filled her with dread. Robin and John had met in the army. Robin had often come to spend a flying week-end with John, and always on those occasions Ann had felt an access of calm pleasure in performing her usual task of keeping things running smoothly. And now Robin's firm was sending him to Nigeria, and he was making a prolonged visit, which might easily be a farewell. Ann's calm pleasure was gone. She realised that the thing which no one seemed to think could come to her had come. She watched him filling in his time with rowing and the amusing playing with paints that he called painting; and she saw the days slipping by one after another with never a sign that his going would not be for her the final closing of the door. John would be going back to his reading for the Bar; Jane, perhaps, would be going to Nigeria; and then old Ann and the old vicar would go on for a few more years together. A few more years would mean the neighbourhood of forty.

Ann went in slowly to see that tea was ready for herself and her father.

John and Jane and Robin were all back soon after tea, and then began the scramble against time to be ready for the dance in Falmouth. The Pembertons' big motor launch was to leave the old quay at seven o'clock and the vicarage party had an invitation to join it. The run across Falmouth harbour was a matter of only fifteen minutes.

Jane was tremendously excited. 'My dress ready, Ann?'

'Yes, dear. You'll find it laid out on the bed.'

'Well, be a sport. Come and help us on with it. And I wouldn't trust myself to do my own hair. You must give us a hand.'

They were all in the drawing-room, and the lamps had just been lit. Ann was sitting on a large downy couch, her father at her side. Robin, strumming at a baby grand, had his back to her; but at that moment he swung round on the stool.

'But Ann is coming too?' he asked.

A strange silence fell upon the room, as though someone had hurled a bomb which had not yet exploded and there was tense waiting for the bang.

'But – ' said the vicar.

'But – ' said Jane.

And John said, 'But – '

It was left to Jane to achieve the sentence.

'But old Ann hasn't been to a dance for years!'

'I'm sure Ann doesn't like dancing,' said John.

'Oh, no,' Jane hurried on. 'Ann always stays in to read to Father. He never goes out at night except to evening service, and he can't be left alone.'

The vicar patted Ann's hand affectionately. 'No, Robin, my boy,' he said. 'We couldn't get on at nights without our Ann. We're at a most fascinating part of Milman's *History of the Jews*, aren't we, Ann?'

'Yes,' Ann said, addressing Robin, who had now come across and stood by the couch. 'Since mother died someone *has* to be with father in the evenings. He hates being alone.'

Ann's heart fluttered rather wildly as Robin positively scowled. 'Well,' he said. 'I'm dashed, you know, if it seems quite fair. Look here; I'll make a sporting offer. It'll be new to me to read Mr Milman on the Jews, and apparently it'll be rather a change for Ann to go to a dance. Let's swop places. I'll read to you to-night, sir.'

'But Ann positively hasn't got a dress,' Jane burst out.

And simultaneously John: 'Oh, but, look here, Robin, old man. You mustn't talk rot, you know. Ann really enjoys this sort of thing. After all, this is your holiday, not Ann's. Ann's got all her life before her to enjoy this place.'

'Yes, of course,' Ann said quietly. 'All my life.' And getting up, she took Jane by the arm and led her from the room. 'Come along, my dear. No more arguing. You're late enough as it is.'

'There, you see,' said John triumphantly. 'It's no good trying to persuade her to go. All our efforts are wasted. She absolutely enjoys bossing us all about.'

Robin ruminated for a while. 'Well,' he said dubiously at last. 'I see clearly enough, John. Ann's a sport of a high order.'

This idea caused John to chuckle quietly. 'My dear boy, Ann is one of nature's old maids. She doesn't know a step invented since the war. In a dance-room she'd be about as happy as Father in Tattersall's ring.'

'Eh, boy, eh?' said the vicar, jerking up a head which was beginning to sag sleepily. 'Tattersall's, eh? Now you two run away and change. I was thinking . . . thinking . . .' And his chin sagged forward again.

So Ann found him when she came down later with the *History of the Jews* under her arm. He was sound asleep and she did not wake him to continue that most fascinating chapter of Milman which they had reached. Nor did she read to herself. She quietly made up the fire and sat down before it. 'She really enjoys this sort of thing . . . All her life before her to enjoy it.' These words of John's were the ones that had hurt her most. But, after all, was he to blame? Was Jane to blame? Was their father to blame? Somehow they had all blundered in the course of the years into this position, this dependence on Ann to be the central pivot turning always in the same way, in the same spot, in order that others might move through a variety of experience. They thought she liked it. She was sure they were honest about that. And, till now, certainly, she had not found it disagreeable, her comfortable and equal progress through the years. She realised that had anyone but Robin Elder been concerned, she would not have felt slighted at being left out of the party. She would, honestly, have preferred to stay at home. The others were not to blame.

But there it was, this new and tremendous feeling that everything in life had to be looked at from a different angle. She felt so profoundly changed that she almost wondered that no one had noticed that she was not the Ann of a few weeks ago. Had Robin noticed? She would have given much to have that question answered. Was his intervention that night merely the impulse of a generous nature, or was it in any way a particular feeling directed to her? She would have given more to have that answered.

But meantime, here was the vicar coming to with a start and exclaiming: 'Splendid, Ann, splendid. Thank you very much, my dear. Most interesting. And now I must be off to bed. You'll stay up for the others, won't you?'

When John proposed in the morning that he and Robin should take a flying trip to Penzance, Robin pleaded to be excused. He was sitting at the breakfast table, pampering the queer taste of Ann's spaniel for toast crusts. He seemed a little absent and preoccupied, Ann thought, and she put it down to tiredness. It had been nearly three o'clock when they got back from Falmouth. Neither Jane nor the vicar was down; Ann, Robin and John had the breakfast room to themselves.

'No; let's have a day's rest, old man,' Robin urged. 'We've been racketing all over the county this last ten days, and I'm quite willing to sit still for a few hours.'

'Better get Father to introduce you to his herbaceous borders,' said John facetiously. 'Or ask Ann to explain all about the brasses in the church. Yes; that's an idea. You know, Ann's the world's greatest expert on our brasses. It's been her life study.'

'I should be very glad – ' Robin began, when John cut in again.

'And, come to think of it, Ann, you certainly must show him the brasses in return for his splendid championship of you last night. Yes, you owe it to him. Young Roper – '

'Oh, come, John, come,' Robin interrupted, crimsoning suddenly. 'Cut it out. That's done with. I was unnecessarily rude to young Roper.'

'Well, never let it be said that the days of chivalry are ended. It was a good sight to see,' went on tactless John. 'You must know, Ann, that Jane was telling young Roper that you had nearly come to the dance yourself. "Good heavens!" says Roper. "Not Ann! You don't say old Ann is having a second blooming?" '

Poor Ann! A rotten age, thirty-five! A fiery tide rushed into her face and her eyes moistened.

'Cut it out, John, you fool, cut it out,' Robin was muttering savagely, kicking his friend's shin vigorously under the table;

but tact, and even sometimes commonsense, were not strong
cards with John Bennison, and he went plunging on as
though relating some really diverting thing that concerned
nobody present.

'Well, this young Galahad happened to be hovering near
with the fair Miss Pemberton, whom he forthwith drops,
and going up with some menace taps young Roper on the
shoulder. "Pardon me, sir," he says, "have I had the pleasure
of being introduced to you?" Young Roper, rather surprised,
eyes him up and down, and then says, "I think not. Don't
know you from Adam." "Then I'm sorry I can't have the
pleasure of punching your nose," says Robin. "And that's
the only reason why I regret not knowing you." And with
that he snaps his fingers under the aforesaid nose and walks
away.'

Ann writhed under a tumult of conflicting feelings: anger
at young Roper's impertinence, shame at John's casual
acceptance of the circumstances, and a throbbing joy at
Robin's intervention. For the second time that night he had
spoken for her when everybody else seemed to consider there
was no particular reason for anybody to speak. She hung her
head over her plate with pretence of being busy with her
food till John pushed back his chair with an unceremonious
' 'Scuse me' and left the table.

'Just going to overhaul the old bike,' he explained. 'See
you soon, Robin. By the way, Ann, got any old dusters?'

For the first time in its existence, so far as any member of
the Bennison family could remember in recalling the circum-
stance later, the institution failed to function according to
plan.

'I haven't finished breakfast yet, John. Ask Jenny. She
may have some.'

Resentment at John's conduct had gradually emerged as
the dominating feeling out of the struggling complexity, and
the words came if not angrily at any rate with a certain

asperity. John paused a moment at the unaccustomed tone, then shrugged his shoulders and went. Ann felt tears rising to her eyes at having been betrayed into hasty speech, and after struggling with them for a moment in silence she too got up and said: 'Pardon me, Robin; I've got a lot to see to. And I must find those dusters for John. And . . . and . . . thank you so much for what you said last night.'

She hardly knew how she got the words out, her face aflame, her tongue stammering; and as soon as they were spoken she walked rapidly to the door. Robin's surprising remark arrested her with the door-knob in her hand. 'I'd see him hanged before I'd get his dusters. Let him get 'em himself. You're not his batman.'

Now if there was one thing more surprising to Ann than to find herself wavering, even for a moment, in her lifetime habit, it was to find herself aided and abetted in her defalcation. She stood irresolute for a moment; and so absurd are life's caprices that in that ridiculous mental perplexity about a duster all her past and future joined issue. Her future won. 'Right,' she said. 'I won't.'

Robin had got up from the table, a light of malicious merriment playing in his eyes. 'Come here, Ann,' he commanded.

She came, wondering. He led her to the window, threw it up, and called to John who was stinking the lawn with the cleaning of an acetylene lamp: 'Hi, John! Seen anything of Ann's tennis racket?'

'Not the faintest idea where it is,' John answered.

'Well, I can tell you. It's in the tool-shed. Run and get it, there's a good chap.'

With some reluctance, John made off and presently returned, grumbling. 'Can't find it. It's not in the tool-shed.'

'Sorry, old boy,' Robin answered cheerily. 'Did I say the tool-shed? I meant the summerhouse. I saw it there yesterday. D'you mind sprinting along for it?'

John came back and handed the racket through the window.

'Thanks. Ann and I are going to have a quiet set or two.'

'What!'

It was a surprised and outraged Jane, just entering the breakfast-room. 'I did think you were going to sit and have a chat with me while I was having breakfast, Ann. Besides, Father hasn't had breakfast yet.'

'Splendid opportunity for your chat,' said Robin brightly. 'You can be looking after your father and chatting and having a first-rate time.'

'I'm much too tired to look after anybody's breakfast but my own,' Jane answered. 'I wasn't in bed till half-past three.'

'No more was Ann, and she's been up an hour.'

'Oh, but Ann's used to early rising. She positively adores it.'

'Aye, aye,' rumbled the vicar, ambling in and smiling rosily round on everybody. 'Wonderful girl, Ann, wonderful girl. Good morning, my dear. Good morning. We'll go through those accounts after breakfast.'

'Oh, but sir,' Robin pleaded, 'I was hoping that Ann might have a set or two of tennis with me. And then she's promised to show me the brasses in the church.'

'Dear, dear, dear,' moaned the vicar. 'Those accounts, you know, those accounts, my boy! One must be business-like. Now, Jane – '

'Yes, most business-like, I'm sure, sir,' Robin answered briskly.

'No, no, she's not. I was going to suggest Jane for tennis.'

'Well, another sporting offer, sir. I'll go through the accounts with you after Ann and I have had a set or two. I'm no end of a man at accounts. Now, Jane, quick, tea –

tea for your father. Come along, Ann. Tennis is splendid on top of a hearty breakfast.'

It was incredible. Ann had played tennis in the morning. The morning, when all sorts of things have to be done if the household sailing is to be smooth for the day; the morning, when Ann, aproned and demure, had for years been seen toiling steadily away at this duty and that; the morning, when it was difficult enough in all conscience to keep pace with the unhurrying but persistent sun. A sense of something insecure in the foundations of existence had entered into the vicarage. The vicar was grave when Robin went in to help with the accounts. The young man glimpsed Jane in an apron and congratulated her on her appearance.

'Quite the matron.'

Jane sniffed.

No one was more shaken than Ann herself. That hesitation at the door-knob had led to so much. And yet she did not regret it. John had gone off somewhere on his bike and had not asked for a push off. The tennis was over. Robin had gone into the study. Ann, obsessed with a sense of freedom, did not return to the house. She strolled through the garden gate across a field, into the churchyard. The swallows had come and with shrill twittering notes were swirling like lithe bent bows about the old tower. Back from the south, back from Africa . . . Nigeria . . .

It was an incoherent and jumbled reverie that she fell into as she stood rooted there looking at the swift beauty of the birds. Robin had said nothing, done nothing, that a high-spirited lad might not have done; and yet . . . Perhaps at thirty-five one clutches at nothings. But there were those two strange interventions on her behalf and Robin's queer outbreak of the morning.

She entered the church. In its ancient and accustomed

quiet she felt that she would recover her poise, get the derailed coach of her mind running again on the old smooth track. But the church failed her. Something stronger than all the old influences of her life were at work within her. She had never before been restless in this place. She was restless now. She sat down and tried to compose her mind, but no sooner was she seated than a swallow, flying through the open door, began to fill the building with a frightened crying. Some fatal command seemed to forbid it to go out again by the way it had come in; and hither and thither it plunged and cried, finding restraining walls whichever way it moved. Now, attracted by the lights of a window, it dashed itself against the glass and recoiled with a loud distress; now it perched for a while palpitating on a beam under the dim roof, only to drop off and go once more with unending clamour, searching, searching, searching, for the freedom of sun and air, the freedom of unconfined journeying above the earth.

Helpless to help, Ann watched the bird and felt that her own heart was a sharer of its case. The narrow walls of her environment had never until the last few days seemed irksome; but now her heart was urgently demanding a way out, freedom to choose her own path in the sun and the air, freedom to love.

At last, with a desperate swirl, the swallow came violently against a wall and fell like a stone almost at her feet. She took it in her hand and saw that its breast was palpitating still. There were tears in her eyes as she turned to carry it out into the sunlight. With the tears in her eyes and the injured bird in her hand, she confronted Robin Elder.

'Poor little thing, poor little thing,' he said; and he put out his hand and with a touch exquisitely gentle unfolded the hand that held the bird. Ann's heart fluttered as wildly as the swallow's breast as she turned her tear-filled eyes to Robin's face. It was as though that unhappy moment had

summed up all the distress of the last few days. She sat on a
seat and cried, honestly and frankly; and Robin, when he
had laid the bird on a sunny bank outside, came and sat at
her side. For a long time he did not speak; and when he did,
it was as though his thoughts, as he had watched her in the
church before she saw him, had run on the same lines as her
own. Indeed, the parable was obvious.

'Ann,' he said, 'I have put the little thing out in the air,
but I'm afraid it's too late.' Then for a while he was silent,
and at last went on: 'I have been watching someone else
lately longing for the sun and air and freedom. Ann, I can
help you to it.'

He bent towards her and took her hand and drew it down
from her face.

'W-why aren't you helping F-Father with the accounts?'
she sobbed.

Robin laughed. 'He wouldn't have me. He said they were
too intricate – altogether beyond me. Nobody but old Ann
could understand them. He's inconsolable about your
scandalous behaviour.'

'I must g-go and h-help him at once.' But she made no
effort to hitch action to her words.

Robin released her hand and stood up, smiling. 'Let it
never be said that I am keeping you from your duty. If you
want to go, go.'

'I d-don't.'

And Ann got up too, and flung her arms round Robin's
neck and cried herself into happiness.

When Robin, with none of the diffidence which young men
are supposed to show, approached the vicar on the subject
of Ann that very day, he began by saying that he had designs
to take one of Mr Bennison's daughters with him to Nigeria.
The vicar put up as good a show of surprise as he could, and

then said: 'You can imagine, my dear boy, what a loss Jane will be to us all.'

His surprise became very real when Robin answered: 'Jane! You are under a misapprehension, sir. I'm afraid I've already developed a family habit and spoken to old Ann about it.'

CHRISTMAS HONEYMOON

We were married on 22nd December, because we had met on the 21st. It was as sudden as that. I had come down from Manchester to London. Londoners like you to say that you come up to London; but we Manchester people don't give a hoot what Londoners like. We know that we, and the likes of us, lay the eggs, and the Londoners merely scramble them. This gives us a sense of superiority.

Perhaps I have this sense unduly. Certainly I should never have imagined that I would marry a London girl. As a bachelor I had survived thirty Manchester summers, and it seemed unlikely to me that, if I couldn't find a girl to suit me in the north, I should find one in London.

I am an architect, and that doesn't make me love London any more. Every time I come down to the place I find it has eaten another chunk of its own beauty, so as to make more room for the fascias of multiple shops.

All this is just to show you that I didn't come to London looking for a bride; and if I had been looking for a bride, the last place I would have investigated would be a cocktail party. But it was at a cocktail party in the Magnifico that I met Ruth Hutten. I had never been to a cocktail party in my life before. We don't go in for much of that sort of thing in Manchester: scooping a lot of people together and getting rid of the whole bang shoot in one do. It seems to us ungracious. We like to have a few friends in, and give them a cut off the joint and something decent to drink, and talk in a civilised fashion while we're at it. That's what we understand by hospitality. But these cocktail parties are just a frantic St Vitus gesture by people who don't want to be bothered.

I shouldn't have been at this party at all if it hadn't been for Claud Tunstall. It was about half-past six when I turned from the lunatic illumination of Piccadilly Circus, which is my idea of how hell is lit up, and started to walk down the Haymarket. I was wondering in an absent-minded sort of way how long the old red pillars of the Haymarket Theatre would be allowed to stand before some bright lad thought what fun it would be to tear them down, when Claud turned round from reading one of the yellow playbills, and there we were grinning and shaking hands.

Claud had something to grin about, because the author's name on the playbill was his. It was his first play, and it looked as though it wouldn't matter to Claud, so far as money went, if it were his last. The thing had been running for over a year; companies were touring it in the provinces and colonies; and it was due to open in New York in the coming year. No wonder Claud was grinning; but I think a spot of the grin was really meant for me. He was the same old Claud who had attended the Manchester Grammar School with me and shared my knowledge of its smell of new exercise books and old suet pudding.

Claud was on his way to this party at the Magnifico, and he said I must come with him. That's how these things are: there's no sense in them; but there would have been no sense either in trying to withstand Claud Tunstall's blue eyes and fair hair and general look of a sky over a corn-field.

That's going some for me, and perhaps the figure is a bit mixed, but I'm not one for figures at any time. Anyway, it explains why, five minutes later, I was gritting my teeth in the presence of great boobies looking like outsizes in eighteenth-century footmen, yelling names and looking down their noses.

We stood at the door of a room, and I was aware of the gold blur of chandeliers, and a few dozen apparent football scrums, and a hot blast of talk coming out and smacking our faces, so I deduced this was the party all right. One of the boobies yelled: 'Mr Claud Tunstall and Mr Edward Oldham,' and from what happened it might just as well have been 'The Archangel Gabriel and one Worm.' Because the moment we were over the threshold all the scrums loosened up and girls descended on Claud like a cloud of bright, skittering, squawking parrakeets, flashing their red nails at him, unveiling their pearly portals in wide grins, and bearing him off towards a bar where a chap in white was working overtime among all the sweet accessories of sin. I never saw him again.

Well, as I say, I might have been a worm, no use at all to parrakeets, but that lets in the sparrows. I was just turning slowly on my own axis, so to speak, in the space that was miraculously cleared round me, when I saw a girl looking at me with an appreciative gleam in her brown eyes. She was the brownest girl I ever saw – eyes, skin and hair – homely as a sparrow, and just as alert.

As our eyes met, there came fluting out of one of the scrums a high-pitched female voice: 'No, Basil, I'm teetotal, but I can go quite a long way on pahshun fruit.'

The pronunciation of that *pahshun* was indescribable; it seemed the bogus essence of the whole damn silly occasion; and the brown girl and I, looking into one another's eyes, twinkled, savouring together the supreme idiocy. Instinctively we moved towards one another, the twinkle widening to a smile, and I found myself getting dangerously full of similes again, for when she smiled the teeth in her brown face were like the milky kernel of a brown nut.

We sat together on a couch at the deserted end of the room, and I said: 'Let me get you something to drink. What would you like? Though whatever it is, it would taste nicer in civilised surroundings.'

'I agree,' she said simply. 'Come on.'

And so, ten minutes after I had entered the Magnifico, I was outside again, buttoning my overcoat warmly about me, and this girl was at my side. It was incredible. This is not the sort of thing I usually do; but it had happened so spontaneously, and to be out there in the street, with a little cold wind blowing about us, was such a relief after the gaudy Bedlam, that the girl and I turned to one another and smiled again. I could see she was feeling the same about it as I was.

Our eyes were towards the dazzle of Piccadilly Circus, when she turned and said, 'Not that way,' so we went the other way, and down those steps where the Duke of York's column towers up into the sky, and then we were in the park. To be walking there, with that little wind, and the sky full of stars huddling together in the cold, and the bare branches of the trees standing up against the violet pulsing of the night – this was indescribable, incredible, coming within a few minutes upon that screeching aviary.

Ruth Hutten was a typist – nothing more. Her father had been one of those old fogies who rootle for years and years in the British Museum to prove that Ben Jonson had really inserted a semi-colon where the 1739 edition or what not has a full-stop. Things like that. Somehow he had lived on it, like a patient old rat, living on scraps of forgotten and unimportant meat. Ruth had lived with him – just lived, full of admiration for the old boy's scholarship, typing his annual volume, which usually failed to earn the publisher's advance.

When he died, the typewriter was all she had; and now she typed other people's books. She had been typing a long flaming novel about Cornwall by Gregoria Gunson; and Gregoria (whom I had never heard of before but who seemed a decent wench) had said: 'I'll take you along to a party. You'll meet a lot of people there. Perhaps I can fix up some work for you.'

So there Ruth Hutten was, at the Magnifico, feeling as much out of it as I did, and as glad to escape.

She told me all this as we walked through the half-darkness of the park, and I, as naturally, told her all about myself. She was hard up, but I had never known anyone so happy. And I don't mean gay, bubbling, effervescent. No: you can keep that for the Magnifico. I mean something deep, fundamental, something that takes courage when you're as near the limit as Ruth was.

To this day I don't know London as well as Londoners think everyone ought to know the place. I don't know where we had supper; but it was a quiet place that everybody else seemed to have forgotten. There was a fire burning, and a shaded lamp on the table. The food was good and simple, and no one seemed to care how long we stayed. I wanted to stay a long time. I had a feeling that once Ruth got outside the door, shook hands and said 'Good night', I should be groping in a very dark place.

I crumbled a bit of bread on the table, and without looking at her I said: 'Ruth, I like you. I've never liked anyone so much in my life. Will you marry me?'

She didn't answer till I looked up, and when our glances met she said: 'Yes, if you and I can't be happy together, no two people on earth ever could.'

This was five years ago. We have had time to discover that we didn't make a mistake.

We were married at a registry office the next morning. The taxi-driver, who looked like one of the seven million exiled Russian princes, and the office charwoman, who had a goitre and a hacking cough, were the witnesses. I tipped them half a sovereign each. I cling to these practical details because I find them comforting in view of the mad impracticality of what was to follow. Please remember that I am an unromantic northerner who couldn't invent a tale to save his life. If I tried to do so, I should at once begin to try it with this and that – in short, with Something. The remarkable thing about what happened to me and Ruth was simply that Nothing happened. If you have never come up against Nothing you have no idea how it can scare you out of your wits. When I was a child I used to be afraid of Something in the dark. I know now that the most fearful thing about the dark is that we may find Nothing in it.

It was Ruth's idea that we should spend the few days of our honeymoon walking in Cornwall. Everything was arranged in a mad hurry. Not that there was much to arrange. We bought rucksacks, stuffed a change of underclothing into them, bought serviceable shoes and waterproofs, and we were ready to start.

Walking was the idea of both of us. This was another bond: you could keep all the motor cars in the world as far as we were concerned, and all the radio and daily newspapers too; and we both liked walking in winter as much as in summer.

Cornwall was Ruth's idea. She had Cornwall on the brain. Her father had done some learned stuff on Malory; and her head was full of Merlin and Tintagel and the return of Arthur. Gregoria Gunson's novel helped too, with smugglers and romantic inns and the everlasting beat of surf on granite coasts. So Cornwall it was – a place in which neither of us had set foot before.

We made our first contact with Cornwall at Truro. Night had long since fallen when we arrived there on our wedding day. I have not been there since, nor do I wish ever to return. Looking back on what happened, it seems appropriate that the adventure should have begun in Truro. There is in some towns something inimical, irreconcilable. I felt it there. As soon as we stepped out of the station, I wished we were back in the warm lighted train which already was pulling out on its way to Penzance.

There was no taxi in sight. To our right the road ran

slightly uphill; to our left, downhill. We knew nothing of the town, and we went to the left. Soon we were walking on granite. There was granite everywhere: grey, hard and immemorial. The whole town seemed to be hewn out of granite. The streets were paved with it, enormous slabs like the lids of ancestral vaults. It gave me the feeling of walking in an endless graveyard, and the place was silent enough to maintain the illusion. The streets were lit with grim economy. Hardly a window had a light, and when, here and there, we passed a public house, it was wrapped in a pall of decorum which made me wonder whether Cornishmen put on shrouds when they went in for a pint.

It did not take us long to get to the heart of the place, the few shopping streets that were a bit more festive, gay with seasonable things; and when we found an hotel, it was a good one. I signed the book, 'Mr and Mrs Edward Oldham, Manchester', and that made me smile. After all, it was something to smile about. At this time last night, Ruth and I had just met, and now we were 'Mr and Mrs Edward Oldham'.

Ruth had moved across to a fire in the lounge. She had an arm along the mantelpiece, a toe meditatively tapping the fender. She looked up when I approached her and saw the smile. But her face did not catch the contagion. 'Don't you hate this town?' she asked.

'I can put up with it,' I said, 'now that I'm in here and now that you're in here with me.'

'Yes,' she answered, 'this is all right. But those streets! They gave me the creeps. I felt that every stone had been hewn out of a cliff that the Atlantic had battered for a thousand years and plastered with wrecks. Have you ever seen Tewkesbury Abbey?'

The irrelevant question took me aback. 'No,' I said.

'I've never seen stone so saturated with sunlight,' said Ruth. 'It looks as if you could wring summers out of it. The fields about it, I know, have run with blood, but it's a happy place all the same. This place isn't happy. It's under a cold enchantment.'

'Not inside these four walls,' I said, 'because they enclose you and me and our supper and bed.'

We fled from Truro the next morning. Fled is the word. As soon as breakfast was over we slung our rucksacks on to our backs and cleared out of the granite town as fast as our legs would take us. December 23rd, and utterly unseasonable weather. The sky was blue, the sun was warm, and the Christmas decorations in the shops had a farcical and in-appropriate look. But we were not being bluffed by these appearances. We put that town behind us before its hoodoo could reimpose itself upon our spirits.

And soon there was nothing wrong with our spirits at all. We were travelling westward, and every step sunk us deeper into a warm enchantment. Ruth had spoken last night of a cold enchantment. Well, this was a warm enchantment. I hadn't guessed that, with Christmas only two days ahead, any part of England could be like this. We walked through woods of evergreens and saw the sky shining like incredible blue lace through the branches overhead. We found violets blooming in a warm hedge bottom, and in a cottage garden a few daffodils were ready to burst their sheaths. We could see the yellow staining the taut green. We had tea at that cottage, out of doors! I thought of Manchester, and the fog blanketing Albert Square, and the great red buses going through it, slowly, like galleons, sounding their warning horns. I laughed aloud at the incredible, the absurd things that could happen to a man in England. One day Man-chester. The next London. The next marriage, Truro, and the cold shudders. The next – this! I said all this to Ruth, who was brushing crumbs off the table to feed the birds that hopped tamely round her feet. 'It makes me wonder what miracle is in store for to-morrow,' I said. 'And anyway, what is Cornwall? I always thought it was beetling cliffs and raging seas, smugglers, wreckers and excisemen.'

We entered the cottage to pay the old woman, and I went close up to the wall to examine a picture hanging there. It was a fine bit of photography: spray breaking on wicked-looking rocks. 'That's the Manacles,' the old girl said. 'That's where my husband was drowned.'

The Manacles. That was a pretty fierce name, and it looked a pretty fierce place. The woman seemed to take it for granted. She made no further comment. 'Good-bye, midear,' she said to Ruth. 'Have a good day.'

We did, but I never quite recaptured the exultation of the morning. I felt that this couldn't last, that the spirit which had first made itself felt in the hard grey streets of Truro had pounced again out of that hard grey name: the Manacles. It sounded like a gritting of gigantic teeth. We were being played with. This interlude in fairyland, where May basked in December, was something to lure us on, to bring us within striking distance of – well, of what? Isn't this England? I said to myself. Isn't Cornwall as well within the four walls of Britain as Lancashire?

We breasted a hill, and a wide estuary lay before us, shining under the evening sun. Beyond it, climbing in tier upon tier of streets, was Falmouth. I liked the look of it. 'This is where we stay to-night,' I said to Ruth. 'We shall be comfortable here.'

A ferry took us across the harbour. Out on the water it was cold. Ruth pointed past the docks, past Pendennis Castle standing on the hill. 'Out there is the way to Land's End,' she said.

I looked, and low down on the water there was a faint grey smudge. Even a Manchester man would know that that was fog, creeping in from the Atlantic.

All night long we heard the fog-horns moaning, and it was very cold.

I hate sleeping in an airless room, but by midnight the white coils of fog, filling every crevice, and cold as if they were the exhalation of icebergs, made me rise from bed and shut the window. Our bedroom hung literally over the sea. The wall of the room was a deep bay, and I had seen how, by leaning out of the window, one could drop a stone to the beach below. Now I could not see the beach. I could not see anything. If I had stretched my arm out into the night the fingers would have been invisible. But though I could not see, I could hear. The tide had risen, and I could hear the splash of little waves down there below me. It was so gentle a sound that it made me shudder. It was like the voice of a soft-spoken villain. The true voice of the sea and of the night was that long, incessant bellow of the fog-horns. The shutting of the window did nothing to keep that out.

I drew the curtains across the window and, turning, saw that a fire was laid in the grate. I put a match to it. Incredible comfort! In ten minutes we felt happier. In twenty we were asleep.

There seemed nothing abnormal about Falmouth when we woke in the morning. A fairly stiff wind had sprung up. The fog was torn to pieces. It hung here and there in isolated patches, but these were being quickly swept away. There was a run on the water. It was choppy and restless, and the sky was a rag-bag of fluttering black and grey. Just a normal winter day by the seaside; a marvellous day for walking, Ruth said.

At the breakfast table we spread out the map and considered the day's journey. This was going to be something new again. There had been the grey inhospitality of Truro; the Arcadian interlude; the first contact with something vast and menacing. Now, looking at the map, we saw that, going westward, following the coast, we should come to what we had both understood Cornwall to be; a sparsely populated land, moors, a rock-bound coast. It promised to be something big and hard and lonely, and that is what we wanted.

We put sandwiches into our rucksacks, intending to eat lunch out of doors. We reckoned we should find some sort of inn for the night.

A bus took us the best part of ten miles on our journey. Then it struck inland, to the right. We left it at that point, climbed a stile, walked through a few winter-bare fields, and came to a path running with the line of the coast.

Now, indeed, we had found traditional Cornwall. Here, if anywhere, was the enchanted land of Merlin and of Arthur – the land that Ruth dreamed about. Never had I found elsewhere in England a sense so overpowering both of size and loneliness. To our left was the sea, down there at the foot of the mighty cliffs along whose crest we walked. The tide was low, and the reefs were uncovered. In every shape of fantastic cruelty they thrust out towards the water, great knives and swords of granite that would hack through any keel, tables of granite on which the stoutest ship would pound to pieces, jaws of granite that would seize and grind and not let go. Beyond and between these prone monsters was the innocent yellow sand, and, looking at the two – the sand and the reefs – I thought of the gentle lapping of the water under my window last night, and the crying of the fog-horns, the most desolate crying in the world.

Southward and westward the water stretched without limit; and inland, as we walked steadily forward all through the morning, was now a stretch of cultivation, now the winter stretch of rusty moor with gulls and lapwings joining their lamentations as they glided and drooped across it, according to their kind. From time to time a cluster of trees broke the monotony of the inland view, and I remember rooks fussing among the bare boughs. Rooks, lapwings and gulls: those were the only birds we saw that day.

It was at about one o'clock that we came to a spot where

the cliff path made a loop inland to avoid a deep fissure into which we peered. In some cataclysm the rocks here had been torn away, tumbling and piling till they made a rough giant's stairway down which we clambered to the beach below. We ended up in a cove so narrow that I could have thrown a stone across it, and paved with sand of an unbelievable golden purity. The sun came through the clouds, falling right upon that spot. It was tiny, paradisial, with the advancing tide full of green and blue and purple lights. We sat on the sand, leaned against the bottom-most of the fallen granite blocks, and ate our lunch.

We were content. This was the loveliest thing that we had found yet. Ruth recalled a phrase from the novel she had typed for Miss Gregoria Gunson. 'And you will find here and there a paradise ten yards wide, a little space of warmth and colour set like a jewel in the hard iron of that coast.' Far-fetched, I thought, but true enough.

It was while we were sitting there, calculating how long that bit of sun could last, that Ruth said, 'We wanted a lonely place, and we've found it, my love. Has it struck you that we haven't seen a human being since we got off the bus?'

It hadn't, and it didn't seem to me a matter of concern. I stretched my arms lazily towards the sun. 'Who wants to see human beings?' I demanded. 'I had enough human beings at the Magnifico to last me a very long time.'

'So long as we find some human beings to make us a bit of supper to-night . . .'

'Never fear,' I said. 'We'll do that. There! Going, going, gone.'

The sun went in. We packed up, climbed to the cliff top, and started off again.

At three o'clock the light began to go out of the day. This was Christmas Eve, remember. We were among the shortest days of the year. It was now that a little uneasiness began to take hold of me. Still, I noticed, we had seen no man or woman, and, though I kept a sharp lookout on the country inland, we saw no house, not a barn, not a shed.

We did not see the sun again that day, but we witnessed his dying magnificence. Huge spears of light fanned down out of the sky and struck in glittering points upon the water far off. Then the clouds turned into a crumble and smother of dusky red, as though a city were burning beyond the edge of the world, and when all this began to turn to grey ashes I knew that I was very uneasy indeed.

Ruth said: 'I think we ought to leave this cliff path. We ought to strike inland and find a road – any road.'

I thought so, too, but inland now was nothing but moor. Goodness knows, I thought, where we shall land if we embark on that.

'Let us keep on,' I said, 'for a little while. We may find a path branching off. Then we'll know we're getting somewhere.'

We walked for another mile, and then Ruth stopped. We were on the brink of another of those deep fissures, like the one we had descended for lunch. Again the path made a swift right-hand curve. I knew what Ruth was thinking before she said it. 'In half an hour or so the light will be quite gone. Suppose we had come on this in the dark?'

We had not found the path we were seeking. We did not seek it any more. Abruptly, we turned right and began to walk into the moor. So long as we could see, we kept the coast behind our backs. Soon we could not see at all. The night came on, impenetrably black, and there would be no moon. It was now six o'clock. I know that because I struck a match to look at the time, and I noticed that I had only three matches left. This is stuck in my mind because I said, 'We must be careful with these. If we can't find food, we'll find a smoke a comfort.'

'But, my love,' said Ruth, and there was now an undoubted note of alarm in her voice, 'we *must* find food.

Surely, if we just keep on we'll see a light, or hear a voice, or come to a road – '

She stopped abruptly, seized my arm, held on to prevent my going forward. I could not see her face, but I sensed her alarm. 'What is it?' I asked.

'I stepped in water.'

I knelt and tested the ground in front of me with my hands. It was a deep oozy wetness; not the clear wetness of running water. 'Bog,' I said; and we knew we could go forward no longer. With cliff on the one hand and the possibility of stumbling into a morass on the other, there seemed nothing for it but to stay where we were till heaven sent us aid or the dawn came up.

I put my arm round Ruth and felt that she was trembling. I want to put this adventure down exactly as it happened. It would be nice to write that her nerves were as steady as rock. Clearly they weren't, and I was not feeling very good either. I said as gaily as I could. 'This is where we sit down, smoke a cigarette, and think it out.'

We went back a little so as to be away from the bog, and then we plumped down among the heather. We put the cigarettes to our lips and I struck a match. It did not go out when I threw it to the ground. In that world of darkness the little light burning on the earth drew our eyes, and simultaneously we both stood up with an exclamation of surprised delight. The light had shown us an inscribed stone, almost buried in the heather. There were two matches left. Fortunately we were tidy people. We had put our sandwich papers into the rucksacks. I screwed these now into little torches. Ruth lit one and held it to the stone while I knelt to read. It seemed a stone of fabulous age. The letters were mossy and at first illegible. I took out a penknife and scraped at them. '2 miles – – ' we made out, but the name of the place two miles off we do not know to this day. I scraped away, but the letters were too defaced for reading, and just as the last of the little torches flared to extinction the knife slipped from my hand into the heather. There was nothing to do but leave it there.

We stood up. Two miles. But two miles to where, and two miles in what direction? Our situation seemed no happier, when suddenly I saw the stones. I had seen stones like them on the Yorkshire moors, round about the old Brontë parsonage. But were they the same sort of stones and did they mean the same thing? I was excited now. 'Stay here,' I said to Ruth, and I stepped towards the first stone. As I had hoped, a third came into view in line with the second, and, as I advanced, a fourth in line with the third. They were the same: upright monoliths set to mark a path, whitewashed half-way up so that they would glimmer through the dark as they were doing now, tarred on their upper half to show the way when snow was on the ground. I shouted in my joy: 'Come on! Supper! Fires! Comfort! Salvation!' Ruth came gingerly. She had not forgotten the bog.

But the stones did not let us down. They led us to the village. It must have been about nine o'clock when we got there.

Half-way through that pitch-black two-mile journey we were aware that once more we were approaching the sea. From afar we could hear its uneasy sound: the voice of a bell-buoy tolling its insistent warning out there on the unseen water.

As the murmur of the sea and the melancholy clangour of the bell came clearer we went more warily, for we could not see more than the stone next ahead; and presently there was no stone where the next should be. We peered into the darkness, our hearts aching for the light which would tell us that we were again among houses and men. There was no light anywhere.

'We have one match,' I said. 'Let us light a cigarette apiece and chance seeing something that will help us.'

We saw the wire hawser: no more than the veriest scrap of it, fixed by a great staple into the head of a post and slanting down into darkness. I first, Ruth behind me, we got our hands upon it, gripping for dear life, and went inching down towards the sound of water.

So we came at last to the village. Like many a Cornish village, it was built at the head of a cove. The sea was in front; there was a horse-shoe of cliffs; and snuggling at the end was a half-moon of houses behind a seawall of granite.

All this did not become clear to us at once. For the moment we had no other thought than of thankfulness to be treading on hard cobbles that had been laid by human hands, no other desire than to bang on the first door and ask whether there was in the place an inn or someone who would give us lodging for the night.

Most of the cottages were whitewashed; their glimmer gave us the rough definition of the place; and I think already we must have felt some uneasy presage at the deathly mask of them, white as skulls with no light in their eyes.

For there was no living person, no living thing, in the village. That was what we discovered. Not so much as a dog went by us in the darkness. Not so much as a cock crowed. The tolling from the water came in like a passing bell, and the sea whispered incessantly, and grew to a deep-throated threatening roar as the tide rose and billows beat on the sand and at last on the sea-wall; but there was no one to notice these things except ourselves; and our minds were almost past caring, so deeply were we longing for one thing only – the rising of the sun.

There was nothing wrong with the village. It contained all the apparatus of living. Bit by bit we discovered that. There was no answer to our knocking at the first door we came to. There was nothing remarkable in that, and we went on to the next. Here again, there was no welcome sound of feet, no springing up of a light to cheer us who had wandered so long in the darkness.

At the third house I knocked almost angrily. Yes; anger was the feeling I had then: anger at all these stupid people who shut down a whole village at nine o'clock, went to their warm beds, and left us standing there, knocking in the cold and darkness. I thudded the knocker with lusty rat-tat-tats; and suddenly, in the midst of that noisy assault, I stopped, afraid. The anger was gone. Plain fear took its place. At the next house I could not knock, because I knew there was no one to hear me.

I was glad to hear Ruth's voice. She said, surprisingly, 'It's no good knocking. Try a door.'

I turned the handle and the door opened. Ruth and I stepped over the threshold, standing very close together. I shouted, 'Is there anyone at home?' My voice sounded brutally loud and defiant. Nothing answered it.

We were standing at the usual narrow passageway of a cottage. Ruth put out her hand and knocked something from a little table to the floor. 'Matches,' she said; and I groped on the floor and found them. The light showed us a hurricane lantern standing on the table. I lit it, and we began to examine the house room by room.

This was a strange thing to do, but at the time it did not seem strange. We were shaken and off our balance. We wanted to reassure ourselves. If we had found flintlocks, bows and arrows, bronze hammers, we might have been reassured. We could have told ourselves that we had wandered, bewitched, out of our century. But we found nothing of the sort. We found a spotless cottage full of contemporary things. There was a wireless set. There was last week's *Falmouth Packet*. There were geraniums in a pot in the window; there were sea-boots and oilskins in the passage. The bed upstairs was made, and there was a cradle beside it. There was no one in the bed, no child in the cradle.

Ruth was white. 'I want to see the pantry,' she said, inconsequently, I thought.

We found the pantry, and she took the cloth off a bread-pan and put her hand upon a loaf. 'It's warm,' she said. 'It was baked to-day.' She began to tremble.

We left the house and took the lantern with us. Slowly, with the bell tolling endlessly, we walked through the curved length of the village. There was one shop. I held up the light to its uncurtained window. Toys and sweets, odds and ends of grocery, all the stock-in-trade of a small general store, were there behind the glass. We hurried on.

We were hurrying now, quite consciously hurrying; though where we were hurrying to we did not know. Once or twice I found myself looking back over my shoulder. If I had seen man, woman or child, I think I should have screamed. So powerfully had the death of the village taken hold of my imagination that the appearance of a living being, recently so strongly desired, would have affected me like the return of one from the dead.

At the centre of the crescent of houses there was an inn, the Lobster Pot, with climbing geraniums ramping over its front in the way they do in Cornwall; then came more cottages; and at the farther tip of the crescent there was a house standing by itself. It was bigger than any of the others; it stood in a little garden. In the comforting daylight I should have admired it as the sort of place some writer or painter might choose for a refuge.

Now I could make it out only bit by bit, flashing the lantern here and there; and, shining the light upon the porch, I saw that the door was open. Ruth and I went in. Again I shouted, 'Is anyone here?' Again I was answered by nothing.

I put the lantern down on an oak chest in the small square hall, and that brought my attention to the telephone. There it was, standing on the chest, an up-to-date microphone in ivory white. Ruth saw it at the same moment, and her eyes asked me, 'Do you dare?'

I did. I took up the microphone and held it to my ear. I could feel at once that it was dead. I joggled the rest. I shouted 'Hallo! Hallo!' but I knew that no one would answer. No one did.

We had stared through the windows of every cottage in the village. We had looked at the shop and the inn. We had banged at three doors and entered two houses. But we had not admitted our extraordinary situation in words. Now I said to Ruth, 'What do you make of it?'

She said simply, 'It's worse than ghosts. Ghosts are something. This is nothing. Everything is absolutely normal. That's what seems so horrible.'

And, indeed, a village devastated by fire, flood or earthquake would not have disturbed us as we were disturbed by that village which was devastated by nothing at all.

Ruth shut the door of the hall. The crashing of the sea on granite, the tolling of the bell, now seemed far off. We stood and looked at one another uneasily in the dim light of the hurricane lamp. 'I shall stay here,' said Ruth, 'either till the morning or till something happens.'

She moved down the hall to a door which opened into a room at the back. I followed her. She tapped on the door, but neither of us expected an answer, and there was none. We went in.

Nothing that night surprised us like what we saw then. Holding the lantern high above my head, I swung its light round the room. It was a charming place, panelled in dark oak. A few fine pictures were on the walls. There were plenty of books, some pieces of good porcelain. The curtains of dark-green velvet fringed with gold were drawn across the window. A fire was burning on the hearth. That was what made us start back almost in dismay – the fire.

If it had been a peat fire – one of those fires that, once lit, smoulder for days – we should not have been surprised. But it was not. Anyone who knew anything about fires could see that this one had been lit within the last hour. Some of the coals were still black; none had been consumed. And the light from this fire fell upon the white smooth texture of an excellent linen cloth upon the table. On the table was supper, set for one. A chair was placed before the knife and fork and plates. There was a round of cold beef waiting to be cut, a loaf of bread, a jar of pickles, a fine cheese, a glass, and a jug containing beer.

Ruth laughed shrilly. I could hear that her nerves were strained by this last straw. 'At least we shan't starve,' she cried. 'I'm nearly dying of hunger. I suppose the worst that could happen would be the return of the bears, demanding "Who's been eating my beef? Who's been drinking my beer?" Sit down. Carve!'

I was as hungry as she was. As I looked at the food the saliva flowed in my mouth, but I could as soon have touched it as robbed a poor-box. And Ruth knew it. She turned from the table, threw herself into an easy chair by the fire, and lay back, exhausted. Her eyes closed. I stood behind the chair and stroked her forehead till she slept. That was the best that could happen to her.

That, in a way, was the end of our adventure. Nothing more happened to us. Nothing *more*? But, as you see, nothing at all had happened to us. And it was this nothing-ness that made my vigil over Ruth sleeping in the chair the most nerve-racking experience of all my life. A clock ticking away quietly on the chimney-piece told me that it was half-past nine. A tear-off calendar lying on a writing-table told me that it was 24th December. Quite correct. All in order.

The hurricane lamp faded and went out. I lit a lamp, shaded with green silk, that stood on the table amid the waiting supper. The room became cosier, even more human and likeable. I prowled about quietly, piecing together the personality of the man or woman who lived here. A man. It was a masculine sort of supper, and I found a tobacco jar and a few pipes. The books were excellently bound editions of the classics, with one or two modern historical works. The pictures, I saw now, were Medici reprints of French Impressionists, all save the one over the fireplace, which was an original by Paul Nash.

I tried, with these trivial investigations, to divert my mind from the extraordinary situation we were in. It wouldn't work. I sat down and listened intently, but there was nothing to hear save the bell and the water – water that stretched, I reminded myself, from here to America. This was one of the ends of the world.

At one point I got up and locked the door, though what was there to keep out? All that was to be feared was inside me.

The fire burned low, and there was nothing for its replenishment. It was nearly gone, and the room was turning cold, when Ruth stirred and woke. At that moment the clock, which had a lively silver note, struck twelve. 'A merry Christmas, my darling,' I said.

Ruth looked at me wildly, taking some time to place herself. Then she laughed and said, 'I've been dreaming about it. It's got a perfectly natural explanation. It was like this . . . No . . . It's gone. I can't remember it, but it was something quite reasonable.'

I sat with my arm about her. 'My love,' I said, 'I can think of a hundred quite reasonable explanations. For example, every man in the village for years has visited his Uncle Henry at Bodmin on Christmas Eve, taking wife, dog, cat and canary with him. The chap in this house is the only one who hasn't got an Uncle Henry at Bodmin, so he laid supper, lit the fire, and was just settling down for the evening when the landlord of the Lobster Pot thought he'd be lonely, looked in, and said: "What about coming to see *my* Uncle Henry at Bodmin?" And off they all went. That's perfectly reasonable. It explains everything. Do you believe it?'

Ruth shook her head. 'You must sleep,' she said. 'Lay your head on my shoulder.'

We left the house at seven o'clock on Christmas morning. It was slack tide. The sea was very quiet, and in the grey light, standing in the garden at the tip of the crescent, we could see the full extent of the village with one sweep of the eye, as we had not been able to do last night.

It was a lovely little place, huddled under the rocks at the head of its cove. Every cottage was well cared for, newly washed in cream or white, and on one or two of them a few stray roses were blooming, which is not unusual in Cornwall at Christmas.

At any other time, Ruth and I would have said, 'Let's stay here.' But now we hurried, rucksacks on backs, disturbed by the noise of our own shoes, and climbed the path down which we had so cautiously made our way last night.

There were the stones of black and white. We followed them till we came to the spot where we found the stone with the obliterated name. 'And behold, there was no stone there, but your lost pocket-knife was lying in the heather,' said a sceptical friend to whom I once related this story.

That, I suppose, would be a good way to round off an invented tale if I were a professional story-teller. But, in simple fact, the stone *was* there, and so was my knife. Ruth took it from me, and when we came to the place where we had left the cliff path and turned into the moor, she hurled it far out, and we heard the faint tinkle of its fall on the rocks below.

'And now,' she said with resolution, 'we go back the way

we came, and we eat our Christmas dinner in Falmouth. Then you can inquire for the first train to Manchester. Didn't you say there are fogs there?'

'There are an' all,' I said broadly.

'Good,' said Ruth. 'After last night, I feel a fog is something substantial, something you can get hold of.'

ONE THING LEADS
TO ANOTHER

I don't suppose you know what it is to be a girl like me. Suppose indeed! There's no suppose about it. You don't.

They talk about emancipation and all that, but I'd like some of them to live with my father for a week. They'd find out how emancipated they were!

When you're a kid it's not so bad, though it's not always a joke for a kid if it comes to that. Don't I remember when our Jack used to change at the Traceys whenever he wanted a game of football. He was in the school team and daft about the game. The team gave him boots and shorts and a jersey, and he'd change at the Traceys, play his game, go back with the Tracey kids to change again, and then come home.

All because games were sinful! When father found out and tanned him black and blue, Mr Tracey came round and told Dad to be reasonable. 'After all, Mr Loftus, we're not living in the middle ages.'

'A pity we're not,' was all Father said to old Tracey, and bawled to me: 'You come in, Carrie. I won't have my children making a playground of the streets.'

There was no other playground, I can tell you, but every Sunday afternoon we went for a walk in the country. We took the tram as far as it would go, wet or fine, and then we walked. Jack and I walked together, and Father and Mother walked about ten yards behind. Father always wore his bowler hat and Mother always carried her umbrella. They never spoke to one another, just marched side by side like soldiers, and Jack and I had to march like soldiers too. If we spoke in loud voices Mother would say: 'Don't shout!' and if we spoke quietly Father would say: 'What are you two conspiring about?'

Once Jack shouted: 'A thrush's nest!' and Father said: 'Never mind thrushes' nests. You're out for exercise.'

When Jack was seventeen and I was twelve, Father came downstairs one day and said: 'Who's been smoking in the W.C.?'

Jack said: 'Is it forbidden?'

I thought Father was going to have a stroke. Not that I knew anything about strokes, but his face went first red, then purple, and he looked as though he was trying to swallow something that was sticking in his throat. At last he said: 'That remark was a defiance, my boy.'

Jack said quietly: 'I just want to know where I can smoke, that's all.'

'You won't smoke as long as you are under my roof,' said Father. 'If you want to smoke you'd better not darken my door.'

Yes, actually those words in the year 1923! 'Darken my door.'

Jack took a packet of cigarettes out of his pocket, lit one and walked out into the passage. It was a fine summer evening. We heard the door bang, and Mother said: 'My lord'll be back soon. Don't worry about him.'

That's where she was wrong; and then they had only me.

As I say, I was twelve then; and when I was seventeen they sent me to a secretarial college. The first day I was there, Mother came as far as the door with me. Before we got there she had shown me where I must buy a pot of tea to drink with the sandwiches she had put up for my lunch. 'And mind you go straight back to the college, and don't talk to strangers.'

She was waiting for me when the day's work at the college was ended, and took me safely home.

I didn't tell her that I had seen Jack. He said he'd screw

my neck if I mentioned his name. But there he was in that café where I'd gone to eat my sandwiches. I walked in feeling very awkward because, say what you like, those places don't like people who order a pot of tea and then unpack sandwiches on the table.

I didn't have to do that, because there Jack was, sitting at a table not far from mine. He got up at once and came across and said: 'Well, if it isn't little Carrie!'

For a moment I didn't recognise him. He was beautifully dressed and had a small dark curling moustache, but I soon tumbled to him, and believe me I was glad!

'You come and eat with me and Doris,' he said, and he took me across to the girl who was sitting at his table. I hadn't known she was with him, and she gave me a thrill, I can tell you. Everything about her was just what I should have liked everything about me to be. But there! I had already begun to wear spectacles, and if I'd used rouge like her, Mother and Father would have thought I'd taken the wrong turning.

But Doris was all right, and even if I had unpacked my sandwiches I'm sure she would not have said anything. But I kept them out of sight, because Jack said: 'Well, what are you having? You'd better have it on me.'

So I had saddle of mutton and red currant jelly and all sorts of things, ending up with an enormous ice in three or four colours. You never saw such a thing. Jack said I had evidently been colour-starved. 'She'd better come round and see us some night, Doris,' he said.

It was only then that it dawned on me that they were married. It seemed incredible. Jack was nothing but a big boy when I saw him last, but there the wedding ring was on Doris's finger.

What a day! What a lunch! I seemed to learn one sur-prising thing after another. Now it seemed that Jack was quite well off. Doris was his boss's daughter; and what I want to tell you is this: Jack never did go home, I never did tell Father and Mother that I was seeing him, but I did see him and Doris and the two children they had in due course, and this went on for eight years.

Of course I'd finished with the secretarial college long ago, and got a job, and the joke was that I was Jack's secretary. Mother was just how I expected her to be when I said I'd been offered a post, and she insisted that she must see my prospective employer before I took the job. So Jack arranged for old Hunnable, his venerable white-haired father-in-law, to conduct the interview, and everything went off well.

Mother almost held my hand as we walked up the stairs and across the office to Mr Hunnable's room; and there was Doris sitting at a typewriter and pretending to be the old man's secretary who was sacked and working out a week's notice. She just had to come to see the fun and to hear Mother telling Mr Hunnable what a good home I came from and how I was unused to the temptations of a city life. She had on the most seductive dress and sheer stockings and lipstick.

'Please leave us alone, Miss Lavallière,' old Hunnable said to Doris, and she had to go, making a grimace at him behind Mother's back for this dirty trick in spoiling the fun for her.

'Sit down, Mrs Loftus,' he said. And then he sighed and pointed to the door Doris had gone through and said: 'I hope your daughter won't give me the anxiety I've had from that one, Mrs Loftus. I suppose a certain freedom must be allowed to young ladies nowadays, but really one must draw the line somewhere, and Miss Lavallière is too often inclined to draw it above the knee.'

Mother bridled at the mere mention of knees, and looked severely at my black lisle stockings and said: 'I've brought Carrie up sensibly, Mr Hunnable. You'll have none of that nonsense with her.'

'They begin well, Mrs Loftus,' said Mr Hunnable. 'But they develop. They develop.'

'Well, you let me know if there are any developments in that line with Carrie,' Mother said. 'I shall know how to deal with it. You remember, my girl, shorthand and type-writing are what you're here for.'

They were, and I had plenty of them. Jack earned his pay, and he made me earn mine. It wasn't easy at first to keep the secret at home, and one night when I blurted out Jack, I just managed in time to convert it into Jackson, and this Jackson thereafter was very useful to me. I told plenty of tales about him. He became a bit of a card; and I think Mother wished I had nothing to do with anybody but Mr Hunnable.

She often talked about him and told me how lucky I was to have such a fine old gentleman about the place; and she was never tired of saying: 'I bet he finds you a change after that slut. I expect she's arrived now where she was heading for. French! Well, a man who has a French girl in his office is asking for it.'

Poor Doris! By then she was the mother of Mother's first grandson.

But to come back to this independence they talk about. Was I independent? I was not. I had to account at home for every penny I earned and every hour I spent. Jack was always urging me to revolt. 'Take a little flat,' he used to say. 'You can afford it now. Don't darken their doors.'

That was all very well, but if I could afford a flat, they couldn't afford to let me have one, because Father was out of work now and I used to give them a pound a week as well as pay for my food. Perhaps I was a fool. Perhaps I wasn't. It depends on how you look at it. I'm not much of a one for leaving people in the lurch, even if you've got little enough to thank them for.

'Well, have a fling,' said Jack, twirling his moustache,

which was more luxurious now because he was altogether a more luxurious person. There he was at thirty, boss of everything. Mr Hunnable had retired, and I was no longer Jack's secretary but chief of a department. But I kept that to myself at home. Yes, I could certainly afford a little flat now.

'Have a fling and show 'em you're the boss,' said Jack. 'If they live on you, make them live on your conditions. Tell you what, Doris and I are going to the Derby on Wednesday. Come with us.'

I was horrified. Of all the things that made Father go mad, horse-racing was the worst. 'The lives it's ruined,' he used to moan. Anyone would think it had ruined his own life.

Doris joined her pleadings with Jack's. 'You'll never have a better chance,' she said. 'Give 'em a real shock. Tell 'em you're spending Tuesday night with Mr Jackson and going on to Epsom early on Wednesday morning. Because that's just what you're going to do – isn't it, Jack?'

'I hope so,' said Jack.

Well, there was Tuesday morning, and there was I eating a cereal breakfast food that was supposed to make you start the day feeling like Jack the Giant Killer, and all it was doing to me, because of my nervousness, was making me feel sick.

'You haven't got much to say for yourself,' Mother said. 'Something on your mind?'

She looked at me as though expecting me to confess the worst there and then; but I just shovelled the last spoonful of that food into my mouth and went upstairs without a word. My suitcase was packed, but I hadn't known till the last minute whether I should unpack it again or take it with me. Now I picked it up with sudden resolution and walked swiftly downstairs.

'I shan't be in to-night,' I said tonelessly, before my courage should fade out.

Mother dropped the morning paper and glanced across at Father. 'D'you hear that? She won't be in to-night! She just informs us. Daughters don't ask in these days. They just announce their intentions.'

Suddenly I hated Mother. I'd put up with so much from her. I'd put up with it for so long. Now I saw her face with a swift clarity that I had not known before. I saw that it was mean and spiteful and tyrannical.

'Well, I've announced *my* intentions,' I said, my voice all at once hard and controlled. 'I've told you I shall be away for one evening. Or would you prefer that I followed Jack's example?'

'Lot of good that would do you,' she sneered. 'I'd like to know where he is now. Wishing he could sneak back home, I'll bet. And you watch yourself, my girl. You remember that French piece that was thrown out of the office. You take warning.'

I picked up the suitcases and strode towards the door. 'And *you* take warning,' I said. 'I'm twenty-five years old. I'm more or less keeping a roof over your head. Any time hereafter that I want to spend a night out I shall do so. And any time that I want to follow Jack's example, I'll do that too.'

She got up and moved towards the door. For a moment I thought her life-long habit of tyranny would be more than she could now resist, and my mouth went dry. Then she sank back into her chair and I was outside. In the street I dropped the suitcase to the ground and stood still, panting. I could hardly realise it. I had won.

Believe it or not, that was the first night I had ever spent away from home, except holidays, when Mother was with me; and to be starting off in a motor-car at five in the morning, as we did the next day, was the sort of hare-brained adventure that I could never have believed that I would be engaged in.

But there we were. Jack said he wasn't going to be caught in the traffic, and we might as well spend the day in Epsom as in London. We were there by six, and the holiday, and the idea that I was going to see horse-racing, and the larks that were singing, made me feel so excited that I just couldn't keep still, but said I'd wander about for a time while Jack was finding a garage for the car. He showed me the hotel where I was to join him and Doris for breakfast.

Then I went strolling up the lane that leads from the town to the Downs, and I couldn't feel that this was anything wrong that I was doing (though I did think remorsefully of Mother now and then), and I felt more like fourteen than like a grown manager of a department twenty-five years old.

Right at the top where the lane opens out into the Downs I was rather alarmed because there were hundreds of men couched under those fine beech trees and the red brick wall. The sun had come out like a resurrection trump and they began to stir. There was a fine commotion round the frowsty tents and the canvas lean-tos. Fires blazed, bacon sizzled in pans, and the dudes among them were at it with razors.

There is a great trough there with the name of Cicero on it – not him that could talk the hind leg off a donkey in the Roman law courts, but the quadruped who won the Derby. Some of these bundles of rags and bones were sousing themselves in Cicero's trough, stripped to the waist, and I thought I'd better go on.

Then I stumbled on a heap that might have fallen off an old-clothes dealer's cart – round as a furled hedgehog, and it grunted as I once heard a hedgehog grunt that I kicked in a field in the dark.

'What the hell!' it said, and that made me jump and start to go on very quickly; and then this bundle unfurled and sat up on haunches and a set of very white teeth grinned at me through a mass of dirty whisker.

'Beg pardon, miss. No offence,' it said. 'Lookin' for an 'orse?'

I said politely that I was not looking for a horse; I was just taking a morning walk, thank you; and then he said: 'Made yer mind up, I suppose. Pasch! Everybody thinks it'll be Pasch. Pasch my eye! Don't believe 'em, lady. Don't waste yer money.'

He got up and came towards me combing his whiskers with long dirty fingers. I began to walk back towards the town and he fell in at my side.

'Listen to me, lady,' he said, 'and avert your eyes. Don't look at the sad wreck of the man I once was. Think of me in my prime. Think of me in silk, turning the scale at seven ten, riding the finest horses that ever flashed past the winning post out yonder.'

He waved his hands towards the Downs and seemed to be deeply moved. 'Stable jealousy!' he muttered. 'Stable jealousy was my undoing. Stable jealousy ended the career of as good a lad as ever bestrode a thoroughbred. And that lad is talking to you now. Epsom, Newmarket, Doncaster, O-ti and Long Shon: a flash of glory, lady, and then the end.'

I relaxed my stride a little and looked at him with sympathy. It seemed deplorable that a great jockey should come to this. I tried to imagine how he would look shaved and bathed and wearing a jockey's cap. He had the bow legs. 'Will you never be able to ride again?'

'Never, lady,' he said with conviction. 'All I can do now is to use my influence to secure information. I am selling this information for a contemptible price.' He began to fumble in his pocket and brought out some dirty scraps of paper. He whispered very quietly: 'What would it be worth to you to know the name of the horse that will win the Derby this afternoon?'

Now, honestly, I had never intended to bet. I remembered

what Father had said about that; but when I knew that I could actually learn the name of the winner my heart began to beat a little swiftly. He saw my hesitation and said: 'Would it be worth five shillings to you, lady? And, believe me, if this horse does not win I am prepared to meet you at this time and place next year, and repay your money.' He added devoutly, 'D.V.'

Well, I went back to Epsom, very excited, clutching my little piece of paper on which was written: 'Bois Roussel.'

'Keep it to yourself. We don't want a run on this 'orse,' was the last thing the little man said to me. But of course I had to tell Jack and Doris of my luck. They were waiting for me in a fine aroma of coffee and kidneys and bacon and new bread – enough to put anyone in a good humour, and the story of my lucky encounter seemed to make the cup of their joy overflow. They sat back in their chairs; they laughed and laughed.

'Oh, Carrie, my dear,' said Jack at last, 'have you never heard of a tipster? In a few hours' time you'll find hundreds of 'em willing to disclose the most Secret, Sacred, Inside Information for a shilling, sixpence, nay tuppence. Five bob really is a bit steep. We shall have to take this girl about a bit more, Doris, and open her eyes to the ways of this wicked world.'

'Yes, indeed,' said Doris. 'You keep off Bois Roussel, Carrie. If you're betting at all, put your money on Pasch.'

'Pasch! Nonsense!' said Jack, arresting a forkful of kidney half-way to his mouth. 'Scottish Union, my girl, Scottish Union. And where I got that from is where the *real* information comes from.'

'Yes, I know,' said Doris. 'It's where you got the winner of the Grand National from.'

Jack blushed, and poured me out some coffee. They continued to go at it, and I said nothing. I'd paid five shillings for my Information and I was going to use it.

What a scene it was when we got there! I'd never imagined such a thing: the bookies going purple in the face, the revivalists singing their hymns, the hot pies and ice-cream and the trampling, jostling, shouting people. Jack had got us places on a wagonette, so that we were high up over everybody's heads, and just before the race started we went down to lay our bets. Doris insisted on backing Pasch, and Jack put his money on Scottish Union. 'Someone's got to keep the money in the family,' he said. 'And what about you? D'you still insist on this supreme folly? Look at that,' he added, pointing to a man who was chalking up figures on a blackboard. 'Twenty to one, Bois Roussel.'

'What does that mean,' I asked, clutching the little scrap of dirty paper that I had kept all day.

'It means that if you put a bob on and *if – if*, mark you – Bois Roussel wins, you get back your bob and twenty more. In short, money for jam.'

I didn't hesitate. I stepped up to the bookie and said: 'One pound, Bois Roussel.'

'One *pound*!' Jack cried. 'You mean one shilling. A pound is what you get *if* you win.'

'One pound is what I said,' I told him. 'I've never betted in my life before, and I don't suppose I ever shall again, so I might as well make a good job of it.'

Jack led me back to the wagonette, and there were the horses cantering along to the start. I thought I'd never seen anything so lovely, and I hoped that the little man who had sold me the Information was not looking at them now. They would bring back too painful memories of his prime at Longchamps and Auteuil. 'There he goes,' said Jack. 'That's Bois Roussel. That's the graveyard of your hopes.' Oh, the lovely horse! The beautiful colours!

I wonder whether anybody else there felt as I did? I wonder whether racing people get bored and blasé? My heart nearly stopped beating, not with excitement, but

E.S.B. F

because it was so beautiful: that restless line of horses tossing the colours about on their backs, then breaking away into the frenzied race that thudded the earth and sent shivers up my spine.

How long does a race like that last? I don't know. It seemed to me at once endless and unendurably fleeting. In no time at all, Jack, who had his field-glasses to his eyes, dropped them and said: 'Good God! That horse has passed Pasch!'

He put the glasses up again hurriedly, and said: 'It's a thunderbolt! It's up to Scottish Union! It's beaten him – beaten him! Bois Roussel!'

Jack's was the only voice I heard shout the name. Everyone else seemed stricken dumb.

And I can tell you I was pretty dumb by eleven o'clock that night. We celebrated. I had never celebrated with Jack and Doris before; I had never celebrated with anyone before. Perhaps those who are accustomed to celebrations would not think that the dinner and the music-hall and the odd drink afterwards came to much. It came to a lot with me, and round about eleven o'clock it came to a realisation that I had a father and mother.

Gone now were my fine emancipated thoughts. Present only to my consciousness was the realisation that a good deal of the wages of sin remained in my purse – 'the lives it's ruined!' and that I wanted to go to sleep on someone's shoulder.

I was aware of Jack stopping the car at the corner of our street, of Doris putting my hat straight, and then of my key and the lock doing a bit of jig-saw work. The next thing I knew was that Father and I were sitting face-to-face in the parlour in a sort of mutual wonder and friendly understanding. 'She's gone to bed,' he whispered, pointing a finger aloft. 'Given you up for the night.'

My voice was a conspiratorial echo of his. 'Been to the

Derby,' I whispered. 'Backed Bois Roussel.' I fumbled my bag open and pressed notes into his hand. 'Twenty to one.'

He looked wonderingly at the money, then put it back in my bag.

'I wouldn't touch winnings on a horse with a barge-pole,' he said firmly. 'Look at me. Look!'

He got up and struck his chest. 'A free man once. What ruined me? Horse-racing. Nineteen hundred and eight. A long time ago, my girl. Talk about your twenty to one! A hundred to one! Signorinetta – the rankest outsider that ever won the Derby. I had a quid on her, and I wish she'd dropped dead on the course. But she made me a hundred pounds, and on the strength of that I married your mother. And I never had the courage to do what Jack did. You go on doing it, my girl. Keep it up. But don't talk to me about winners. Go to bed now. Want a hand?'

I managed without. But it had been a full day, and I dreamed that the little man with the whiskers had turned into Father who was dressed like a jockey and was riding Signorinetta hell for leather with Mother riding after him on Bois Roussel. The last I saw of them, they had flashed past the horse-trough labelled Cicero and were pounding down the lane towards Epsom. Then I woke up and I wasn't feeling too good.

SHE WANTED DIAMONDS

Of all the houses! Not even gas, to say nothing of electric light, in this year of our Lord!

Alice Forbes turned up the wick of the cheap tin lamp that stood on the dressing-table. It began to smoke, to smell, to smear the glass chimney. She cursed and turned it down again.

When you knew the house was going to come down, because it had been condemned as unfit for human habitation, you could understand that no one was going to bother to put in gas or electric light or anything else. But why did *she* have to live in a house that was unfit to be lived in? What did Myrna Loy have on her, anyway?

Now, if this were Myrna Loy's room, Myrna would come through that door, touch a couple of switches (if there were not someone to touch them for her) and the whole place would fill with a soft radiance. Although this was a bedroom, there would be a fire burning – fancy that! a fire in a bedroom! – and there would be no sound as Myrna advanced across the deep carpet towards the polar-bear skin spread before the fire. She would stand there, pensively tapping the fender with her foot as the firelight gleamed on the cold icy folds of her dress. The curtains would be drawn, and though there was so much light, it would all be filtering through silk shades. And there in the background would be the bed – immense, white, with silk sheets and a marvellously embroidered counterpane, and a switch so that you could put out the last light when you were in, and another that called a servant.

Alice got up from the bed whose mean covering was stretched over a straw-stuffed mattress. The lamp was smoking again. She cursed it, as she knew how to curse, turned it a little lower, and looked at the ghost of her face in a small inadequate mirror. She smeared the lipstick with her fingers, rubbed some powder on her chin – it was the devil how her chin would shine – and turned again to the bed. She thought she looked all right. She shoved the film-fan magazine under the mattress – Mum hated those magazines, 'putting ideas into your head' – and put on her cloak. It was plum-coloured, with a grey fur collar, cheap as muck; a shower of rain would ruin it. But, barring accidents, it would look all right.

She blew out the lamp and crept down the echoing wooden stairs. Dad and Mum were in the kitchen. Dad looked fagged out, poor old thing. She'd like to do something for him. He never jawed her, as Mum did. He had his boots off, and as he sat in a broken-down old wicker chair his feet were on the fender. Dad was always resting his feet. No wonder, tramping round all day with a little pan and brush, sweeping up the orange peel and waste paper and what the horses left behind. What a job for a man! She'd bet Myrna Loy's father would never have to do that.

Mum was at the other side of the fireplace, darning a pair of Dad's socks. He didn't half get through them! You could put a fist through the hole that stretched across Mum's darning mushroom.

'Well, and where are you off to, your ladyship?' Mum asked. She didn't say it nicely, either. Always surly. 'Why don't you stay in sometimes of a night and do a bit of darning or something?' That was what she meant. And you'll catch me doing it, Alice thought. You'll see me staying in this place that's been condemned because the walls are rickety and the woodwork's rotten, and that hasn't got so much as a bath.

'I'm going out with Joyce Sanders,' Alice said, hoping her attitude was full of easy nonchalance.

'Palley de Dance again, I suppose,' Mum sniffed.

'Right, as usual,' said Alice; and Dad said, taking his old clay pipe from his mouth with his twisted rheumaticky hand that shook a little: 'Let her get some fun while she can.'

'Fun!' said Mum. 'I don't know what they call fun nowadays. We didn't have that sort of fun when I was a girl – out till eleven o'clock or midnight. *And* we dressed according to our station. You can't tell a lady from a skivvy nowadays.'

You cannot, Alice thought, unless you see where they live. Put her in the right place – let her just walk across that bedroom of Myrna Loy's – and she'd look as good as the next. She pulled her cloak about her and wished she had orchids. She could carry them. 'You're the sort of girl who ought to wear orchids.' That's what someone had said to her. Never mind who. That was over now – the dirty dog. She knew his sort.

She tapped her foot on the fender, standing up very straight and tall. There was not enough light to shine on her lustrous hair; but it was lustrous and she had just sneaked time to have it dressed before coming home. She knew it looked all right, dark and shining above her dark shining eyes. Dad put out his shaking hand and stroked the cheap velvet of her cloak, wistfully. 'You look grand, Alice,' he said.

She could have cried about Dad. 'You go to bed early,' she said, 'and have a good night's rest. Well, Mum, I'm going. I've got a key.'

Joyce Sanders was waiting by the tram stop. The wind was blowing very cold, and Joyce was holding her coat tight about her body. Her flimsy pink dancing skirt was fluffing round her feet in the wind. Alice looked at Joyce standing there under the arc lamp as she came up. I like Joyce, she thought, but she's not a patch on me. Say what you like, she hasn't got what it takes. Can't you see she's a factory girl having a night out? Of course you can. I'll bet no one would know I was a servant girl just by looking at me. 'Hallo, Joyce! You look a treat.'

'Don't be so daft,' Joyce said. 'Do I look all right?'

'Absolutely Marleen,' Alice answered her, thinking: Poor Joyce! I wish she could do something about that awful skin. But there! You have to have a friend. It was safer to go about in two's.

The tram roared up, nearly empty. The conductor barred their way, grinning. '*Next* tram for Buckingham Palace, ladies,' he chaffed. 'This one's only for the boorjwassie.' Cheeky hound! He wouldn't talk to me like that if I wasn't with Joyce.

'Good night, chickens,' he said when they got off. 'Watch out for the foxes.'

Joyce laughed and waved her hand to him as the tram went away – the silly little fool. He was just her class.

In the ladies' cloakroom of the Palais de Danse Joyce powdered Alice's back. 'You do look lovely, Alice,' she said. 'D'you think I could wear a dress like that?'

Not if your back's anything like your face, Alice thought; and she said: 'Why not? Nothing like showing a bit of the real piccaninny to fetch 'em.'

'I don't think Albert would like it,' Joyce said.

You *get* your Albert before you begin worrying about what he likes and doesn't like. I've never seen him take you home yet, or bring you. Of course, you couldn't *say* a thing like that, but there's no harm in thinking. Alice leaned close to the mirror to give a final touch to her lipstick. And Albert, anyway! My God! Albert! Had you seen him? Yes, thank you very much.

Jasper Merridew's Hot Rhythm Boys were knocking it up properly. 'Come on,' Alice said, and they went out together to the floor.

The disk made up of red, green, yellow, blue and gold segments was revolving before the spotlight. It was lovely – just lovely.

There were a number of dancers there already, and the Rhythm Boys were making them respond. The trap drummer was all over the place – whang! boom! ping! – and Jasper Merridew himself was half turned to the dancing floor, his oiled curly hair shining, his white teeth flashing. He was the only man there in tails and a white tie. It wasn't often you saw so much as a dinner-jacket at the Palais de Danse. Mostly, the boys wore their Sunday best and dancing pumps.

The dance ended with a spatter of sporadic clapping. Albert Hopkins let go the girl he had been dancing with and came across to Joyce and Alice, wiping his hot forehead. He addressed Alice: 'These boys know it all. They had me yearning. How's tricks, kid?'

'It wouldn't be fair to play with you,' said Alice. 'I've got all the aces.'

'Just tell me what you want out of life and it's yours,' said Albert. 'Speak up, and don't skimp it.'

'I want diamonds,' Alice said, 'and all that goes with 'em.'

'I'll write to Barney Barnato,' said Albert. 'And in the meantime, I'll marry Joyce.'

'Not really?' Joyce exclaimed.

The silly little fool.

A flood of moony light filled the room, the band began to play a blues; and Albert said: 'Come on, Joyce. Leave her to her dreams.'

Not of you, anyway.

'Good evening. If it's not an impertinence to ask, may I have this dance? Sorry to burst in, but I don't know a soul here.'

Alice turned round very slowly. There was something in the voice. He was wearing a dinner-jacket! He stood there

with his hands in his coat pockets – you know that elegant
way, just the thumbs showing – legs slightly apart, superbly
at ease. She gave herself time to take him in thoroughly: the
stripe of broad braid down the leg of his trousers, the dancing
pumps, not cracked like so many of them here; the silk
handkerchief, with a thread of black in its white, peeping
out of his breast pocket. He was about as tall as she was,
but stouter, and there was an exciting foreignness in the
brown suffusion of his eyes and the crinkly lie of his hair.

Alice smiled and said: 'Delighted!' They moved into the
dance.

He danced excellently. A vague, almost imperceptible
scent exhaled from him.

I'll bet he's foreign, Alice thought, with a queer excitement. 'We haven't even been introduced,' she murmured.
'My name's Alice Forbes.'

'George Burnson,' he said in that voice that was hardly
above a whisper. 'Like to know something more about me?'

'Uh – huh.'

'I couldn't help overhearing what you were saying when
I was standing behind you, admiring your back.'

'I expect I was saying something very silly.'

'Not at all. You were saying you wanted diamonds.
Nothing silly in that. You and diamonds. Quite appropriate.'

He held her with a disturbing sense of intimacy, and his
voice suggested secrets between them alone.

'It struck me as queer, because I'm in diamonds.'

'You mean you *sell* diamonds?'

He laughed softly. 'I handle them every day.'

This was roughly true, for George Burnson was a pawn-
broker's assistant.

'How wonderful!' Alice murmured, picturing Mr George
Burnson running cascades of jewels through his hands, as
she had seen Ali Baba do in a pantomime.

'That was lovely,' Burnson said. 'Thank you.' He joined perfunctorily in the applause and led her off the floor. 'What about a bit of supper.'

'Oh, I'd love it. But you can't get much here.'

Mr George Burnson laughed softly, disparaging the ices and the coffee and biscuits which was all the Palais de Danse ran to.

'I didn't mean here. I could run you to a little place. My car's outside.'

He looked confident that he would not be refused, standing there with one hand lightly on her arm. She hesitated for a moment, thinking of Joyce. It was against the code to desert a friend. 'I'll come,' she said.

It was not a splendid limousine. It was a small open two-seater that couldn't have cost much second hand. But it was a car. Alice's cloak was not much of a protection in it.

'I'll drive very slowly,' Burnson said. 'You know, what you want is furs.'

Yes; that would be grand. Furs were one of the things that went with diamonds. 'I shouldn't have brought this old knockabout if I'd known I was having company,' Burnson improvised. 'However, it's not far, you see. Here we are.'

It bore the same relation to a fashionable restaurant that the car did to a limousine. But Alice didn't know that. 'I guess this is how Myrna Loy feeds,' she laughed.

'When she's lucky,' said Burnson. 'And I reckon when Gary Cooper's lucky he's allowed to take out a girl like you.'

'No, I don't suppose he'd ever take out a working girl,' Alice said. 'After all, I'm only a lady's maid.'

She thought she'd got over that very nicely. You had to tell a boy who you were and what you did, and lady's maid was near enough. Boys hated to hear that a girl was just a servant. And a daily help at that. Lady's maid suggested high heels and a little white apron, a rustling in a boudoir, gentle and delicate operations.

Alice ceased for a moment her task of polishing the big round mirror of Mrs Dugdale's dressing-table. She was pleased enough with her opening skirmish with George Burnson and unrepentant of her deception. The first vision of Burnson steeped in diamonds had faded, for she was a realist. She wondered what 'something in diamonds' might really mean.

She had got rid of him last night very neatly. Of course, he had wanted to take her home, and she had insisted that it must be only to 'the corner of the square'. He had dropped her at the corner of one of the great London squares, and then she had walked purposefully, as though towards an objective, till his two-seater was out of sight. Bus and tram soon took her home. They were to meet again in a week's time. 'And then,' Burnson had said, 'we'll go to a *real* place. Wear your furs!'

She did! Burnson met her at the corner of that fashionable square where he had left her a week ago. He had done a deal, and not for the first time, with his brother, the garage mechanic. Half a guinea wasn't much for the loan of a Bentley.

'And you watch what you're doing with it,' said Ike Burnson. 'I don't want to lose my job.'

'I'm putting money into your pocket, ain't I?' demanded George, whose speech deteriorated when he was not engaged in conquest. 'And I can drive, can't I?'

'If you keep both hands on the wheel.'

George grinned. 'They're both off when I want 'em off.' He waved airily, and drove to his encounter with Alice. There she was, and, by the lord, she was an eyeful.

When the car drew up to the kerb, Alice strove hard to be calm. She succeeded. It was not easy. She had had to make a lightning adjustment in her estimate of George Burnson. He had said, the last time they met: 'I shouldn't have brought this old knockabout if I'd known I was having company.' Nevertheless, she had expected to see the old knockabout once more – if he had not been obliged to sell it in the meantime. The Bentley sliding so silently to a standstill knocked her off her perch.

As if the furs themselves had not been enough of a problem! She had said she'd wear them, and wear them she would.

Mrs Dugdale, the widow who employed her as a daily help, had gone away for a week. Alice was the only servant. She had a key of the house and let herself in each morning.

She sat on her favourite seat, on the long stool before Mrs Dugdale's mirror, engaged in her favourite occupation: studying her face and dreaming of fantastic backgrounds for it. Then she noticed the safety-pin lying on the carpet under the mirror. She stooped to pick it up, knocked her head, in rising, under the long table on which the pots and brushes and bottles were arranged, and then said: 'Well!'

She hadn't known about that drawer. Whacking her head under the board must have opened it. She pushed it to, fumbled beneath, pressing with her fingers, and presently found the hidden catch. The drawer again slid slowly open.

Alice found that her lips were dry and her throat was throbbing. She left the drawer open and went on with her work. Then the telephone bell rang. Nothing unusual in that; but she jumped sharply, as though a policeman had suddenly put a hand on her shoulder and said, 'Now then, what's all this?'

She ran downstairs and answered the telephone. 'No, Mrs Dugdale will not be back for a week.'

She returned to the bedroom very slowly, her own words echoing in her mind. 'Mrs Dugdale will not be back for a week.'

She began to fumble in the drawer, and then she found

the necklace. She knew nothing about jewels, but she liked the look of the stones against her neck when she tried it on. She took out the box from which she had extracted the diamonds, dropped them into it, then shut the drawer. They were now outside, on the table, almost by accident, it seemed, but her cheeks were burning, her throat was dry again, and she did not look at herself any more in the glass.

She pawned the necklace that night. The next day, at Mrs Dugdale's, she did even less work than usual. She mooched about, now wondering what sort of fur coat you could get for twenty pounds, which was the sum she had raised on the necklace, now terrified at the idea of spending the money at all. So long as she had the money and could go back at any moment and redeem the necklace, she felt safe. She knew that it was the second step, spending the money, which would create a real chasm over which she might not be able to return. And she did not spend it. She suddenly thought of Mrs Dugdale's fur coat. She and Mrs Dugdale were much of a size. Just as the car belonging to some client of Ike Burnson's employer knocked Alice off her guard, so Mrs Dugdale's fur coat knocked George off his. He stepped from the car, raised his hat, and, taking a chance, kissed her. She did not resent it. They got into the car feeling very pleased with themselves and with one another. The taximan beating his arms across his breast at the corner thought they were a swell couple. He was no older than Burnson. He wished he could dress like that and drive round with a nice little piece in a fine fur coat.

If Burnson had analysed the situation at all, he would have said that the first encounter with Alice was reconnaissance, and the second one the occasion to improve to the full the situation which he had discovered to be favourable. The eating house to which he had taken Alice a week ago would not do this time. It must be the real thing. It was, in fact, a long way from the real thing, but it was as near to it as Burnson's imagination and experience could go, and Alice was more impressed than she would have admitted.

This, at last, or so it seemed to her, was what she had always dreamed about. This was something that could have been filmed, and she couldn't say more than that. There was a foreign waiter who took away Burnson's hat and coat, who pulled out a chair for her, helped her off with her fur coat and laid it reverently over the back of her chair. The carpet was soft; the lights were discreet; there was a band.

Burnson took up the menu. 'Will you leave this delicate operation to me?' he asked.

Would she not! It would have paralysed her.

They ate, and then they danced, and then Burnson ingratiatingly suggested 'a little run round'. There was a place, it seemed, called the 'Red Squirrel' where they might call in and have a drink. 'Not so very far,' Burnson said.

It seemed far enough to Alice, and when they had had their drink and gone on again London was a long way behind. Burnson turned the car off the high road. Then he brought it to a standstill, switched off the headlights and the light within the saloon. Alice switched it on again. Burnson frowned. Some of them were like that and some weren't. When they were, you played the diamonds trick. He had never yet failed to get the diamonds back. There was always some excuse: a new setting or what not.

He smiled and said in his suavest way: 'I was getting a bit tired. 'V'you ever driven?'

Alice shook her head.

'Takes it out of you at night. I thought we'd rest a bit.'

'Why not,' Alice agreed. 'We can rest with the lights on.'

'It's my eyes, you see. They get dazzled looking at the road. However, keep it on. There's something I want to show you.'

His left arm slipped round Alice's waist. His right hand slipped into the pocket of his jacket, and brought out an oval leather case. Expertly, his thumb pressed the catch. The lid flew open. Alice gave a little cry and the necklace sparkled in the dim light.

'I thought they'd please you,' Burnson said. Gently, he pulled open the neck of the fur coat and snipped the necklace round Alice's throat. She put up her hands and fingered the diamonds. 'I must see them,' she said, and Burnson noticed with satisfaction that pleasure made her voice husky. 'My bag. Where's my bag with the mirror?'

They both looked for it, Alice with increasing agitation. Burnson cursed under his breath. Blast the bag. Things were getting side-tracked. 'Are you sure you brought it?' he asked.

'Sure? Of course I'm sure. I used it in that Squirrel place. That's where I must have left it. We must go back at once. Every penny I've got is in it – my key – everything.'

'Oh, presently, presently,' Burnson grumbled. 'They'll keep it for you. Someone'll hand it to the manager.'

'What a hope. They looked a handing over lot to me. Come on now. We'll come back here.'

She flashed him a meaning smile and, mollified, he switched on the headlights and started up the engine. With one hand Alice held the collar of her coat tight round the necklace. The other unobtrusively closed upon the oval case that was lying on the seat.

The crowd at the Red Squirrel had thinned. The table at which Alice and Burnson had sat was both unoccupied and isolated. She marched swiftly towards it, Burnson at her heels. She spoke very quietly, fiercely and swiftly. 'Listen, you dirty thief. There was no handbag, or only a cheap one that I dropped through the car window. There's a waiter coming. Order drinks, and sit down, and keep your mouth shut.'

Burnson's face crumpled. He grasped a chair back, and she gave the order firmly herself. 'Two Martinis.'

'Drink them both,' she said, when they came. 'They'll do you good. You look as yellow as you are.'

He swallowed the drinks and looked at her, not speaking. 'I wanted you here,' she said in a low, intense voice, 'because there are lights and company. One slip up from you and I'll scream. So you're in diamonds? Like hell you are. You work in the pawnshop where you pinched this necklace.'

Burnson licked his dry lips and began to speak. 'Listen, Alice. I – '

'Shut up,' she snarled. 'Don't Alice me. I know because I pawned it. Even ladies need a bit of ready money sometimes, but they don't like going to pawnshops. They send their maids. Twenty pounds I raised for her on this. And now I'll tell you what's going to happen. When she gives the money to redeem it, I'll take a walk, put the money in my pocket, and go back with this necklace. Thank you for twenty pounds, Mr Burnson.'

Colour came back to his face. His hands clenched. 'You thief! You swindler!' he said.

'Not so loud,' Alice advised him. 'You know whether you can afford to shout. I'd like to know where a pawnshop assistant got a Bentley from.'

She watched the sweat break out on his forehead, and knew she had scored.

'I should get that car away quickly,' she advised him. 'As to the necklace, I must leave you to get out of that as best you can. I reckon it'll cost you twenty pounds, plus interest. You'll have to show the ticket, of course. I'll post it to the shop, addressed to Mr George Burnson.'

He wetted his lips. 'Bernstein, please.'

'It doesn't surprise me. Well, I reckon that's all. We'll walk to the door together for the sake of good form, and I'll wave you an affectionate farewell. And I shan't leave this place until the lights of your car have disappeared into the far distance.'

Bernstein put on his hat and coat. 'Blast you! Blast you!' he whispered.

'Certainly, darling,' she said in a penetrating voice. 'It's been a lovely evening. Harold has promised to pick me up.'

Harold turned out to be a lorry driver making for Covent Garden market. Alice, half asleep as they jogged towards town, suddenly laughed at the thought that she had played a real film scene without realising it. And everything was marvellous. Mrs Dugdale got back her coat and her jewels, and Alice got twenty pounds.

She thought of Dad, resting his feet in front of the fireplace that was nearly falling out of the kitchen wall. She'd seen some boots lined with lambskin. They did up with zip-fasteners. And she'd buy something for Mum – perhaps.

The lights slid by, mirrored in the shining tarmac.

THURSDAY NIGHT

Mind you, I'm not such a fool as I look. And, anyway, I don't think I even look such a fool as I did fifteen years ago. After all, I've had to exercise a certain amount of authority during the last five years. That sort of thing has its effect. When Mr Vicker's bell rings now, I go straight in with a smile. There's no one else in the department does that. I used not to myself. There was always that hesitation – you know, that sort of quick look round your mind for something you'd done wrong or forgotten to do right. But now I go straight in and say, 'Yes, Mr Vicker?' It's sheer routine.

And so I believe it's true to say my eye has a straighter glance – perhaps keener, even. I don't know whether my chin is firmer, or whether I only imagine it. But say what you will, promotion tells on a man, tightens him up. That might easily tell on the chin in time. We shall see. Mine had a tendency to recede, and my upper teeth protruded a little. Mind you, it was nothing much. Still, I wonder now and then whether it's a little better. It's not the sort of thing you could ask people about. But I was comparing a snap that Elizabeth took of me the other day with one she took at a choir picnic sixteen years ago. That was the summer before we were married. Looking at the thing as dispassionately as I can, I should say there was a shade of improvement.

I suppose culture tells too, in the long run. It may not make you beautiful. Look at the busts of Socrates, and he was pretty cultured considering when he lived. But it does give something, say what you will. It firms the face somehow.

And of course, during the past fifteen years I have gone in for culture a lot.

Don't misunderstand me. I'm not setting up to be any great shakes. I don't want to be considered a bigger character than I am. But then I don't want to be considered a smaller one either. It was fear of that that started all this business of Thursday night. I felt a man had to preserve his integrity, if you'll allow me to put it that way. Perhaps it sounds a bit pedantic. But what I mean is I hated the idea of being utterly absorbed by Elizabeth. You know what I mean. They have excellent intentions, these women, and Elizabeth's intentions were as good as anyone's. Don't think I'm saying a word against Elizabeth. But in those days I wasn't so self-reliant as I am now. I was twenty-five, and my looks hadn't hardened or firmed at all. My glance was very wavering, and it was through spectacles. Not that I mind that now, because after all the glance is the thing, and I think in certain lights spectacles give a sort of hard glitter that isn't at all unattractive. That is, if the glance itself is right.

But there it was. In those days it wasn't right, and that's all there is to be said about it, and the chin wasn't right either. Whatever you may think about it now – and I should like your honest opinion some day – it certainly was not right then.

And it was just because of this that I wouldn't let Elizabeth dominate me. It would have been so easy to slip under and, once under, should I ever have got up? After all, a man must have a certain *quality* if he is to see his weaknesses as clearly as I did, and then act to overcome them.

It was a novel I had been reading that opened my eyes. The author might have known my very case. The book was about a young man with limitless possibilities but no will to realise them. Then there came along a woman of great vital force. As long as I live I shall never forget the phrase the author used. Something about just as blotting-paper absorbs a blot of ink. I can't quite remember. But I made up my mind I must never be absorbed like that. That's what I meant about integrity. After all, a man owes something to his own soul. You can't get away from that.

Elizabeth was a typist in a coal merchant's office, but I'd be the last to hold that against her. She was a pretty cultured girl. She could read simple things in French like *Lettres de Mon Moulin*, and as for English, she didn't waste much time on the *Meg's Paper* sort of thing. She read real books, like things by Priestley and Walpole. And in the choir she could read music better than most of us. I suppose it was all these things that called to the best in me. Mind you, I hadn't gone in for culture much myself at that time, but the feeling for it – the call, if you know what I mean – must have been there, though dormant.

Well, it was one thing to be attracted by Elizabeth, but another to be absorbed by her; and from the start she showed a tendency towards absorbing me. The first time we were out together after getting engaged was on that choir trip when she took the snap. We went to Brighton, and then we all got on a motor coach and went up to Devil's Dyke. I had never been there before, and I'm instinctively touched by natural grandeur. I don't know how people can do any work at all, say, in the Alps. I should just stand there and stare with a lump in my throat. And that's how it was up there on the Devil's Dyke. That great plain, you know, rolling away at your feet, with all the little villages, and Chanctonbury Ring and all that, and the thought that it had all been going on age after age. You know, ancient Britons, and tumuli, and that sort of thing. I can tell you, I found it pretty moving, and I wanted to stand there and let the thing sink in, as it were, a sort of well, if you know what I mean, to draw on now and then.

Mind you, all this wasn't articulate. I couldn't have put it into words then if you'd paid me. Now that I'm forty, I can look back and analyse my own emotions. But all I felt then was the shock when Elizabeth put her arm through mine and started drawing me to one of those little clusters of furze bushes that grow there. It was pure possessiveness. It was an attempt to dominate me, to have me all for her own without any thought of the emotions I was feeling. I drew myself up and said: 'Excuse me, Elizabeth, I'll join you presently.' I allowed a decent interval to pass, just for the sake of form, though the spell was broken, and then I joined her.

I might as well not have done. She was not nice to me at any time for the rest of the day, although when we got to her parents' house in Camden Town she did ask me in to supper. But I refused – politely, mind you, for I am one for punctilio – and then I went to my bed-sitter not far from Euston Station and thought the matter over most carefully. I decided that I had acted rightly, went to bed, and slept soundly.

The next morning I was doing my exercises in front of an open window. Now, when I believe so deeply in *mens sana in corpore sano*, I find it difficult to realise the state of my mind then, when the healthy body was all that mattered to me. Anyhow, it is interesting to reflect that the simple exercises I did then, evolving them out of my own mind, are being advocated to-day by advanced thinkers. I don't want to overstress the point, but there again it seems to me *is* a point that goes to show I had the root of the matter in me.

Well, there I was, not completely nude, because I believe that even in private we should observe the decencies, but wearing only cellular shorts, standing on my hands with my feet resting high up on the door, and my eyes staring between my arms at a point on the opposite wall. I used to maintain this attitude as long as possible. It seemed to me to give poise to my shoulders, and I hold that a man who is about to become a woman's mate owes it to her to bring a fit body to the altar.

It was at that moment that I thought of the Thursday night idea. I came back to my feet with a slow rhythmic motion that I had taken some trouble to master, and sat down to look at it in all its aspects. I have since learned to do this with all my thoughts, but that was the first time when I consciously engaged in what one may call thinking scientifically.

The idea involved deceit, and for a long time that troubled me. Let me be frank with myself, because at my age a man should be able to look at his own naked soul. It involved deceit about wages, and also a deliberate lie. If I was not to be like that blot of ink in the novel, I must have one evening a week in which I could do just what I pleased, and I must have some small sum of money so that the evening could be profitably spent. So my scheme simply was to tell Elizabeth that I should be engaged at the office every Thursday night till ten o'clock, and when she inquired about my wages, as she was sure to do sooner or later, I should tell her that they were a pound a week less than they actually were.

Let me tell you frankly that a mind untrained in acute thinking, as mine was then, is aghast when a problem of that sort first crops up. Now I should have no hesitation in seeing at a glance the paramount claim of human personality which, after all, is the most important thing there is. Then I saw it more crudely. It was black and white. Could I tell Elizabeth a deliberate lie?

Once more, don't let me make excessive claims, but it seems to me that what are now modern methods sprang instinctively to my help. I didn't, of course, use the words they use to-day. I didn't call it seeking Guidance; but that, in effect, is what it came to. I was so agitated that I hadn't dressed. I knelt down by the bed in my cellular shorts. I always wore these, summer and winter, and still do, because aeration of the skin has a tonic effect. It braces the outlook. Fortunately it was a mild summer morning or I might have suffered from my temerity, for normally I am not the man to take risks with my health. I think health is *given* to us, if you know what I mean, and therefore we should regard it as something sacred. It was this instinctive piety that forced me to my knees and made me empty my mind, so to speak, so that if any whisper came I might humbly receive it.

When it did come, I was gratified to find that it was in accordance with my inclination, and that greatly strengthened me in the course I have been following now for fifteen years.

Being married, as they vulgarly say, though I don't much care for such expressions myself, isn't all pie. I think this is more happily phrased by the saying that there must be give and take. Elizabeth was never a one to give, and I should be ungenerous if I didn't at once admit that this has been in many ways to my advantage. Only the other day she calculated the amount she would have given to beggars in a week if she had heeded their importunity, and then she multiplied this by the number of weeks of our married life. It was an impressive sum.

But this is by the way, and I only mention it because of my habit of looking well round a question – a habit that has deepened since I took to expressing my thoughts on paper, rather surprising myself at a natural aptitude which I had hardly suspected.

It is rather the give and take of the mind which I wish to stress. In this Elizabeth shows no resilience. (I think the use of that word resilience, coming just there, shows what I mean about the knack of writing.)

Well, to begin with, there was the question of where we

were to live. I was an orphan. To be precise, I still am, and I regret it more and more, because, though I was nothing when my poor parents were alive, I can say now, in all modesty, that they would not be ashamed of their son. Both of Elizabeth's parents were living and her three sisters and one brother were living with them. They were anxious that we too should live with them after marriage. There seemed to me to be many advantages in this. We should save a certain amount of money; and, what is more, we should lead as it were a community life. I rather dwelt on this point with Elizabeth one Sunday as we were walking through Regent's Park, because the community to me seems so frightfully important. Mind you, I believe in the individual – in what I call integrity – but only within the corporate life of the hive, as it were. As it happened, there actually were bees in Regent's Park that day, and I was able to make the point effectively, because, say what you will, a practical illustration helps. Like the flowers and 'how we began' teaching in schools, which is all to the good. Pistils and stamens are a tremendous help and I shall not hesitate to use these enlightened methods if Elizabeth ever gives me a child.

But Elizabeth said bees had nothing to do with it: she preferred birds who set up in nests of their own; and she said this so prettily that I admitted that she had turned the tables on me. She said: 'A little bungalow out Harrow way would do me as well as anything,' and as a matter of fact (or *as a fact*, as a stylist would say) that was what we found.

We called it Chanctonbury, and it was a pleasing enough residence, with cretonne curtains and central heating and all that sort of thing. Say what you like about the suburbs, they are better than the slums, except that in the suburbs you have so much of this hire purchase business. We got Chanctonbury that way, and I can tell you it was a surprise to me at the end of the year to find that I'd paid off almost nothing at all. It had all gone on meeting the interest. You don't think of these things.

We had to cut it pretty close at first, but we managed. I was getting five guineas a week then, and of course I told Elizabeth it was four, because I had not weakened about the Thursday night scheme. I was working for Bildmat Limited (Cables, Bilma, Piccy), and that's short for Building Materials Limited. I used to have my cheque paid into my banking account every week, and I opened an 'A' account into which a pound went automatically.

We were busy at Bildmat, what with wood from Scandinavia, and steel from Germany, and materials for concrete, and made-up doors, and bricks, and everything. I was in the general office then, a pretty poor fish, I am free to confess, though marriage gave me a little spurt of confidence that permitted me to turn some of the crude jests that were made after the ceremony. I remember one chap used to chant: 'Where was Archie when the lights went out?' (Archie is my name, but naturally I sign cheques and letters and suchlike Archibald). Another clerk, who is now under me in the concrete department of which I am the head, piped up: 'The light wasn't out, fathead. Archie likes to see what he's doing, don't you, Archie?' Generally speaking I am not one for answering this sort of coarse innuendo. Silence is the best answer, but anyway I retorted on these chaps pretty shrewdly: 'In his own bed, young feller, if you *must* know, and his wife in hers.' For that was the simple truth. We agreed on twin beds from the beginning. I've never held any of this against these men, though they are now my subordinates. I expect them to call me Mr Tomlinson, but that's all. Generosity is a sign of strength.

It was a pretty lucky thing that we were so busy at Bildmat from the very beginning. On the first night of my return there after the honeymoon, which I foolishly spent at

Ramsgate, not knowing then the virtue of small and un-known places where one gets close to Nature, who, after all, is the great reviver. I brought some work home from the office. I need not have done this, but it was a pretty clever move, and it gratified me to find that my brain was cool and clear and able to handle the situation which I was determined to create. For, of course, Elizabeth said: 'I *did* think I'd have you in the evenings after being in that rotten office all day.'

I wiped my spectacles on a little piece of wash-leather that I carry in the case (*etui*, I think is the French word, and on the whole a more pleasing one) because experience has shown me that wash-leather was the best thing for this purpose. A handkerchief is so rarely completely clean. Well, I wiped my spectacles, which is a little idiosyncrasy of mine in a situation of that sort because it gives you an air of pondering the matter, and when you put the spectacles back it has a look of resolve. I did this, and then said, though with a smile to take the sting out of it: 'Rotten, Elizabeth? It would go hard with us if Bildmat were not there to provide our bread and butter.'

'I wanted to go into Harrow for the pictures,' Elizabeth said, and I must admit that she said it in a sulkier way than I liked. Still, I kept a firm hold on myself. For what it's worth, it does happen to be a fact that situations rarely run away with me. 'Why should you not go to the pictures?' I asked. 'You know, Elizabeth, that the last thing I wish is to dominate your actions. Because I have to work is no reason why you should not be enjoying those pleasures which a husband delights to procure for his wife.'

I meant that at the time because the pictures did seem to me then to be a rational form of amusement. But under-stand, please, that I am writing of fifteen years ago, and 'pictures' now mean the great works of our galleries. Elizabeth never grew up with me in these matters, but we found a way out of it when we got to know young Willie Walmsley. He was always willing to take Elizabeth to the pictures, and I could pursue my studies at home.

But that night she just said that going by herself didn't seem the same thing. Then I played my trump card. 'My dear Elizabeth,' I said, taking off my spectacles and wiping them again, 'this business of bringing work home will not trouble you after to-night. It has long been the bane of us Bildmat workers. But, as it happens, Mr Vicker has this very day found a solution. He proposed to the staff that, instead of taking bits of work home night after night, we should agree to stay on till ten one night a week. Everyone thinks it a splendid idea, and we have decided that the night shall be Thursday.'

'Well, I don't think it's a splendid idea,' said Elizabeth. 'If Mr Vicker has got more work than the staff can do, let him employ more men. The fat old miser.'

Mere loyalty to the community in which I worked forbade me to allow that to pass. 'That remark,' I said severely, though keeping heat out of my voice, 'is both unjust and in-accurate. Mr Vicker, so far from being fat, is a lean man, with a face sharpened by business acumen. If he employed more men, he would have to spread out the salaries of the rest of us, and where would Chanctonbury be then?'

It was not a very pleasant evening, and when we retired to bed (or, to be accurate, which is the first duty of every writer, to our beds) there seemed to be a great space between them. This was a psychological fact that often interested me – how far apart our beds seemed some nights, how near on others. I felt that it justified the experiment of single beds. Observations of that sort were beginning to interest me, a sign of the mind's awakening to something more than the surface of things, and I couldn't have made such an obser-vation in a double bed. I speak without actual experience, but I should say that on a cold night a man and woman would tend to cling together, however deep the mental or emotional cleavage. This would be to allow the mere body the upper hand.

In the morning a letter came on which I relied to put things right between me and Elizabeth. I had typed it in the office, and by a simple subterfuge which I need not go into induced the office boy to sign it 'J. G. Vicker'. Elizabeth, of course, didn't know Mr Vicker's writing, but she would see at a glance that this wasn't mine. After the boy had signed it, I typed 'Managing Director' under 'J. G. Vicker'.

Well, I read this, and then tossed it negligently across the table to Elizabeth. There it was, headed 'Bildmat Limited (Cables, Bilma, Piccy)', and it couldn't help convincing her. It read:

My dear Tomlinson,
    I send this grateful line to thank you for the way you supported my policy at the office meeting this afternoon. These changes are not easy to put through, but your timely and forceful speech helped, and probably turned the scales. I was struck by your touching reference to your wife and your certainty that, though you are but newly married, she would see this thing with a practical eye. Believe me, my dear Tomlinson, speaking as a man of experience, such women are rare. She must be a grand little helpmeet and I send her my heartiest wishes. Well, here's to many happy Thursday nights in the mutual service of Bildmat. Ever yours sincerely,
J. G. Vicker,
Managing Director.

I could see Elizabeth was touched. 'He seems very familiar with you,' she said. I wiped my spectacles and answered:

'There is such a thing as gratitude in the world, my dear.'
Then I hurried off to my train (North Harrow, Met.).

Well, Thursday nights were all right after that. Till then, I
had always hurried home to my bed-sitter and then gone on
to choir practice, or to meet Elizabeth, or done a bit of quiet
reading, though of course it wasn't the sort of reading I'm
now accustomed to do. But the idea of using the time to
develop my personality had never occurred to me before,
but that's what I had to do now. So when I left the office
at 5.30 I went to an A.B.C. and had a pot of tea and toast
and two boiled eggs and then I began to walk about the
town. It was a fine September evening, and I had a pound
in my pocket, but I didn't spend any of it that night.

The first thing you discover when you start on this business
of making something of yourself is how little you know, but I
would say to any young man who finds himself in my
position: Don't be discouraged. Persevere.

Of course, I may not have been a typical case. I have
already indicated one or two little things which suggested
talents that were there, though not awakened; but even
apart from this, I think anyone can pick up a lot of culture
in London.

Even I was a bit at sea that first night. I walked about
trying to look at the buildings with an architectural eye,
because it's all wrong the way beauty may be about us
and we taking no notice of it. Now, when I can tell at a
glance an Ionic, Doric or Corinthian column, it is pretty
appalling to reflect on the state I was in then.

I kept round about the centre of the town till dusk came
on, with an eye ever alert for the human comedy which we
take too much for granted. I watched the people going into
the theatres, arriving in cars and taxis. The women were
wearing beautiful clothes, and I said to myself that a wise
man would get beneath these things. (That last sentence, I

see, is open to what the French call a *double entendre*, but if anything else of that sort occurs in these lines, dismiss it. I am, as I have said, one for punctilio, and insulting women does not come naturally to me.) What I mean is simply this, that I felt there was something my mind should grasp beneath the appearance of these things. All these rich people, all these poor people: what about it? These thoughts were crude and vague, the mere beginnings of an awakening consciousness. Later on, when I joined the Left Book Club, I was surprised to find how many grievances an intelligent man ought to have that I had not been aware of, but I took care to counterbalance this by reading everything on the other side. I believe in a well-balanced mind.

When the theatre crowds were all inside, I wandered towards Hyde Park. It was dusky now, and the park seemed delightful. I had never been there before in the evening, and, keeping my mind alert for pieces of real knowledge, I was struck by the number of attractive young women who courteously wished me good evening. It made me feel jocund and debonair, and though one, whose cheerful greeting I returned, actually began to walk along with me in a friendly way, I made her feel at last that I was by nature a solitary.

And, curiously enough, I began to feel a great desire to be back with Elizabeth. This recurred throughout the weeks ahead, though with diminishing force, and at last my Thursday nights became the most precious part of the week. I was actually sorry when the time came for me to set off home. Mind you, I don't reproach myself for this. Man, after all, is a complex creature, and I don't suppose I'm any simpler than the rest. And throughout the rest of the week Elizabeth would get the benefit of the deepening personality within me. Women who try to dominate men don't realise that they are impoverishing their own souls.

But that first Thursday night I was seized with this desire, so I hurried towards the Marble Arch, listened for a while to the speakers, and then crossed the road to Baker Street. I used to find it impossible to walk in that street without thinking of Sherlock Holmes, but that sort of light nonsense was knocked out of my head when I began to read the great Russians. I read Dostoievsky and Tolstoy and all of them, and I think I got their message. Mind you, I don't claim to have entered into the fullest possible spiritual communication with them, but I did get the rough dominating idea – that things are pretty grim. I think we should all remember that.

Well, that night I hurried along Baker Street, foolishly thinking of Sherlock Holmes, and then I reached the station and was soon at North Harrow.

That was how those Thursday evenings began. Right through September and October I did no more with them than that: just walking about and letting the great stream of life flow over me. I didn't ever spend the pound that I had put aside, and as time went on I liked to think of that money accumulating there in the 'A' account. I'm going to step ahead a bit here, although I know I shouldn't. I took the Laureate School's course in fiction writing, and they were very down on any break in the continuity of a narrative. So I know that what I am doing is not orthodox, but a writer, after all, must trust his instinct now and then. After all, tradition isn't everything, though I admit the Laureate School is right to insist on it. It suits most people. But the exceptional man must break away now and then, so I'm going, as I said, to step ahead and tell you about that 'A' account.

After I had been married a year, Mr Vicker raised my wages by five shillings a week. One of those clerks who are now my subordinates said: 'I'd throw it in the old devil's teeth if I were you, Archie,' which is a typical instance of unreasoning passion at work. Don't think that I considered Mr Vicker was treating me well. Far from it, but I was not a very cultured man at that time. My increases of pay began to be on a higher plane *from the moment my own personality began to be on a higher plane*. I venture to underline that phrase. I think it is significant.

Well, I felt diffident about asking Elizabeth to accept that extra five shillings, because she might think it strange that Mr Vicker, who had written to me so familiarly, should give me so small an increase. So I had the money paid into the 'A' account.

A year after that, a senior clerk left and I was, quite justly, given his position. That carried an extra pound a week. Remember, I had now been married for two years, and I had enjoyed more than a hundred days – nearly four months – of untrammelled development. I was able to look at Elizabeth dispassionately, and, as I have said, she had not travelled with me. I had taken a grave dislike to the cinema, while her passion for it had deepened; and I was able now to compare the novels she read with those of the great Russian masters. With Strindberg too. We had got into the choir of the local chapel, and this interest in music was still a bond between us, especially when we were working hard, say, on a cantata. Then something of the old feeling came back. Don't misunderstand me. I still loved Elizabeth, mind you. I love her to this day. But love is deep and wide and embraces many a *nuance*, as the French would say, though I am not sure that those are right who hold the Latin races to be past masters in the art of love. I may claim to have some insight into the matter myself. As I see it, my love had now passed beyond mere passion. There was a comradely element in it, perhaps something even a little fatherly. I surprised myself calling Elizabeth 'Little Woman', and when she said sharply, 'Don't talk to me as though I were a child,' that startled me. It opened my eyes in a flash. When you've looked into psychology you see the hidden meaning of a thing like that. I *was* treating her as a child. My love was becoming fatherly, because I was mentally and, though I say this modestly, perhaps spiritually a generation ahead of her.

That was why I didn't give her the whole of that pound increase. I had five shillings of it paid into the 'A' account, and once I had started on that course I did the same every time I had a rise. I have had a few in the course of the last fifteen years, for Bildmat has flourished; and when I became chief of the concrete department five years ago the rise was something pretty substantial. Every time I put a good share into 'A' account, and now, even allowing for what I have spent on deepening my culture, there's more than a thousand pounds in it.

And when I say, 'What I've spent,' you begin to see that I wasn't always satisfied with just walking about and observing things. As soon as the autumn was over I began to make Thursday night a night for classes. As I have said, you can pick up a lot of culture in London for nothing. I began to look out for all the Thursday night opportunities. There was a series of talks on 'Counterpoint' in a Golder's Green chapel. I attended them every Thursday for six weeks, and then I found a course at Camberwell on 'The Great Composers'. There are plenty of free concerts to be had too, if you know where to look for them; and by the end of that winter I could tell Mendelssohn from Wagner with the next man. I could go into a room where music was being played and, without looking at the programme, say 'Mendelssohn' or 'Wagner' or perhaps 'Sibelius' just like that. And that's what a cultured man should be able to do.

It was mostly music that winter, and in the summer there were bands in the parks or hardening my muscles on the Serpentine for please don't think I had forgotten the part the body plays in making up the Whole Man. Then when winter came on again I concentrated on art. It's astonishing how many people there are talking on art up and down London.

E.S.B.   H

I heard all I could, and in my lunch-times I went to the National Gallery or the Wallace collection or looked at the picture shops in Bond Street. The Tate was a bit off the track for the lunch-hour, but I got there once, though Mr Vicker was furious when I got back ten minutes late. I explained where I had been civilly enough, but he merely said: 'Don't yammer. Where's that file?'

The National Portrait Gallery attracted me more than most, because the art there is combined with biography and I could fortify myself by looking at the men who had made good in other days. It was a profitable winter, and my only regret was that at the end of it I was not able to tell a David Cox from a de Wint as quickly as a fully cultured man should.

Naturally, I took these occupations home with me. They engrossed all my evenings, as well as my Thursday nights. Fortunately we became acquainted with Willie Walmsley at this time. Elizabeth often went to the cinema with him, and she went a lot to his house to play bridge. I don't want to disparage things which other people find attractive: I speak merely for myself when I say that a good deal of the time that goes on bridge could be better employed. But since Elizabeth wanted bridge, I was pleased she should have it with Willie. His father and mother were great players, and they made a four several times a week.

I like Willie. On his own plane he is an attractive character, though he gives more time to pleasure than a man should if he is to develop all round. He's rather like those men in the old melodramas: fair and blue-eyed and always laughing. They are supposed to be very attractive to women, but that of course is just the sort of idea that would derive from melodrama. In fact, a woman is attracted, even when she doesn't know it, to the character with the greatest magnetic pull. That's what these mere pleasers neglect: the magnetism of a deep personality. Not many people have seen the significance of that word 'must' in Tennyson's line: 'We needs *must* love the highest when we see it.'

Well, feeling like this about it, I wasn't going to dominate (save in so far as my character couldn't help doing it) the behaviour of Elizabeth. I allowed her a good deal of freedom. This year she has taken up skating at the Wembley rink. Willie skates very well, and fortunately he has a car which saves Elizabeth a lot of trouble. And, though I try hard to fight against the selfishness in my own nature, I have to admit that it suits me to be left alone with my books.

At least, it suited me. Because now we're up against a real point. Consider what I have been doing for the last fifteen years. Art and music, literature and astronomy, political economy and civics, modern languages and a dip into Latin, because I would be the last man to deny that the ancients have something to give us, though I am not yet quite sure what it is. Mind you, you can't have it both ways. I took a long course on psychology which has done much to give my mind the poise and quickness that I have kept in my body. I admit my eyesight is not what it was, and my hair is a little grey at the temples. Still, that is not unbecoming in a man of forty, perhaps the contrary.

But what I must face is this. I am a little fatigued. I don't take to a new subject with quite the leap that I used to know. This was very marked last Thursday, so much so that for the first time in all these fifteen years I suddenly resolved to go straight home. Rather to my surprise, I found Willie and Elizabeth sitting side by side on the sofa looking at an album of photographs. I had thought they would be playing bridge at his parents'. However, Willie explained that his mother had a bad headache and so the game was off. He had just come round to let Elizabeth know and had stayed to look at the photographs.

That just shows the value of a mind that waits to hear the evidence before jumping to conclusions. Though I have long given up reading trashy novels, I know that is just the sort of situation in which many a man makes a fool of himself through not waiting for a rational explanation.

'You've changed a lot more than Elizabeth, old man,' Willie said, looking at that old snap of the choir picnic. 'You're quite the senator these days.'

I think we are all too ready to take these things as idle compliments. I didn't see why I should. It seemed to me Willie was speaking the truth as he saw it. I should have liked to ask him about my chin, but you can't very well do a thing like that. I just wiped my spectacles on the wash-leather – that old trick has lasted all these years – then I said: 'Elizabeth, I must say, wears well.'

That, again, is the simple truth. Elizabeth is a handsome woman, dark, very slender and rather tall and three years younger than myself.

Well, that was some days ago and when I asked myself why I came home in that way I was forced to this answer: *The first part of my task is done.* I have given myself a cultured mind in a sound body, and *for what*? An instrument is worthless unless it is used. I have still to make up my mind in what direction to expend my force.

However, the Thursday nights are over. Before leaving the office I posted myself a letter which Elizabeth shall read to-morrow:

My dear Tomlinson,

As I informed the men this afternoon, Bildmat will no longer require the attendance of the staff on Thursday nights. I look back on these occasions – rather more in-formal, somehow, than our day-work – with genuine regret that they are over. The larger staff made possible by the increasing prosperity of the firm makes them no longer necessary. In all this you have rendered yeoman service, nor do I forget what we owe your devoted wife.

Yours, in all sincerity,

J. G. Vicker.

Please forgive that word 'Yeoman'. It is senseless. The Laureate School would have dropped on it at once; but it is the sort of word that Mr Vicker would use.

Well, this is the last day of the year, and here I am sitting in my chair at Chanctonbury. When I got in, there was a note on the mantelpiece from Elizabeth.

'Gone with Willie,' it said.

At first it seemed to me a little inconsiderate. She might have waited till I had had my supper, but I am not, after all, one of those helpless men who can't knock together a poached egg and a bit of toast. I have always been one for cultivating little practicalities alongside the big things. I expect they have gone to some so-called carnival somewhere or other. They went at this time last year. It makes them very late.

But it has given me a chance to write this record of an effort that I look back on with a proper pride. I am drawn to municipal work. On the whole, I think that would be a good outlet for all that is stored in me. I believe as deeply as ever in the community and work for the community. After all, there is a great need of trained minds in municipal service. Mind you, I don't disparage the work that is being done, but I am not the only one to remark the absence of men of deep culture from this field.

I suppose Harrow will soon become a borough. I should wear the chain with pride. Perhaps I shall grow a beard.

There is the question of time off, of course. I shall mention that to Mr Vicker to-morrow. A man of genuine patriotism would see the point. He may even regard the idea with pride.

It wouldn't be a bad thing for the office. 'Oh, meet Mr Tomlinson, head of concrete, Mayor of Harrow.'

Then there's that £1,000 or more in 'A' account. I should think that Chanctonbury, which is now paid for, ought to bring in a thousand, because, mind you, I haven't let the place decay. It's a pretty little property with a lot of improvements since I came here. The garden shows what horticulture can do in a small space when scientific thought has helped artistic discrimination.

That would give us, say, £2,000.

If we paid that down, without a building society load of interest, we'd get a house that a man could live in with dignity.

It's gone midnight now, but I don't suppose I'll see anything of Elizabeth and Willie for another hour. They'll be first-footing and all the rest of it. Well, things will be very different now for Elizabeth. And for me, too. Mind you, I'm not boasting, but it only shows you that a man can make what he likes of his life, and other people's too.

3.30 – Elizabeth not yet back.

MACHINE FOR LIVING

John Willie Barraclough stood at the window, looking down into Cheapside. Not Cheapside, London. Cheapside, Bradford, in the West Riding of Yorkshire. John Willie could both see and hear the tall trams laboriously clanging up the hill that was Cheapside. They ground round the corner by the Midland Hotel and then went hell-for-leather up the hill, as though fearful lest, should they stop half-way, they would never make it. That was one of the things John Willie Barraclough liked about Bradford. You couldn't go anywhere without clambering uphill or sliding downhill, unless you walked along Manningham Lane, or Valley Road, or Leeds Road.

'A good place, Bradford,' John Willie would say; and Sugden, his partner, always said: 'Ay, 'appen it is – for goats.'

They had known one another for a long time, had John Willie Barraclough and Eli Sugden. They had been in a weaving shed together when boys, and they had been partners for more than thirty years. Barraclough and Sugden, Manufacturers, it said on the brass plate fixed to the smoke-blackened front of their premises.

Nearly every morning from ten to eleven you would find John Willie and Eli in the Beanstalk Vegetarian Café; not that either of them was a vegetarian, but the Beanstalk happened to be the place where the best coffee was to be had and where the connoisseurs of dominoes forgathered year in, year out. Buried in a great desert of towering warehouse blocks, approached over roads where stone setts were so worn, so ground into grooves, so shiny on wet days, that they looked like the primeval setts first laid down when God said, 'Let there be Bradford!' The Beanstalk Vegetarian Café with its glowing fires, its old-fashioned upholstered benches, its private nooks, its ineradicable flavour of good coffee and good tobacco, was the very soul and centre of comfort, well-being and good fellowship to all its frequenters. You could give John Willie the Athenaeum and Brooks's with the Café Royal and the Monseigneur thrown in, and he would say: 'Ay, Ah reckon nowt to the likes o' them places. Give me t'owd Beanstalk.'

He was a somebody in the Beanstalk; and, if it comes to that, he was a somebody in Bradford. He had been President of the Chamber of Commerce and of the Liberal Club; he was the sort of man the *Yorkshire Observer* interviewed when it wanted views on what the Budget would do to the wool trade.

John Willie considered the trams charging up the hill, considered the grey, lowering sky that seemed to press down upon the railway station roof from which only the road and the trams separated him. 'Ah reckon there'll be snow before t'morning, Eli,' he said.

' 'Appen there will, an' then,' Eli answered listlessly.

John Willie swung back into the room, stood with his back to the fire, and considered the face whose every hair and wrinkle he knew as well as his own.

'What's ailing thee, lad?' he said. 'Tha's taciturn.'

Eli Sugden fiddled with a ruler, drew random lines on a scribbling pad, and at last answered: 'Anno domini, John Willie – that's what ails me. Ah'm goin' to chuck it oop.'

For a moment John Willie was too flabbergasted to answer. Then he sat down at the opposite side of the 'partners' desk' and said earnestly: 'Coom now, lad; don't be damn soft. Tha's nobbut a year older'n me.'

'Nay, it's no good,' Eli answered. 'Ah didn't choose this, John Willie. It's been shooved on me. Doctor's orders.' He laid a hand dramatically on his heart. 'It's there, lad. She's missing too many ticks.'

John Willie Barraclough looked wonderingly on Eli Sugden with whom, for so many years, he had done so many things.

'That's a reight rum 'un,' he said. 'To think o' thee wearin' out, Eli.'

'Ay,' said Eli. 'It cooms – an' then.'

'Ay,' said John Willie, 'it does.' He got up and reached for his hat and overcoat. 'Well, Eli,' he said with a false heartiness. 'Us'll talk it ovver in t'mornin'. 'Appen thi doctor's mistaken.'

' 'Appen 'e isn't,' said Eli. 'I know t'owd ticker better than 'e does onny day.'

John Willie pulled his coat collar up round his ears as he stepped out of the dark passageway into Cheapside. The cold was bitter. The sky was low and black and seemed overcharged. Even as he turned up his face to look at it, the first light snowflake fluttered down and caressed his cheek. He turned into the great open space of Forster Square. It was like a pool into which all the hilly streets that centred there poured the tramcars that now congested it. All over the square people were herded like sheep in iron pens, waiting for the trams, and the snow began now to fall upon them thickly.

John Willie's home was less than a mile from where he stood, but he never walked it nor went by tram. He entered the Midland railway station whence, infrequently, he set out for London, and never with any diminution of a tense, childlike expectancy. But he wasn't going to London now: he was going to Manningham, the first station along the line.

The journey occupied about two minutes, and John Willie always travelled first class.

He just had time to open his *Argus* before the train was pulling up at the station. He was not surprised to see his daughter's photograph: 'Miss Enid Barraclough, an exhibition of whose oils and water-colours will be opened at the Crewe Hall on Thursday.'

This was Tuesday. Enid would be coming up from London to-morrow, John Willie reflected, as he stuffed the paper into his pocket, turned out of the dingy little station, and trudged up the steep road where for thirty years he had lived. To-morrow: he must let Mrs Bairstowe know about that, so that she could get the bedroom ready.

The snow was falling heavily now. The road was white. The boys would be coming soon with their toboggans to hurtle down it from top to bottom. Eh, it was a grand place to live in, was Bradford, he reflected. Winter sports in every side street off Manningham Lane. He and old Eli Sugden had done their share of it fifty years ago.

He stood for a moment at his gate watching the flakes falling through the light of a street lamp and settling on the black twigs that clawed up from the sooty trees. Then he pushed the gate open and walked soundlessly over the snow up the cunningly twisted path that led through rhododendron bushes to the door of Throstle's Nest.

It was a massive, monumental house, built of stone that the years had blackened beyond redemption. There were big flat windows on either side of the heavy porch, and an attic storey was above the two floors. It often occurred to John Willie that it was an immense place for an ageing widower who lived alone. John Willie junior had never been troubled by Anno Domini. Arras, 1917, had done for him and a lot more of the West Yorkshires; and his mother had not long survived him. Enid, a late-born child, was only seven then;

and now she, too, had been gone for five years. Mrs Bairstowe and John Willie often talked about Enid, and John Willie had never seen the point of that buzzing off to London. 'All these careers for women, an' Lord knows what all,' he grumbled. 'Nay. Ah reckon nowt to it.'

But there it was. Throstle's Nest was not what it had been when young John Willie had been barging in from the Grammar School, and Enid had been mewling in a pram, and he and Edith would spend a whole month arguing about where to go for the summer holidays; and then go to Morecambe again. But he could never persuade himself to give up Throstle's Nest, just because all those things *had* happened in it, and because Captain J. W. Barraclough, M.C., had spent his last leave there, and because Edith had given the place its name. Proud she had been of it, as any girl might be who had worked at Manningham Mills and then found herself running a house with stables at the back.

John Willie put his key in the lock, pushed open the door, and breathed in the deep satisfaction that his home never failed to give him. 'Solid Coomfort.' It was a fine spacious hall with a fire crackling on the hearth. He liked that – for his visitors as well as for himself: a fire to hit you in the eye as soon as the door was opened. Welcome. The house was very quiet. It felt warm through and through. John Willie threw his hat and coat on to a chair and was chafing his hands at the fire when a parlourmaid, trim as a little yacht, sailed up to him with a telegram on a salver. He hated such finicky ways. 'Why can't she just hand damn thing to me,' he thought, but Mrs Bairstowe knew all that was to be known about such matters.

John Willie tore open the telegram, and then raised a great shout: 'Mrs Bairstowe! Mrs Bairstowe!' and as the housekeeper came unhurriedly from her room: 'Our Enid's comin' home to-night – not to-morrow – to-night. "Bringing Denis", she says. Oo the heck's Denis?'

'We shall see,' said Mrs Bairstowe safely.

'We shall an' all. Get rooms ready. Ah'll go an' wash misel.'

John Willie sat in his bedroom, with his back to the big double bed in which Edith had died. He still used it. Here, as in the hall, a fire was burning. Solid comfort. He believed in it. Edith's photograph, and Enid's photograph, and Captain J. W. Barraclough's photograph, with a few ribbons on the tunic, stood on a chest of drawers.

'Photos, nowt but photos now,' he said. ' 'Appen I'd better get one of Eli Sugden.'

He stood there kicking at a large piece of coal when Enid tapped at the door and came in. She lifted the curtain and peeped out at the snow wuthering through the dark. 'Thanks for the fire in my bedroom,' she said.

'Tha needs it a night like this,' said John Willie. 'Thi young man's got one, too. Tha's looking bonny, lass. Is it for him or me?'

The firelight gleamed on Enid's burnished hair and on the burnished satin of her clinging dress. ' 'Appen for both of you,' she said, provoking him.

'Ah don't reckon much to him,' said John Willie. 'A long stick o' nowt.'

'You wouldn't, would you?' said Enid, laying on his shoulder a long hand with fingernails stained and lacquered. 'You'd like me to marry a big jannock lad, smelling of tops and noils. Whatever they are. I never could learn about your old woollen trade.'

She tapped a cigarette on her nail, and John Willie gave her a light. 'What's tha mean,' he said, 'marrying? Tha can't marry a man I've never seen or heard of. Who is he, onny road?'

'He's Denis Thompson, and he's going to be a very famous architect.'

'Just by hoping to be, like?'

'No. Now don't be Northern and pig-headed, Daddy. Denis works just as hard as you do; and he doesn't spend half of every morning in the Beanstalk Café.'

'Hey!' shouted John Willie, 'you leave Beanstalk alone, lass. There's many a good stroke of business done over the bones. That's business-men's cloob, that is.'

Enid stroked his hair, which was very white and getting thin. 'I don't want to do you out of your old dominoes,' she said soothingly. 'Take a box with you when you retire. You'll find some crony to come in and play with you.'

John Willie's whitey-yellow Viking moustache bristled with annoyance and his gold-rimmed spectacles flashed in the firelight. 'Retire!' he cried scornfully. 'Me retire! Tha's talkin' daft, lass. Oo'd run Barraclough and Sugden – with Eli Sugden crocking up too! There's a bit o' news tha's not heard. Eli's heart's gone wonky. 'E's chucking oop.'

Enid pulled up a footstool and put it alongside her father's chair. She settled herself at his feet and took his hand in hers. 'There, you see,' she said. 'That's what comes of going on too long. Why don't you give it up, Daddy? Give it up now, while you've still got a chance to enjoy things. Go and live away in the country – out at Ilkley or somewhere. That's what I came home to ask you. You will, won't you?'

'Well, of all the interferin' – Look 'ere, my lass, oo d'you think's goin' to keep you if I retire, eh?'

'Oh, you're all right,' said Enid comfortably. 'You can't pull off that stuff with me. You're a warm man. You could retire to-morrow and still my allowance wouldn't be a fleabite to you. But the point is, I shan't want it, any-way.'

'Not want it! Tha's daft, lass. I never knew a woman yet who didn't want all she could lay her fingers on. Oo's goin' to keep thee? An' it costs a pretty penny by the looks o' thee to-night.'

'Denis will keep me.'

John Willie laughed harshly. ' 'Im!'

'He made three thousand last year.'

'Ee – well – that's talkin', that is,' said John Willie.

'I thought it would be,' said Enid. 'Come on, now. Let's go down. And you turn over what I've been saying about retiring. Denis will design you a lovely house.'

'That's a good bit o' mee'ogany, that is,' said John Willie, smiting the massive dining-table. 'Lasted fifty years an' good for another five 'oondred.'

'But who wants a table to last five hundred years?' Denis demanded. He was a damn talkative young man, John Willie decided; a young man with a devilish self-confident grin, and red hair cropped as close as the grass on a lawn. His ears stuck up in aggressive points, and he talked twenty to the dozen, his thin face pale.

'Take this house,' he said. 'Whoever built it had the same idea that you've got about tables. Built to last. It looks like a cavalry barracks. Every intelligent idea in architecture for the last hundred years has passed it over. Just because it's built to last. A house shouldn't be built to last. A house should be a machine for living. It should be capable of change as ideas in living change. Look at your great fire-places, belching out smoke as though this whole filthy town weren't already blackened like a high road to hell.'

' 'Ere, 'ere, 'arf a minute,' said John Willie, 'wot's all this about a machine for livin'? When you've lived as long as I 'ave you'll know the only machines for livin' are men and women. An' this 'ere 'ouse is wot it is because it's *me* – see, *me* as lives in it. Every stick an' stone of it is built into me, an' I'm built into every stick an' stone of it. Don't you lay your 'ands on it, lad.'

He glared at Denis Thompson as though that pushful young modern were taken in the very act of pulling the place down stone by stone. He hurled a cigar-case across the table.

'Tak' one o' them, an' listen to me. This is *my* machine for livin', see. On that door you'll see marks me an' Edith drew when young John Willie and Enid was growin'. An' over the fireplace there's a photo o' Morecambe that looks daft to you, no doubt. But not to me, because it means summat. An' on that sideboard there's a wine-glass without a stem. See it? Chook it away, says you. No. Let it stay there. I smashed that one day when I let out a clout at young John Willie. It were only time I ever laid 'ands on 'im, an' I can see t'pain an' woonder in 'is eyes now. Ah went oopstairs an' cried an' never laid 'ands on 'im again. That's what wine-glass means. An' everything in the 'ouse means summat. The very stones in t'path mean I've trod 'em 'ollow day in, day out, for thirty years. All you can build, mi lad, is a 'ouse. It's you and me, an' the likes of us, as makes it a machine for livin'. An' sometimes it don't 'appen at all.'

Denis pulled negligently at his cigar. 'Oh, come, sir, that's the romantic view.'

'An' don't call me sir,' said John Willie savagely. 'That's one of the things I like about Bradford. We've got none o' that bunkum. Put on your 'at an' coom with me. I'll show you summat.'

They climbed the white silent hill of the street. The snow was no longer falling. In Manningham Lane they got on to a tramcar which landed them on the cold heights of Heaton. John Willie knew his spot well. He often came there on a bright starry night, or on such a night as this. He led Denis Thompson over the dumb snow till infinity stretched before them. The ghostly landscape slid away from their feet down to the valley which was sown with lights. Then beyond the valley it lifted itself to the heights of Idle and Eccleshill, and from that point to the right and to the left you could see the necklaces of light where the great roads ran, looping and climbing and twisting upon the face of the hills. And beyond those hills were other hills, their lights receding and receding till you seemed to be gazing upon a universe of stars, bright major planets and dwindling stardust set in due order in one stupendous harmony.

'An' beyond what you can see,' said John Willie in a vibrant voice, 'there's Baildon Moor, and beyond Baildon Moor there's a great moor stretching on to Ilkla, and there's as much as you want beyond that.' He looked for a silent moment at the pallid land lit with its wonder of stars; then added: 'Them's the Yorkshire hills, mi lad. Built to last.'

Denis crushed a cigarette butt into the black wall on which he leaned. 'I wonder,' he said.

'You don't,' cried John Willie. 'You don't woonder. That's what's the matter with all of you. You don't know what woonder is.'

In the morning the snow was sludge. John Willie, with stout goloshes over his shoes, squelched through it from the station to Cheapside. Eli Sugden was not in the office. The partners' room seemed desolate, and when the moment came at which he was accustomed to go to the Beanstalk Café, John Willie felt low and dispirited. He didn't go. He sat there staring at a few letters on his desk, taking up this and putting down that. He would have telephoned to Eli but, like himself, his partner would not have the telephone in his house. When he was at his most desperate, Marsden the manager came in to say that Mr Sugden was in a taxi downstairs, and would Mr Barraclough go down to see him? John Willie hustled into his overcoat, seized his hat, and ran down to the street.

'Mornin', John Willie. 'Op in,' said Sugden; and to the driver: 'Beanstalk.'

John Willie rubbed his hands gleefully. 'Well, Eli, what's t'meanin' of this, lad?' he asked.

'It means Ah'm not climbin' thi damn stairs any more,' said Eli. 'Doctor's orders.'

'But there's stairs at Beanstalk.'

'That's another matter. Doctor said nowt about them.'

Over the dominoes he said: 'Ah'm goin' for a cruise. That's latest. A long cruise lastin' all winter. Tha's better join me, owd lad. Ah reckon yon Marsden can mak do till we're back.'

'Tha's not serious, Eli?' said John Willie.

'Never more so,' Eli answered. 'What dosta do, when all's said an' done, but sit on thi behind and pretend to run a show that Marsden and the clerks is runnin' for thee?'

'There's summat in that,' John Willie assented.

'Well, then,' said Eli, 'what's to stop thee?'

'Nowt,' said John Willie.

'Well, we'll get our tickets, an' then.'

Enid and Denis spent the day arranging the show of pictures in the Crewe Hall. They came home through a raw sleety night to find John Willie trudging restlessly up and down the drawing-room. 'Ah, so tha's coom,' he exclaimed. 'Well, Ah've got some news for thee, lass. Ah'm goin' to tak' thi advice.'

'That *is* news,' said Enid.

'Not altogether, mind 'ee,' John Willie added. 'Ah'm not sayin' Ah'll chuck it altogether. But Ah'm goin' round t'world. With Eli Sugden.'

He stood there with his back to the fire, his thumbs in his waistcoat armholes, and a cigar sticking jauntily out of his mouth. He looked at her defiantly; and she could not resist something overwhelmingly comic about him. She broke into a peal of laughter.

'Go on,' he said, 'laugh. But tell us what tha's laughin' about. What's funny?'

'You and Eli Sugden. You'll never do it. You'll never get

out of England. You'll never get out of Bradford, wherever you are.'

'Ay, an' there's summat in that, too,' he conceded. 'Ah don't reckon these 'ere foreign places'll 'ave mooch to show me. Ah wouldn't be goin' at all if it wasn't for Eli. No, not a yard out of Throstle's Nest.'

'Don't you take any notice of me, Daddy,' Enid soothed him. 'You go. You've earned it. And when you're away, think of what I said last night. Give it up altogether. Denis and I have been talking about you to-day. Haven't we, Denis?'

'We have that, sir. Making some grand schemes for you.'

'A little house, Daddy. What do you say to that? You don't want to go on living in this great place, plumb in the middle of all the dirt and smoke. What about a nice little house – say at Ilkley?'

John Willie scratched his head doubtfully; then conceded: 'Well – Ilkla's none so bad. Theer's t'moors an' a good train service. An' 'Enry Moscrop lives there. Ah like 'Enry.'

'There!' said Enid triumphantly. 'Denis said we'd have to push and push all night, and now I feel a slight stirring at the first shove.'

'Go an' change thi dress for dinner,' said John Willie. 'There's too mooch o' thi moother about thee.'

So when he and Eli Sugden set out on their memorable journey, it was understood that Denis Thompson was to design and build a house for John Willie Barraclough, the place to be ready when the voyage ended in the spring. All through that voyage Enid received not a single letter, but from here and there a postcard.

'I don't reckon much to this place. Going on soon,' he wrote from Kingstown, Jamaica; and next there came a card from San Francisco, comparing the place unfavourably with Morecambe. From Hawaii his sole communication was:

'Eli Sugden much better,' on a card portraying girls wearing a little grass; and from a Japanese port he vouchsafed the information: 'English consul here knows a Bradford man.' There was a card from Sydney, which said: 'This place is in Australia, where the wool comes from.'

And as John Willie Barraclough and a renewed Eli Sugden crept northward towards India, the house at Ilkley was rising in grand style, to the consternation of the town's soberer inhabitants and to the great joy of Enid and Denis. It was all very well, Denis argued, for John Willie to decry the modern 'Machine for Living'. He had never seen the sort of thing that was in Denis's mind. Once he saw it, he would be convinced, as every intelligent person must be convinced, that here was the only sort of house for any reasonable being to dwell in.

On a day in early April Enid came up to Ilkley in response to a telegram saying that everything was now ready for inspection. From rising ground they looked down upon the house standing in its small garden: upon its flat roof and wide expanse of glass, its polished steel in place of stone mullions, its walls of pink concrete. They went inside and inspected the electric switches in the kitchen, the lighting flush with the walls everywhere, the chromium book-shelves, the chairs of red leather and twisted steel. In each room one picture was posed over the electric fire, which, like the lighting, was flush with the wall. The hardwood floors were sparsely carpeted, and the carpets were covered with quaint designs, like mottoes in shorthand.

'Rather gorgeous, this, I think,' said Denis, when they came to the dining-room. He patted the table approvingly, loving with his fingers the smooth glass of its surface, and indicating, with the touch of a switch, how the light shone through it, bringing out a pattern of zodiacal signs that were lightly engraved.

Enid stood dumb. 'You like it?' he asked.

'Oh, yes. I like it, but somehow I can't see Father eating from it.'

'You don't have to,' said Denis. 'We shall have our flat in town, and personally I prefer antiques. But as an experiment – pretty nifty – eh?'

'Yes,' said Enid faintly; and added: 'You've still got before you the experiment of getting a cheque out of Daddy for this.'

John Willie, weather-browned, and looking as tough as hide, thought Throstle's Nest had never been more enchanting than that morning two days after his return when he stepped out of the front door accompanied by Enid and Denis. The black branches of the trees were decorated with green, tender shoots, and among the rhododendrons a few daring daffodils were blowing trumpets. Eh, it was good to be back in Bradford after all those daft foreign towns.

He was in high spirits all the way to Ilkley, and only when Denis had cunningly led him to the point whence he could look down on the new house did his spirit receive a shock. He looked at the thing with its bright pink icing, and said: 'Eh, Ah don't know about Ilkla after all. Not if that sort o' thing's goin' on. Ah don't like that on Yorkshire moors. It's like confetti on your moother's grave.'

'That's the new house,' said Denis weakly. 'You see, sir, the point about it – '

'Give me t'key,' said John Willie firmly. 'Now, you two, stay 'ere. Ah'll inspect this alone.'

He strode off down the hill, and Denis and Enid sat on a lichened boulder and watched him disappear through the front door. He returned in half an hour, carefully lit a pipe, and inquired with a backward nod of the head: 'And 'ow mooch did that lot cost?'

'It's very moderate, sir,' Denis answered. 'The whole thing, all in, furniture and everything, five thousand.'

'Five thousand, eh?' said John Willie. 'Now isn't that strange, lass? That's joost t'sum Ah was goin' to give thee for a wedding present. Ah'll write thee a cheque right away.'

He did so, using the boulder for a table.

'Theer!' he said. 'It's thine. It'll mak a nice little place for week-end parties. Ah don't like it. Ah don't like thi damn coolture. Give me coomfort. Ah'm goin' back to Throstle's Nest, an' Ah'll ask Mrs Bairstowe to wed me. Ah feel ten years yoonger since that trip.'

He took up his stick and set off determinedly towards the station. Denis and Enid followed, more slowly.

CORPORAL STRIKE

The long white gate hung askew between the brick gate-posts. One of the hinges was broken; and the paint of the gates was cracked and blistered where it wasn't gone altogether. But the gate-posts were lovely: rich red brick that had stood there for a hundred years or more, and now were patterned over with lichen, green and orange and sulphur-yellow. On each post was a great eagle in white stone, wings outspread. They, too, were weather-stained; they had the loveliness of things with which the seasons have for long had their way. One was headless.

The gravel path upon which the gate opened was grown thick with weeds, and the rhododendrons and kerrias and hollies that made the shrubbery intruded upon it. They had not been pruned for years. I could not see the house – only its chimneys. They were lovely Elizabethan chimneys, each a separate work of art; and they stood smokeless against the autumn sky of milky blue.

The notice which said that the house was for sale had itself decayed. Someone had propped it against one of the gate-posts, and I saw that it had fallen because time had rotted its foot.

I had walked for a long time and seen no one. There was no one to be seen now. The lane from which the gate opened stretched before me, bordered with little trees that were all bearded with moss. They must have had a hard life through many winters with the wind roaring among them from the sea that could now be glimpsed in the distance, spread out and as unruffled as a blue silk coverlet.

The whole scene had the melancholy beauty of decay. I should have turned from the gates had not a thin plume of smoke caught my eye – smoke of so pale a blue that it was almost invisible once it had risen above the dull evergreens and taken the sky for background. It was such a little trembling wisp of smoke that it seemed to come from the ghost of a fire; and when I had put irresolution aside and crunched over the gravel, and come to the lawn before the house, it was, indeed, a poor sort of fire that was burning there.

It was lit at the edge of the lawn, and an old, bent man, with a besom of twigs, was feebly brushing towards it the beech leaves that even now loosened themselves and spun down through the still air.

After a moment of surprise at seeing me there where, clearly, a visitor did not often come, he straightened his old back, leaned his besom against a lovely stone urn, and asked, with a pathetic pretence of being businesslike and brisk, if I wished to see over the house. He was, he explained, the caretaker. He and his wife, and nobody else, had lived in the house for years. He had a look at once so eager and so wistful that it was with regret I told him that nothing but curiosity had brought me inside the gates. Ah, well, he said, for all that, I would perhaps like to see the house and drink a cup of tea.

And so I found myself in the drawing-room from which so much had been taken but which, nevertheless, was gracious still. It was on the sunless side of the house, and a scrap of fire tinkled in the grate. Before it sat an old, shawled woman. Her face, cut like a cameo against the white panelling, reminded me of Whistler's painting of his mother. She was as calm as that, and seemed as far beyond the possibility of turmoil. On the mantelpiece was a photograph of Karen, full-length, poised so lightly that it seemed as though she were about to fly off the earth.

I didn't know, of course, then, that it was Karen; but I learned about her that night. They were so out of the world, that old couple, that they listened to my talk as to travellers' tales; and, sitting there, with my rucksack at my feet, I let the hours go by, a willing captive in that pensive, lovely room. And then they said that I must not go, that I must stay the night; and so it came about that I heard of Karen.

It was nearly midnight when the old man preceded me with a candle up the wide oak stair. When he was gone, I leaned from the window, and saw how all the house was set about with great trees; I felt how deeply one might come to know there the sense of imprisonment. I could imagine that, perhaps from this very window, with owls calling as they were calling now, Karen had leaned out into the night and shuddered as she heard the voice of Corporal Strike howling in the darkness.

' 'E was very 'ansom, midear,' the old man said. He was as fair as that to Corporal Strike, though he had killed him. Very handsome and muscular, swarthy as a Spaniard. I had come that afternoon across the ferry, so I knew the setting in which Karen and Strike had first come face to face. From the fields on the other side of the tidal river you slithered down a path through a wood and there you were at water's edge with that steep wooded bluff rising behind you. The ferryman's cottage lay across the water, a little white huddle under a crown of thatch, and you yelled to call his attention. On a still summer day you needed full lungs to get that call across; and the night when John Tregaskis brought Karen home was a March night of raving wind and surging water.

Karen, you may be sure, didn't mind that. It was an appropriate end to the mad adventure of loving Jack Tregaskis. They had met in Munich, the Danish governess with the blue eyes and the corn-gold hair, and the Englishman with nothing on earth to do but wander the world and spend his father's money. You would have thought they had little enough in common, but you don't want much in common to fall in love. One thing at least they loved besides one another, and that was music. They were both exalted when they met. They were walking from a concert hall and the great harmonies of a Bach fugue were crashing in their heads. You can imagine anything in a moment like that. To Jack Tregaskis Karen's eager figure, hurrying along under the lime trees, seemed to embody all the music's poise and elegance, and to her he seemed the epitome of its strength and depth.

For he did not take long to know her; and there they were, sitting at a little tin table under the trees, drinking coffee, and feeling at ease, each in a strange land, but each at once merry and comfortable with the other.

Then Karen said that she must go, for the Baroness, her employer, did not permit her to be out too late. So Jack Tregaskis learned of her dependent position, but it was not of that he thought as he lingered there, but of her eyes that were the colour of chicory flowers, and of her hair that was the colour of ripe corn, and of her body that swayed away from him under the light of the street lamps as gaily as corn sways when the wind is in it.

It was inevitable that he should think like that, for all his background was of country scenes. He was born in the house with the eagled gate-posts, as his forebears had been for generations. Beauty and solitude were his birthright, and with them he inherited the headstrong blood of all the Tregaskis men. You can see their tablets still – as I did the next day when I walked out of that house – in the nearby church: captains and admirals, many of whom had died in battle or shipwreck, few in their beds. An old rogue who had sailed with Drake was the first of them – Sir Harry Tregaskis, who built the lonely house that so many centuries had left still uncompanioned.

One letter to his father was enough to convince Jack Tregaskis that never would the old man's blessing light upon

Karen. A nobody, picked up in a foreign town. A fly-by-night, no doubt, out for such wandering fools as Jack, who had better come home while yet he had a pound in his pocket. So the old admiral flamed his thoughts upon paper, and Jack could picture him, stumping furiously upon his wooden leg up and down the gravel paths of the house he never left: the house where now he was alone, his wife long dead, his daughter married, his son abroad.

But Jack did not come home. To be in Munich, and to be young, and in love with Karen: what could an old man's anger weigh against that? So he took the way Tregaskis men had always taken: he did as he pleased, and it pleased him to marry Karen and damn the consequences. And then, because breed was strong in him, he must hurry home, convinced that, seeing Karen, the old man would be conquered.

Karen was a gay and merry soul. She had never seen England before, and she spoke English badly, but all was joy to her as they journeyed through the drear March day. The wind rose as they went west. The train swayed across great viaducts, plunged through forlorn valleys drenched with rain, and the windows streamed. A high wind was raging through the little town to which they came in the dark of the evening, and out in the harbour which they must cross on a ferry the sea was noisy and turbulent. On the ferry they did not go below. They stood side by side in the bows with the seas hissing about them, and the darkness over them, and the wind howling.

When they came to the village across the harbour Jack announced simply, 'Now we must walk,' and Karen as simply said, 'Come on, then.' So they slipped and slithered in pitchy darkness up through some fields; then downwards towards the little wood at whose foot was the wide river. There Jack went first, holding with one hand to a rail, and Karen kept a hand upon his shoulder. She could not see.

She could only feel him stumbling before her into the darkness.

The tide was running in, with a great wind pushing it into confusion. Across the welter, seemingly the only thing alive in the world, was the tranquil yellow light in the ferryman's cottage.

'We are at the end of the world,' said Karen.

Jack put an arm around her, taut in a rain-polished white mackintosh, and kissed her wet face and blown hair. 'Not yet,' he said.

Then he let out a great bellow which the wind caught and tore to tatters so that it died upon the water. He yelled again and again, and at last in the darkness a slit of light suddenly came and went alongside the window as the door was opened and shut. Then they saw a lantern bobbing down the cottage path, and it seemed miraculous, with the wind reverberating through the river valley, that it could live for a moment.

But it did; and soon it seemed to be of its own accord, leaping across the tumult of the water. It was a long time, so inky black the night was, before they could make out the boat or the rower.

'Come on, Strike,' Jack Tregaskis shouted. 'I'll give you a hand with her.'

'Good evening, zur,' Strike yelled through the wind. 'It's a long time since I heard your voice. I suppose the bad news 'ave brought you home.'

'What news?' Jack threw into the teeth of the wind. 'I've heard no news.'

'The Admiral, zur. They say he be dying.'

'What!'

'Ay, zur. So I 'ear. Taken very sudden to-day.'

Poor Karen stood stricken at the water's edge, all the gaiety gone from her, lonely as she had never felt lonely before. What share did she have in all this? – in this wild

winter country which now, swiftly, seemed inimical and
forlorn; in this tragedy of the sudden death of a man she had
never seen. Strike held aloft the lantern, and the light fell
on Jack's face, gone grey and anguished. Silently he helped
her into the bucking boat. He took an oar at the bows, and
Strike, with the lantern on the thwart beside him, sat amid-
ships. He was a wild figure, in the fullness of his youth, bare
to the waist, with his smooth brown hairless skin glistening
in the rain. They pulled out into the tug of the current and
the lash of the wind; and as the man bent to his oar Karen
was repulsed by the pride of him. He grinned, exulting in
his strength, his white teeth flashing in the lantern-light, his
muscles strong as steel cables, his whole body a grand
machine that seemed as oblivious of the slapping waves and
drenching rain as if it had been inanimate.

'It be no good wearing clo'es a night like this, zur,' he
shouted over his shoulder. 'If I'm to be wet to the skin, let's
wet the skin and nothing else.'

'Pull, man,' Jack snarled; and Strike fell silent, grinning
at Karen.

When they were across, Jack leapt ashore and held the
heaving bows. Karen stood up, and Strike without ceremony
or question took her round the waist and stepped overboard.
In the darkness of the howling night he pressed her tight to
his naked body and murmured: 'You be light, midear –
light as a li'l bird.'

She strained away from him and did not answer. He waded
through the edge of the hissing water and put her down high
and dry.

In a fainting voice she said to Jack: 'Is it far?' For the
first time, it seemed to her that they had come a long way.

'Three miles,' he said, almost harshly. And when they had
panted three miles through the wet windy dark and come
to the great gates with the eagles poised proudly upon them,
Jack knowing every step of the way, Karen stumbling

blindly at his side, she said tragically: 'Now we are at the end of the world,' and Jack answered: 'Yes, now we are.'

What must she have felt, standing there in the blustering dark, with the great trees weeping all round her, and listening to the sudden alarm that shrilled through the house when Jack hauled at the bell-pull?

'She came in out of the dark like a ghost.' (This is how the old man told me the story.) You never saw such a pale little thing, her hair clinging to her face and her shoes wet through.

'"God 'a mercy, Mr Jack," I said, "we didn't know you were in the country."

'"How is my father?" he asked, very short.

'"Very bad," I said, "but still alive."

'Then he threw off his hat and his overcoat – just threw them down to the floor – and rushed upstairs. "Look after my wife," he shouted.

'And that was the first we heard about any wife. So we brought her in here – into this very room where you're sitting now. I was the butler in those days, you know, sir – twenty years ago – and my wife was the housekeeper. And a fine, bustling house it was. A staff of fifteen indoors and out. My wife put her in the chair here by the fire, and took off her mackintosh, and pulled off her shoes and stockings, and rubbed her feet. When I came in with a bit of food and a hot drink on a tray, she was lying back with her eyes closed. She didn't eat anything.'

The old man died that night. He never saw Karen, never heard of her; and she never saw him. She saw the relatives, who came and stared, and attended the funeral, and went away after the will was read. Everything that mattered was Jack's; and perhaps they wondered whether things would have been like that had the old man known of the marriage to Karen.

The storm in which she had arrived sobbed and moaned

about the country for days. It faded out the day the old man was buried: a wet, troubled March day, full of fits and starts of the tired tempest; and the next day it was spring.

Then Karen was happy. Everyone was gone; the house was hers and Jack's; and though he was moody and pre-occupied with affairs of the estate, all the country about was hers to walk in: a country whose corners sheltered violets and primroses and whose hedges were fledged with the early green of hawthorn.

She didn't mourn. What was there to mourn about? Jack was hers, and this wonderful country was hers; and in a yellow skirt and green jumper, looking as fresh as the daffodils themselves, she wandered alone under the blue sky.

She met George Strike. He was whistling down a lane, swinging his stick at the grasses. He raised a finger in half salute, and she went by, head in air. Strike's eyes darkened, and he shouted after her: 'Don't 'ee know me?'

She stopped then, and he took a step which brought them again face to face. He looked her gay clothes up and down, and said: 'Bain't 'ee in mourning? Bain't 'ee one of the family?' and laughed insolently.

The implication of the words did not strike her. She merely turned the cold light blue of her eyes upon the violet-blue of his, and said: 'I do not like you. You holt me too tight.'

With that she went, and Strike went too, his handsome face twisted with anger, but with a loud laugh on his lips. And in the pub he told how she had said, 'You holt me too tight.' 'I did, too,' he boasted. 'The foreign piece.'

He met Karen often that summer. They did not exchange another word, but when she came up from the beach where she bathed, she would find him lying among the whins on the cliff path, and she knew that he had been gloating upon her, and that he placed himself just there on her return so that she might know she had been watched.

That secret, sardonic surveillance might have become too

much for her. She might have complained to Jack, though she would have felt it a thrust at her pride had she been compelled to do so. But it seemed to her then so little a thing. How could it weigh against the great felicity that was hers, against Jack himself, and her joy in the lovely land that all through the summer belied the tragic promise of her first acquaintance?

And then, suddenly, it became a great thing, for that was 1914. It was incredible, there, where nothing violent seemed thinkable, to feel the swift rain of blow on blow. War! Jack gone! And before the year was out, Jack missing. Then, with the year's end, silence. No word from Jack. No word about Jack. And Corporal Strike muttering in the pub about the foreign piece. ' "You holt me too tight." That's what she said. The foreign piece. I'd like to "holt" her again, the foreign piece!'

The boys went swinging up the road with a fife and drum band. Karen ran down to the gate to see them pass, and Corporal Strike, in charge of the route march, shouted, 'There she is – the German piece! And is she married to him? I wonder.' Then as the head of his little column drew level with the gate, he commanded: 'Eyes left!' And every head swung away from Karen, went by averted, as though she were something too unclean to be looked upon.

He was indispensable, was Corporal Strike. Others came and went, shipped overseas and died; but Strike remained at the camp, so physically beautiful, so superb a trainer, that for long they would not let him go. And every day he marched his men by the gates. 'Look at the eagles!' he shouted. 'German! German eagles!' And they took up the mud of the road and bespattered the spreading wings; and not only the soldiers but the villagers spat out 'German eagles' when they went that way. Some threw mud and some threw stones, and the wings were chipped and scarred.

Karen did not go down to the road again. She remained

in the great house, a prisoner, and her garrison, one by one, deserted. Men and maids alike, they went as the weeks drew on. Some were driven to the colours, some would not remain with a German, some would not serve a woman who, after all, had arrived in a queer fashion. There had been no wedding among the Tregaskis tombs and effigies, and that was how a woman should come to the Tregaskis family. There was something all wrong about a woman who had appeared in a night, and was dancing round the country like a rainbow the moment old Admiral Tregaskis was dead.

And so they went; and soon no one was left but the old man and woman who told me the story; and a boy who saw the gardens run to decay under his hands, and the weeds grow up in the paths; and a little maid whose relatives lived far away.

It became difficult to get food. Karen was the last to be served from the village shops. She loved the evening. Throughout the day the bugle calls rang from the camp. She would listen for 'Lights out' and the 'Last Post'; and then she would clap her hands and say, 'Now we can be quiet!' Then she and the old people would sit together in the drawing-room. They at least had plenty of fire: there was no lack of wood. 'You must call me Karen,' she would say. 'We are friends.' And, difficult as they found it, those stiff English folk, bred in the tradition of deferential service, they called her Karen, and they were, at first, her friends. Then they loved her.

They loved the gaiety that now and then came back to her, making her a woodland thing of light and happiness; and they loved her the more for the ache that came when her sorrows were too many, and she would sit at the piano, white and tragical, beating out great harmonies that stirred their marrow. They came to love her like their own child.

The first time she cried was on one of her nights of gaiety. She talked of Denmark and her happy childhood there. She told them how she had left the country because she had no longer a relative – not a soul in the world. She was gay about the pompous old baroness she had worked for, and she talked of Munich and Jack, and how, soon, they must hear from him.

It was then that they heard a banging at the door and the voice of Corporal Strike, drunk and obscene, howling in the darkness. Karen knelt on the hearthrug and covered her ears with her hands, and the tears rolled down her face. 'Oh,' she sobbed, 'our nights – our beautiful nights! Now he will spoil our nights. We can no more forget.'

And then Corporal Strike disappeared. He went the way of all the others, overseas; but though he was gone, his handiwork remained. Each new draft of recruits learned of the German woman, the recluse behind the stone eagles; and to bedaub the eagles became a traditional joke. So Karen remained a pale prisoner behind the spattered gateway, and when the lush spring drew on, she became more deeply captive. The weeds in the paths, and the stretching arms of untended trees, and the flower-beds unthinned and riotous, made a green prison, and in it she languished.

When the sun grew strong again she said one day that she would go and bathe. The old people were glad of that. They hoped that it was a sign of reviving life and interest; but when Karen came back, pale and panting up the weedy paths, they saw at once that something was wrong. She threw herself into a chair and stared stonily at the fireplace. This time she did not cry. She said in a shaking voice: 'Even the sea – the clean sea – is denied to me.' She never cried after that.

She had gone to the beach and swam out and out. She was a glorious swimmer, and she must have rejoiced, after all those months of captivity, in the clean exhilaration of sun and solitude and salt water. She swam for a long time, and rested, floating with the blue beneath her, gazing up at the blue above where the gulls glided with heavenly beauty. Perhaps she had begun again to find something to live for; and then she swam ashore.

She had begun to dress when a file of soldiers scrambled down the steep pathway that gave the only access to the cove.

'Hi!' one of them shouted. 'This is reserved for the troops.'

Then someone recognised her. 'It's the Bosche!'

They closed in, warily, inquisitively, and Karen stood there, half-dressed, clutching her clothes, shivering and speechless. A lout picked up a handful of sand, but someone shouted: 'Drop that!' He added: 'But keep out of this, miss.'

Then Karen started to run, her heart pounding. The cliff path was steep, and she slipped, falling face-downwards and cutting her cheek on the shaly scree. She lay there for some time, pressed to the ground, her fingers digging into the earth. Then she climbed into the fields, wounded to the soul, and finished dressing.

'You must not go alone next time, Karen,' the old man said. 'I shall come with you.'

She did not answer for a while; then she said: 'No, you shall not. Next time I shall go again alone.'

What could they do? They could not lock her up. They had written to Jack's sister, hinting that things were not well with Karen. But Mrs Charwood had troubles of her own, as who had not in those days; and it was a long way to the North of Scotland where she lived. She wrote a sympathetic letter, and was sure that there would soon be news of Jack, and that things would straighten themselves out in God's good time.

So there was nothing to do except wait with growing anguish for the day, which they were sure would come, when they would find Karen's bed empty and Karen gone. They had not long to wait. It had been a night of glorious moonlight; and Karen was a splendid swimmer. She must have swum on and on under the sky where now there were no gulls flying, nothing at all but the empty and unregarding glory of the moon.

'And so,' the old man said, 'I had to kill Corporal Strike.'

The old woman sitting there calm and austere as a Quaker in meeting, nodded her head: and, when I look back on that moment, I recall that to me, too, the old man's remark seemed unsurprising, a logical and necessary continuation of his story.

Karen was never seen again, nor was Jack Tregaskis. Mrs Charwood, the nearest relative, instructed the old people to remain in the house in order that it might be kept in good condition. So there they stayed, and the war ended, and some men came back and some did not. Corporal Strike came back. The job at the ferry had passed into other hands, and Strike, in any case, seemed disinclined for work. He was more handsome than ever, but devilish in his disposition. He poached and fished and boozed, running on gaily with the war's momentum of ferocity and violence till, like many another, he ran himself out and came against the hard fact of poverty. Then, with great adaptability, he began to turn his hand to any job about the countryside. He did bits of carpentering and bricklaying, white-washing and paper-hanging.

'And so,' said the old man, 'the time came for which I had been waiting.' It was on an autumn evening in 1919 that Strike passed by the gates and found the old man standing there, looking up and down the lane. The eagles were still bespattered, and that was the fact which drew Strike into conversation. 'Many a handful o' that muck I threw myself,' he boasted, and went on to speak of Karen's disappearance. 'I s'pose she'd finished her spying job,' he said, 'and went back where she belonged.'

Perhaps that was it, the old man agreed; but that was all

dead and done with now, and the sooner they got back to their old ways the better. There was plenty to be done, and if Strike cared to do it, there was work waiting for him. The brick pillars of the gate needed pointing, and the eagles themselves were so loose on their bases that a high wind, catching their outspread wings, might bring them down. And he persuaded Strike to climb to the top of a pillar and feel for himself how the eagle rocked on its base.

Strike agreed to do the work; and in his loud-mouthed way told everyone about it at the pub. 'There were Strikes here as long as there were Tregaskises, and maybe longer, and I dare say we'll be here when there bain't no more Tregaskises above ground. But I'll put the old eagles straight for 'un. Fair rockin' they be, not safe to touch.'

'You see,' the old man explained to me patiently, 'I had been loosening them for a long time, so that a touch would send them over.'

And so, when Corporal Strike arrived the next day with all that he needed for the work, he did not get far with it. He died instantly, and never knew that the sudden agony that flamed through him, coming upon him as he knelt at the base of the pillar, was the eagle's beak smashing through his skull.

'I had a mallet,' said the old man, 'so that if he were not killed at once I could finish him. But it wasn't necessary. I left him there for some passerby to find. It was fortunate that he had told everybody how loose the eagles were. You may have noticed, sir, that one of them has no head? This is it. It smashed when it fell on Corporal Strike. I filed the base smooth and keep it here.'

He took from the mantelpiece the head with the hooded eyes and the curved cruel beak that Strike had so often affronted.

'We like to see it there.' And the old woman nodded

placidly as though it were a momento of a visit to Scarborough.

It was only in the morning that the whole thing seemed to me fantastic, incredible. Were these dreams, on which those two old people, cloistered from the world, nourished the emptiness of their days? Or was it all true, and had the necessity of confession welled up, not to be denied?

I do not know. I took the trouble to discover that in 1919 an inquest had been held on George Strike, who died in the circumstances that had been described to me. I took the trouble to look at the Tregaskis tombs and at the memorial tablet which reported that John Tregaskis had been reported wounded and missing in the Great War, and that his death had been presumed.

But of Karen there was not a word. Yet who, after all, would bother to put her on record, and what manner of record could there be concerning one who came so swiftly, stayed so briefly, and so strangely went away? It could not with certainty be said whether she was living or dead. She was, by then, a wraith, a nothing, like the lovely but insubstantial radiance into which she had gone.

VI'LET — 1940

Being up so early pandered to Vi'let's sense of self-importance. It was all for *her* sake that the bed in the opposite corner
of the room was already empty. Usually, when Vi'let got
up at eight, in order to be at school at nine, her father was
still in bed. Sometimes he was still in bed when she went
home for her midday meal. At other times, passing the
Labour Exchange on her way from school, she would see
him standing outside with Madge Connolly's father, Dora
Locker's big brother, and a crowd of other men. He had
bad brown teeth, and one was missing from the middle of
the top row. He lounged there with his thumbs inside his
belt, and a fag-end stuck to his lower lip. Whenever Vi'let
thought of her Old Man, it was either as this Labour
Exchange prop or as a figure recumbent in bed. It seemed to
Jos Lovell that whether he stayed in bed or went to the
Labour Exchange made precious little difference. There was
no work, anyway.

But already that morning Jos was up. Vi'let could hear
him in the next room, and she could hear her mother too.
Vi'let got out of bed and walked across the cold oilcloth to
the window. She didn't need to pull the curtains because
they were nothing more than frayed webs of cheap Notting-
ham lace. You could see through them. Vi'let looked out
on to the Paddington street. She had never seen it like that
before. It looked pitch-dark, and yet it wasn't dark. The day
was in it like a ghost, and the chimneys on the other side of
the street were standing against a sky that seemed as if it
were quivering with ecstasy.

Vi'let could not for worlds have said anything about this,
but she stood at the window, looking at the first dawn she

had ever been conscious of, and loving it. It was something new about her street, the street she had been born in, the street she knew in its stifling summer heat, when the raddled women sat on their doorsteps, and in its winter misery when the fly-blown corner shop seemed an oasis of cheer, a haven of light and comfort. Not once in her thirteen years had Vi'let spent a night out of the street: the street with its lovely lines, its beautifully proportioned houses, that once had harboured comfortable families, and that now was crumbling internally like a cheese that the mice had got into. Vi'let and her Old Man and her Ma were among the mice. They nested in two rotting rooms under the roof, where the servants of old time were tucked away.

'Come on now, our Vi'let. You get yer things on quick. Brekfust's ready. And don't forget yer gas-mask.'

That was Ma. Vi'let turned from her contemplation of the dawn back into the dark room. She couldn't see her clothes, but she knew where they were and had no difficulty in bundling the few meagre things around her plump body. There was no reason on earth why Vi'let, who had been fed on fish and chips at the age of one, should have a plump body. But Nature sometimes freakishly defies even a London slum, and Vi'let was not only well made: she was beautiful. And she was beginning to know it. She pulled her dirty old skirt down over her head, and ran in to the rich alluring smell of bread frying up in some fat that was left in the pan from yesterday's bacon.

At the same moment as Vi'let, Mrs Holsworthy was looking at the dawn. There was no reason why she should be up at such an hour. She knew that the child to be quartered on her would not arrive till noon or later; but she was excited. An evacuated child. What an ugly expression! And it represented an ugly fact: the dirty meanness of modern war. Mrs Holsworthy knew that the child she was to receive would come from London, where untold filthiness might at any moment descend from the sky. Her heart burned when she thought of it. She loathed the idea of war: she loathed meanness and cruelty of any sort. She was shocked as she listened to some of her neighbours discussing the coming invasion of London children. Mrs Greene-Waterer said frankly that she had put some mattresses in the loft over the old stables: she would put her guests there, and see that they stayed there.

Mrs Holsworthy's peaceable nature made it difficult for her to argue with her neighbours but, blushing hotly, she did venture to say to Mrs Greene-Waterer, 'We must give them love as well as lodgings.'

Mrs Greene-Waterer put down her teacup and looked round Mrs Holsworthy's drawing-room. 'A bull in a china shop, my dear,' she said, 'will probably be nothing to one of those in this house.' Her gaze swept the Waterford glass, the Copenhagen porcelain, the Lalique plaques, the demure figurines of Bow, of Chelsea. Mrs Holsworthy's heart fluttered at the thought of harm coming to one of these things. She was given to rather expansive remarks, and she once said with lovely generality, 'I adore beauty.' Her glass and china; her furniture and her garden: all her lovely things had meant more to her than ever since her husband died ten years ago. But children could be taught to love these things and to respect them. Edna was only three when Mrs Holsworthy became a widow, and Edna was as neat and dainty about the house as a little fairy.

Mrs Holsworthy watched the pale sky with the elms dark upon it. The great lawn which ran down to the rose-garden was a still pool of tranquillity. A few birds were restlessly stirring, and the sky was turning from pewter to silver. It was going to be a grand day. Mrs Holsworthy could already sense that.

She sighed with happy anticipation, pulled her wrap

about her, and tiptoed to Edna's room, which opened off
her own. Edna was asleep in her little white bed that had a
small bookcase alongside it containing all the beautiful books
that Mrs Holsworthy had taught her to read: *The Wind in
the Willows. Alice in Wonderland. The Pilgrim's Progress. Lob
Lie-by-the-Fire.* There was a toby jug on top of the bookcase.
Edna had bought it herself in the antique shop in the village.
Mrs Holsworthy didn't think it was very good, but she said
nothing about that. She was glad that Edna was beginning
to collect things, and that she already did not speak merely
of roses, but of Caroline Testout, Madame Abel Chatenay,
and Chaplin's Pink Climber.

There was a second little white bed alongside Edna's.
Edna had been told about the coming guest. Guest was the
word Mrs Holsworthy used. She hated *evacuated child*. She
talked beautifully to Edna about the virtues of hospitality,
and she was sure Edna understood. She smiled now in the
grey dawn light to see that Edna had moved the bookcase
so that its contents were accessible from either bed.

She could not go back to bed now, so she stole out on to
the landing, where she almost collided with Hopkins, the
parlourmaid.

'Oh, Madam! You startled me! Up so early!' said the girl.

'This is the happy day!' said Mrs Holsworthy. 'This is the
day we receive our little guest!'

'Yes, Madam,' Hopkins answered. 'You should get back
to bed for an hour or so, Madam. I'll bring you up some
tea at once.'

The Old Man and Ma both walked with Vi'let through the
hushed streets. The Old Man was thinking that he wouldn't
be out of work much longer now. They'd soon want him.
He was only thirty-four. With Vi'let holding on to his hand,
he slouched past the fag-end of open space where the
German field-gun was. Nineteen-nineteen, that came there.

He could remember it very well. He was still a kid at school. They'd all been marched out when the gun came, and there was a lot of jaw about patriotism. He and the other kids used to play on the gun: climb to the top of the barrel and slide down. They were always being chased off. Now it was one of Vi'let's favourite playing-places, and no one bothered to chase the kids off it any more. People even asked to have it removed. Now, in the still pale light, the gun suddenly looked significant to the Old Man of thirty-four. There was a pile of sand dumped alongside it on the waste patch, and chaps were filling sandbags. Everybody nowadays was filling sandbags. George Connolly, who hadn't had a job for months, got one yesterday, filling sandbags to barricade one of the posh clubs in Pall Mall. 'What about yer own bloomin' 'ome?' the Old Man asked him. George said, 'What I made on that job'd just about fill a bucket on Brighton beach,' and added cryptically, 'An Englishman's 'ome is 'is sand-castle.'

The Old Man and Ma didn't go beyond the gun. They had agreed to leave Vi'let there. They didn't want any sentimental partings. They hated her going. They didn't know where she was going to. Nor did she. The children went where they were sent; those who received them took whom they were given. It was the only possible way.

So the Old Man said: 'So long, Vi'let. Write to us,' and Ma said nothing, but stood and stared after Vi'let, carrying, as ordered, a change of underclothing, food for one meal, and a gas-mask. She also carried a brightly covered penny paper called *Smart Society Stories*. The Old Man gave her a penny a week, and for a long time now she had spent it on *Smart Society Stories*. At the corner she turned to wave, but the Old Man and Ma were walking away, their backs towards her.

Now that she was alone, Vi'let's sense of self-importance grew. It was not yet seven o'clock, and the streets were full of children hurrying to school, their parents with them. Like Vi'let, all of them carried three bundles: one containing food, one containing clothing, and, slung over their shoulders, a square brown cardboard box containing a gas-mask. None of them had learned much at school about modern history: they were learning now.

Vi'let, at any rate, was learning fast. Looking at all the children trotting along so docilely in the dawn, and at Miss Bates, the old moustached teacher whom she hated, scuttling towards school with a white, anxious face, and at the two policemen and one policewoman walking gravely up and down the bleak gravelled yard of the school, she felt that all this was happening for her sake. She was an Evacuated Child. She had heard the phrase and loved it. Germany was going to send planes to pour bombs upon London, and so the children had to be evacuated. And she was one of them. She, indeed, was the only one of them in her own imagination. Perhaps no one else there – not the teachers or the policemen, the parents or the children – had so dramatic a sense of history as Vi'let had at that moment. Canute bored her; you could keep Henry VIII so far as Vi'let was concerned; and she would have made a present of Magna Carta at any time to anyone who wanted it. Now, for the first time in her life, without knowing that she knew it, Vi'let knew what history meant: It meant what happened to Vi'let Lovell.

This sense did not appal her. It gave her indeed a sense of liberation. A few of the children and some of the mothers were snivelling together quietly in corners. Vi'let looked at them with wonder. She had never felt so important, never felt so ready to assert herself against that which she hated above all else: those in authority.

The tiniest creatures – the five-year-olds – blinking and yawning for sleep denied, their gas-masks bobbing on their shoulders where cherubs sprout wings, headed the march to the station. Three hundred children trailed after them. Hardly a head was turned to watch them. Already 'evacuation' was an accustomed idea. This new Flight out of Egypt to avoid the Massacre of the Innocents might have been a customary scene of the modern world.

Mrs Holsworthy, who knew everyone worth knowing in Grassingham, had been given a tip by the stationmaster that the children for that village would arrive at noon. Cook had asked where the expected child would take lunch, and Mrs Holsworthy had replied with as much asperity as her kind heart permitted, 'Why, with me and Miss Edna, of course.' Then she hurried away to see that Edna was dressed for the journey to the station. 'It will seem so *welcoming* if we are both there to meet her,' she had impressed on Edna the night before; and now there Edna was, wearing her Girl Guide clothes, which also had been an idea of Mrs Holsworthy. 'Girl Guides look such sports,' she said, 'and that's what we want, isn't it, my dear? We don't want to seem stiff and severe.'

Edna agreed, though she didn't like being a Girl Guide. She was a pale, fair child, blue-eyed and shy, who would prefer any day to curl up with a book on the sofa rather than traipse through the woods making an unnecessary fuss of cooking poor meals over a fire coaxed out of bits of damp moss. She had been doing that only yesterday, and had come home feeling overtired and rather shivery. She had none of Vi'let's plumpness, and none of Vi'let's beauty. When Edna stood in the bath, Mrs Holsworthy sometimes winced to see her shoulder-blades. You could almost take hold of them, as though they were handles, and lift her up. As for her features, their uncomplaining patient docility was all there was to them. She was just Vi'let's age.

'I'm ready, Mother,' she said now, eager to please, careful to say nothing of the cold spells that had come over her all day and of the small insistent headache that nagged above her eyebrows.

Mrs Holsworthy took Edna's hand and they made a final round together: the nursery where childish things were beginning to be put away and reproductions of masterpieces were taking the place of pictures of lambs and squirrels; the bedroom where the second little white bed was a replica of the first, pale blue silk eiderdowns and all; the dining-room where three places were duly laid. Then they went into the garden, where the late roses and early Michaelmas daisies were still dewy in the pearly autumn sunlight, and Bassett, with his green baize apron, stood lost in admiration before a blaze of wine-red dahlias that were his especial glory.

'Well, Bassett,' said Mrs Holsworthy, 'you've got everything looking lovely for our little guest.'

Bassett nodded towards his dahlias. 'I hope she'll keep her hands off these. I know some o' that sort.'

'It's very strange,' Mrs Holsworthy said, leading Edna out of earshot, 'how the working people – though, mind you, I hate that expression because we're all working people in our way – oh, dear, Edna, what a sentence! What an example after all I've said about simple speech! – but I was going to say, it's strange how they expect the worst of their own class. We mustn't be like that. If we expect excellence, usually we find it.'

'Yes, Mother,' said Edna dutifully, suppressing a shiver.

'Yes. Well, now. The car's ready. Let's be off.'

Three hours in a train seemed an eternity to Vi'let. She had only once been in a train before, and that was when she had gone with the Bible Class to Southend. Being an Evacuated Child was exciting at first: watching the Paddington slums slide by the window, and then the suburbs come with big gardens full of flowers and apple-trees hung all over with reddening fruit, and new factories with trees and lawns around them, and a far-off dark tower on a hill that the teacher with them said was Windsor Castle. Then there were rich green meadows, full of little streams, and, after what seemed to Vi'let a very long time indeed, there were great bare hills running up to the sky with hardly a tree on them, and the informative teacher said that these were the chalk downs and that the earliest sort of men who ever lived had their villages on them.

Vi'let wouldn't listen to that sort of thing: it seemed like a lesson. She put her head out of the window and watched the steam blowing along the train in a long white streamer and the opalescent sky with the rooks flying across it in ragged companies. It was all as strange to her as the Antipodes to Cook or the Indies to Columbus: so strange that she drew in her head and took refuge in the familiar. She opened her lunch bag and munched her bacon sandwiches as she read *Smart Society Stories*. Lady Augusta had just made the handsome chauffeur an honest man when the train dribbled to a stand-still in Grassingham station.

There was quite a reception committee to meet the half-dozen children who were put out at Grassingham. They were signed for like cargo; and then Vi'let, standing on the platform with the others, watched her train slide itself sinuously round a curve and leave her stranded.

So this was where an Evacuated Child was sent to! There was a white railing along the platform, with flowers blazing on one side of it and a stream sliding among mint and cress on the other. There was a basket full of pigeons, and on a siding a truck full of cattle, lowing piteously. And all around, as far as you could see, were fields and hills. Vi'let, a half-finished sandwich in her hand, her gas-mask slung in its box over her shoulder, stood non-committally, a rather fierce young animal, awaiting developments.

Mrs Holsworthy, standing there with the small group of Grassingham people, clutched Edna's hand a little tighter as her eyes fell on Vi'let. The cheap blouse, the short torn navy-blue skirt, and sagging black stockings and broken shoes, could not dim the vitality of that small alert figure. Vi'let's uncovered hair was almost blue-black. Her face had a wild brightness, and her body already showed the contours of young womanhood. Mrs Holsworthy looked at the other children: all smaller and younger than Vi'let, all tired and dispirited with the early rising and the long, unaccustomed journey, none with this girl's eager challenge. She waited in almost painful suspense as names were called out. 'Violet Lovell.'

Vi'let's hand went up with schoolroom readiness, bacon sandwich and all. 'Mrs Holsworthy,' said the committee-man.

Mrs Holsworthy relaxed and smiled. 'Gracious' – that was the word she would most have liked to hear applied to herself. Now in the most gracious way she knew she came forward, stooped, for she was a tall woman, and put an arm round Vi'let's waist. 'My dear,' she said, 'you are coming home with me. I hope you'll be very happy.'

'Mind my gas-mask,' said Vi'let.

Mrs Holsworthy often said with satisfaction that she was sensitive to atmosphere. She could tell what people were thinking about her and whether they liked her. She tried hard to make out what Vi'let was thinking about her, but she was aware of nothing but a sort of alert reserve. Vi'let was watching everything and taking everything in, but she was giving nothing away. She sat next to Mrs Holsworthy, who was driving. Edna was at the back. Never before had Vi'let sat in a motor-car, never had she looked upon such scenes as now unrolled themselves. Grassingham was little more than one long street, incredibly ancient, notoriously beautiful. The inn, the church, the half-timbered shops and houses, the exquisite butter-market and the village green, had all been painted again and again by Arthur Holsworthy, R.A., whose house, a mile beyond the point where the long street ended, was perhaps the loveliest thing even in Grassingham. But Arthur was now in the churchyard which, also, he had immortalised in some North Country Municipality's art gallery, and there was his widow, driving slowly so as to deploy at a seemly pace all this celebrated loveliness before Vi'let's eyes. And she felt that Vi'let was not responding. She was seeing all, and withholding judgment.

Mrs Holsworthy liked her for this. She was accustomed to hear the gush begin as soon as Grassingham burst on a visitor's gaze, and continue till the Chantry, her house, was reached. But Vi'let said nothing, except, suddenly: 'I gotta send a postcard 'ome as soon as I get there. That's the orders.'

'I think Violet might wait till after lunch, don't you, Edna?' said Mrs Holsworthy. 'I don't expect the orders are so desperately strict, do you?'

'Well, Mother,' said Edna, with the patient reasonableness of a grown-up person, 'if Violet had received those orders, I think she ought to be allowed to carry them out. She will feel happier when she has written to her father and mother.'

Vi'let looked round at the child seated behind her. She had not till now taken much notice of Edna, who was not the sort of girl to attract attention. Edna smiled encouragingly, and suddenly Vi'let said: 'Stop! I want to get in be'ind with 'er.'

'My dear, we're nearly there!' Mrs Holsworthy protested, a little hurt, but Vi'let began to fumble with the doorhandle, and perforce the car had to be brought to a standstill. Vi'let climbed out, took her bundle of underclothing, her gas-mask, and *Smart Society Stories*, and installed herself alongside Edna. Almost as soon as she was seated the car swept through a pair of gorgeous wrought-iron gates, along a short curving drive, and came to a stand before the long white house with the pillared portico from which you looked down the celebrated Chantry lawn.

'You see,' said Mrs Holsworthy, smiling forgivingly as she slid out of her seat, 'the changeover was hardly worth while.'

'That's all you know,' said Vi'let. 'Where can I write my postcard?'

'Show Violet the library, Edna, dear,' Mrs Holsworthy said. 'I'll see how lunch is getting on.'

To Vi'let, a library meant only one thing: a gloomy public building in which unemployed men found warmth as they read the daily papers. She was surprised when Edna led her into a small, delicious room filled with books and with pictures by Arthur Holsworthy, R.A., and seated her at a table looking down the lawn towards the rose-garden. Weeping willows edged the lawn, and rising in the middle of the rose-garden was a marble Aphrodite gleaming amid the tremulous spray of a fountain.

'Is this a park?' Vi'let asked.

'No, no,' said Edna. 'It's our place. We live here.'

'Can't nobody come in, so long as they keep orf the grass?'

'Our friends come in, of course, and they can walk any-where.'

'Cor! Thanks for lettin' me write my postcard at once. Ma and the Old Man'll want to know. 'Ere, you can 'ave this. It's a treat, the story in there.' She handed *Smart Society Stories* to Edna, and wrote her postcard.

Dear Pa and Ma: This is a house in a park, with one woman like the districkt visitors that Ma don't like and one kid very pale but all right. I'll all right, and if ever I'm unhappy I'm coming home. Vilet.

Lunch in the Chantry dining-room was a strange experi-ence for Vi'let, but she got through it. There was good food to eat, she had a mouth and an appetite, and sensibly decided that nothing else mattered. Mrs Holsworthy rained encouraging remarks upon her, urging her to eat this and that, to feel at home, not to be shy. Edna, seeing that Vi'let was eating with no need of encouragement, that she was as much at home as was possible in the circumstances, and that she was anything but shy, said nothing, passed dishes, and occasionally gave Vi'let her pale, friendly smile.

As soon as lunch was over, Vi'let said, 'Let's go and walk on the grass.'

'All in due season,' Mrs Holsworthy smiled. 'I shall be ready in about ten or fifteen minutes.'

'I mean just me an' 'er,' said Vi'let.

'Would you like to go alone?' Edna asked. 'I've got rather a bad headache.'

'Edna! My dear!' Mrs Holsworthy reproved her. 'One doesn't allow a headache to interfere with the duty of hospitality.'

'I'm sorry, Mother.'

'Sorry be blowed,' said Vi'let. 'Don't be daft. If you've got an 'eadache, take an aspirin an' 'ave a lay-down. An 'eadache's a rotten thing.'

'It isn't much,' said Edna. 'Come along.'

Vi'let didn't do any of the things that Mrs Holsworthy's neighbours and Bassett had feared. She didn't dig up the celebrated lawn, or uproot the growing dahlias, and she was bored to death when Edna told her all about Mrs Herbert Stevens, K. of K., and Frau Karl Druschki. All this detail didn't interest her a bit, but she loved the space and the sunshine. At the end of the garden there was a wild patch where hazels and alders and willows grew; and on the edge of it she threw herself down and said, 'I'm going to 'ave a good lay in the sun.'

Edna sat at her side and took *Smart Society Stories* from the pocket of her Guide's uniform. The picture on the cover enthralled her. A chauffeur, with the large and luminous eyes of a gazelle, was embracing a lovely girl in evening clothes who leaned back swooningly against the body of a limousine. Beneath it she read: 'I may be only a chauffeur, but, by God, Lady Cynthia, you have stirred in me the passions of a man.'

Edna had never seen such a picture before. Never before had she read such a story. *The Wind in the Willows* was nothing to it. She read on, enthralled, till Mrs Holsworthy, who had succumbed to the sunshine in a deck-chair on the portico, roused herself and went to see what the children were doing.

Her little guest, as she persistently called Vi'let in her mind, was sound asleep, stretched out on her back, her short ragged skirt half-way up her thighs, revealing enormous holes in the knees of her stockings. Edna, tense and bright-eyed, was holding one of those papers that Mrs Holsworthy felt should never be seen in the hands of Arthur Holsworthy's daughter.

She said in a low, vibrant voice: 'Edna! What are you reading?'

Vi'let struggled to wakefulness, sensed the discord passing between mother and daughter. Mrs Holsworthy had taken the paper from Edna's hands and was regarding it with distress.

'This is hardly suitable reading, my dear,' she said. 'Have I been neglectful? Have I failed to provide you with all the books you needed?'

'That's a good book, that is,' said Vi'let. 'Lady Cynthia marries the chauffeur in the end.'

'You hardly understand, I think, Violet, my dear. You and I must have a little talk about reading some time. Shall we?'

'I don't know about that,' said Vi'let shrewdly. 'I've 'eard of little talks before.'

'Well, at any rate,' Mrs Holsworthy suggested pleasantly, 'let's go along and see if we can find some tea.'

'You see, Violet, my dear,' said Mrs Holsworthy, after tea, when she had Vi'let to herself at last, Edna having gone to lie down, 'it's a question of beauty.' She was sitting in a deep chair in the drawing-room, smiling her most gracious smile, and the ragged child stood at her knee. 'The paper you gave Edna to read was not beautiful. I have always taught her to read only beautiful things. When you go to bed to-night you will see the beautiful books she has. It would be nice if you read them yourself. I hope you will. You have a splendid opportunity here. You might begin with a book called *The Wind in the Willows*.'

'All about old Ratty and Badger?' said Vi'let. 'I read that years ago, when I was a kid.'

Mrs Holsworthy was jarred. She knew nothing about the resources of council-school libraries. 'Then perhaps we'll start you with *Alice in Wonderland*,' she said hopefully.

'Lummy! That's an old 'un. I was the Mad 'Atter in a school play when I was nine. I know all them books, Mrs 'Olsworthy. I'm past that stage. That's the trouble. I like to read about real life.'

'But don't you feel those books are more *beautiful* than *Smart Society Stories*?' Mrs Holsworthy persisted.

'Reel life needn't always be beautiful,' Vi'let answered. 'Life isn't very beautiful for the Old Man and Ma, but it's reel enough. D'you always love one thing better than another just because it's more beautiful?'

'I honestly think, my dear, that I can say I do,' Mrs Holsworthy answered, finding her smile more difficult.

'Then you ought to love me more than Edna,' said Vi'let. 'I'm beautiful and she isn't. But it would be nonsense if you did. So I suppose you're talking nonsense.'

This syllogism left Mrs Holsworthy speechless, till Vi'let

herself came to the rescue. 'I s'pose there's beauty *and* beauty,' she said.

'Yes, that's it,' Mrs Holsworthy assented, surprised to find how glad she was that the child had given her a way out.

'There's all this stuff you've got in glass cases,' said Vi'let, dismissing almost with contempt the Waterford glass and Copenhagen porcelain that Mrs Greene-Waterer had trembled for. 'There's all that, and there's our street like I saw it this morning. I like our street.'

'But surely you don't like it better than all this – beauty?' Mrs Holsworthy faltered over the word she was beginning to distrust.

'You bet I do,' said Vi'let. 'I 'ope they'll soon smash 'Itler an' let me get back. But I like Edna. I'd like 'er to come back with me and see a bit of reel life.'

Mrs Holsworthy blenched at the thought, and defended herself with the remark, 'Life is real here, too, you know, Violet.'

Vi'let considered this, examining her fingernails. 'Ay,' she conceded, 'as reel as it can be when you don't 'ave to worry about the rent.'

Edna got over her headache and her shivers, as she usually did, and she and Vi'let spent their days together. Bathed each night, dressed in some of Edna's clothes, with her blue-black hair shining from the brush, Vi'let was a handsome child. Mrs Holsworthy recovered from the disconcerted feeling that her conversation with Vi'let had caused her. She found that she got on better by leaving the conversations to Vi'let and putting in a word here and there. She heard of trouble and discontent among people who had received children. She had none. She displayed Vi'let to Mrs Greene-Waterer with pride.

Only once did Vi'let reveal what was in her heart. She

said to Edna: 'Your Ma's surprised at me. She would 'ave liked an 'Eathen to be kind to.'

'Nonsense,' said Edna. 'She's very fond of you.'

'She would have been fonder if I was an 'Eathen,' Vi'let persisted. 'She wanted to work a miracle.' She dismissed the serious note with a laugh. 'She's disappointed because I'm a bloomin' miracle already – no thanks to 'er. If it wasn't for you, I'd write and ask Ma to 'ave me 'ome.'

Edna accepted this quite simply, which was what Vi'let liked about Edna. 'Tell me some more about your home,' she said. Mrs Holsworthy had never said that. The two children lay on the grass in the sunshine, and Vi'let told some more about her Paddington street, and the Old Man and Ma, and the man on the floor below who bashed his wife, and about fish and chips and threepenny seats in the cinemas.

One thing which bound the children together was that each found the other incredible. It was incredible to Edna that Vi'let had never, before coming to the Chantry, ridden in a motor-car, or bathed in a bath, or lived in a house with a garden; and to Vi'let it was incredible that Edna literally did not know the meaning of fish and chips, that she had never been in a cinema, or attended a school with an asphalt playground. And, finding each other incredible, they were surprised to find daily that the incredible things were of no account, and that the chief thing was that they liked one another very much.

Edna's mother was married to Arthur Holsworthy for five years before the child was born. During those five years she was terrified. Barrenness seemed to her a reproach, and she persuaded herself that she was barren. She besought her husband to adopt a child. Someone from the poorest class, someone they could themselves transform into that ideal being which was her dream. He would never consent. The coming of Edna stayed for a time the vagaries of Mrs Holsworthy's mind in that direction. But when no more children were born, and the doctor told her that no more would be born, she, who was made for generous motherhood, felt her fears return. If Edna should die! That was her life's nightmare, and again she plagued her husband to adopt a child to be Edna's companion. Again he would not, and he died, and she lived with her fear. It was buried now, but it was there, and, though she was not herself fully aware of it, this was her reason for her exultation when she saw the splendid healthy Vi'let, and for her foolish fluttering efforts to impart to the child her own notion of good. She did not know that in doing this she had disparaged Vi'let's notion of good and alienated the child. She rejoiced to see her and Edna so happily at ease, and imagined that, Edna being all hers, Vi'let must be thus bound to her too. Edna's illness stampeded the fear that was dormant in her mind, brought it rushing to her consciousness, and between the duties of the sickroom and the courting of Vi'let's affection she wore herself almost to a shadow.

The illness began with another of Edna's bouts of headache and shivering. She went to bed early, and Vi'let insisted on going too. Vi'let sat up in bed and read to Edna from Kingsley's exemplary volume, *The Heroes* – an edition, as it happened, illustrated by Arthur Holsworthy. This was not Arthur's only legacy to his daughter. He had bequeathed her a house without a telephone. He disliked telephones, and so, even to this day, when his memory was still cherished at the Chantry, though dead elsewhere, there was no telephone in the house.

That was why Vi'let ran for the doctor. She read from *The Heroes*, stumbling gallantly over the Greek names and feeling bored to tears, till she saw that Edna was asleep; then she switched out the light and was healthily asleep herself in five minutes.

She was awakened at one in the morning by restless tossing and moaning in the next bed. She put on the light and was alarmed by Edna's flushed face and weary eyes. 'I feel bad, Violet. I feel very bad,' Edna said; and Vi'let professionally put a hand on Edna's brow and said: 'You're as 'ot as fire. I better call your Ma.'

She bustled into the room next door, clicking on the light. Mrs Holsworthy started up in alarm, to see this sturdy young apparition at her bedside. 'Edna's bad – very bad,' she said. 'You better get a doctor.'

Mrs Holsworthy slipped on her dressing-gown and went in to Edna's bedside. She was so frightened that she did not hurry. She was accustomed to Edna's little illnesses. She usually treated them herself, thus diminishing their importance in her own mind. To admit that they were serious would have given rope to her fear.

She laid her hand, as Vi'let had done, on Edna's forehead. 'A feverish cold,' she said, white to the lips. 'She must stay in bed to-morrow.'

'You better get a doctor,' Vi'let persisted.

Mrs Holsworthy tried to laugh. 'My dear! Drag the doctor out to treat a cold! He wouldn't thank us! You don't feel you need a doctor, do you, Edna?' Her voice trembled.

Vi'let began to hustle into her clothes. 'For Gawd's sake!' she exploded. 'Arskin' 'er!'

Edna and Vi'let had passed a lovely little house in the long Grassingham Street a few days before. A man had come out and stepped into a waiting car. Edna said: 'That's our doctor. He lives there.' So Vi'let knew where she was going to. She was dressed even while Mrs Holsworthy was protesting that there was no need to do anything. 'She'll be quite all right in the morning. You'll see. It's nothing but a cold.'

'So much the better,' said Vi'let. 'No 'arm will have been done.'

She sounded so resolute and self-willed that, distracted as she was, Mrs Holsworthy could not help looking round and smiling at her. 'You're obstinate, aren't you?' she said, 'as obstinate as they make 'em.'

'If Edna 'ad been my child,' Vi'let said, 'I'd 'ave 'ad the car out and been there an' back by now. But that's your look out.'

Obstinate she might be, resolute she might look; but what Mrs Holsworthy did not then guess was that she was desperately afraid. Lying in bed at nights, even with Edna at her side, listening to the crying of owls and the fretting of branches, she was aware of the alien and inimical life that surrounded her. Now she ran as she had never run before. It was a moonless night, and the country darkness was something the town-bred child had no name for. Shop lights, street lamps, neon signs, made every hour of the night feverishly awake in the life she knew. Now she was in a darkness that was absolute, so that, running full lick down the short curving drive, she crashed into a bush whose thorns gashed her face. It taught her caution, and she went slowly, eeling her way, till she reached the mile-long road that led to Grassingham. Then, in the middle of the road, she ran again: ran hell for leather from the sound of hooting owls, and the deep sighing of cows couched behind hedges, and the shrill squeal of a snared rabbit. She did not know what made any of these sounds, but they were dread in the monstrous darkness.

When she reached the High Street her fear was not abated at the sudden flash of a car's headlights. *Smart Society Stories* were fond of kidnapping, abduction, the swift rending away by any means of the young and innocent. In the silent street, all the heady rubbish she had imbibed fed the terror that was growing in her. She reached the doctor's house, ran to the porch, and crouched there, waiting for the lights to flash by. But the car slowed, stopped, and a man came towards her, towered over her with huge menace. She shrank down on the doctor's doorstep, ready to shriek at his touch; but he did not touch her; he spoke.

'Well, my dear. Something wrong? You looking for me? I'm Doctor Martin.'

It was long afterwards before Mrs Holsworthy could bear to hear anything of that night. Then Dr Martin said: 'I never saw anyone so near to collapse. The kid was nearly dead with fright. So I talked to her as though everything were O.K., and she came to with a gasp and rattled off, as if she had been rehearsing it all the way: "Come to the Chantry at once. Miss Edna's dying." '

He shoved her beside him in the driving seat. After he had seen Edna he turned, and she was standing there, gripping the rail of her own bed with the knuckles white through the skin. ' 'Ave I saved 'er?' she asked.

He was already tired to death with a night's work, but he managed to smile. 'It won't be your fault if you haven't,' he said. 'Now hop into bed. I'm going to give you a drink.'

She did as she was told, and gulped down the sedative. He waited for a few minutes till she relaxed and wavered towards sleep. 'That's the stuff,' he said, and when her eyes closed he said to Mrs Holsworthy: 'And when I say "That's the stuff," it goes for this kid.'

Dr Martin was at the Chantry very early in the morning. He brought a nurse with him, and Vi'let's bed was moved into a small back room. And the next day there were two nurses, and one was on night duty and one on day duty. Vi'let was not allowed in the room at all, but Mrs Holsworthy was in and out at all hours of the day and night. On the third day Dr Martin brought another doctor with him, and Vi'let, peeping through the slit of her bedroom door, saw them talking gravely together on the landing and shaking their heads. She saw Mrs Holsworthy come out of the bedroom and speak to them, then rush away crying.

Vi'let knew then that Edna was going to die. She did not cry, but a black misery filled her heart. That's how life is, she thought, which was something Ma was always saying when things went wrong. There she was, sent out of London because she might be killed: and there was Edna, killed anyway in this house where everything was supposed to be safe. You might as well be in one place as another.

She stripped off all the clothes that had belonged to Edna, and put on her blouse and short ragged skirt and torn stockings. She packed her spare underclothing in a bundle, as the instructions had told her to do, and slung her gas-mask over her shoulder. She would have liked to say good-bye to Edna, but she knew that she had said good-bye to Edna when reading *The Heroes*. She didn't care whether she ever saw Mrs Holsworthy again. Mrs Holsworthy had wanted to burn all these clothes she was wearing now, and Edna had said: 'I wouldn't do that, Mother. I know you never like parting with old clothes yourself.'

'Well,' said Mrs Holsworthy, 'clothes that have some association, of course, that remind one of some beautiful thing – '

'These remind me of Ma and the Old Man,' Vi'let objected. 'I want to keep 'em.' And she did.

She sat on the bed in the back room, thinking of these things, waiting for a favourable moment to slip out and away. She wasn't clear about how she'd get to London, but no doubt she could cadge lifts, and if she couldn't do that, she'd walk. Anyway, she couldn't stand Mrs Holsworthy any longer. 'If I was dying,' Vi'let thought darkly, 'I wouldn't thank Ma to be all over some other kid, like she's all over me. Not that Ma would.'

Then she heard Mrs Holsworthy on the landing, moaning in that new soft voice of hers: 'Violet. Violet.' There was something in the way she pronounced the name, with a parting of all three syllables, that made the child furious. She shrank back now towards the window, watching the door with a stony rebellious face. Mrs Holsworthy, haggard with three days' vigil, came in, shut the door, and stood with her back to it. She looked greedily at Vi'let, and said, 'Why are you dressed in those clothes?'

'I'm goin' 'ome,' said Vi'let. 'I want to see my Ma.'

Mrs Holsworthy looked at her as though she were walking in her sleep. 'No,' she said quietly. 'You are not going home, Violet. God is taking Edna from us. You must stay.'

She smiled, and Vi'let thought the smile the most horrible thing she had ever seen. She began to whimper. 'I'm goin' 'ome to Ma.'

'No,' Mrs Holsworthy repeated. 'You must stay. You are never going home again, Violet.'

She came slowly across the room, holding her hands out towards the child. Vi'let cowered till she felt the hands on her shoulders. Then she stiffened and resisted, and at the first movement of her repugnance Mrs Holsworthy's grip tightened frantically. They struggled together, the strong child and the haggard woman, and as they struggled Mrs Holsworthy hissed and gasped her desire. 'You are all I have. You must stay. Oh, Violet, my love, my love. I have always dreamed of you. I have always desired you.'

Vi'let was frightened now. She could not make head or tail of such a woman. She resisted when Mrs Holsworthy locked her closely in her arms and tried to kiss her. She strained back her head, thrust with chest and arms, and at last broke free. 'Look, you old fool!' she cried. 'You've bust me gas-mask.'

The square cardboard box was broken, trampled under their feet. The hateful thing of talc and rubber was lying on the carpet, the snout amputated. Mrs Holsworthy looked at it stupidly, 'Oh, Violet!' she cried.

'Don't you begin again!' Vi'let cried, falling exhausted on the bed. 'You keep orf. You keep your paws to yourself. I hate you – see! Hate you!'

Mrs Holsworthy gave her a fond smile. 'Sleep,' she said. 'I'll come back.'

She went trailing out of the room.

WHY?

This had all happened before, and it was incredible, thought Martha, that it could be happening again.

The summer sun was streaming down, and the white-washed wall of the Brasserie Laporte shone like a great sheet hung out to dry. Martha could see it as she panted down the lane from the house. Its whiteness almost blinded her.

When she came, stumbling in her haste, to the end of the lane and turned to the right, there was a big cool hole torn in the sheet: the doorway into the yard of the brasserie, with a plane tree, now dark and heavy with foliage, on either side.

Bossette, the big black full-bellied mare, almost filled the hole, standing there patiently in the green shade of the trees, the flat, clumsy cart behind her, the beer casks, as full-rounded as her belly, in the cart.

It was a sight so familiar and reassuring that Martha pulled up short, the puckers that the dazzle of the white wall had put about her eyes eased out, and she passed a plump dark hand across her face as though wiping away a night-mare vision.

Then the terror gripped her heart again; she ran forward squeezing past Bossette and the cart into the brasserie yard. At the far side, Louise was straddled on a barrel, her long, skinny black legs bandied to grip its convexity. Jules was in the barrel, which lay on its side. He had backed in stern first.

His tangled hair emerged into the sunlight, and Louise was leaning forward slapping at it. 'Back! Back!' she was shouting. 'Good dog. Back!'

Jules shook his six-year-old head, growled savagely, and

snapped at Louise's hand. Then he saw his mother, crawled out, and ran at her legs on all fours, yapping, barking.

Martha bent swiftly, caught him by the scruff of the neck, and pulled him to his feet. Louise had leapt off the barrel. Martha seized her hand, and as she did so the sharp pain smote her anew.

Even thus – could she ever forget that moment? – even thus, when she was ten, as Louise was now, her mother had seized her hand, pulled her out of the little garden of the labourer's cottage on the turnpike road, and, with nothing but a spade and the clothes they stood up in, had fled down the road, screaming 'Les Bosches! Les Bosches!'

No, Martha would never forget it. It was later in the year than it was now, but it was lovely weather.

She would never forget the chrysanthemums blooming in the gardens, and the harvests whitening in the fields, and the dust rising up under the pale autumn sunshine as they all hurried westward: the little ramshackle carts, the goats bleating, the cows and the sheep, the withered old men pushing their prams full of pots and bedsteads, bolsters and frying-pans, the patient old women, the sturdy young mothers, trudging forward with babies at their big breasts, her own thin voice crying, 'Mais pourquoi, maman? Pourquoi? Why do we fly?' and the dust, dust, dust, a gilded cloud moving with them as the sun sank and the mutter of the following guns deepened.

She would never forget it. She would never forget her own infant cry: *Pourquoi?*

She had run out of the house immediately on getting the telephone message from Emile. No good to stay, he had said. No good to wait for him to return.

Fly! That was what his trembling voice urged: fly with the children. He would manage to join them, somewhere, somehow.

And there she was, one hand holding Jules by a convulsive

grip on the coat collar, one hand holding Louise's hand, squeezing it like a vice, making the child's bones ache.

She let them go when she reached the flat cart that stood there blocking the archway. It was so much a part of her life, this archway.

Fifteen years ago – but it was evening then, and the walls, that had been white as long as she could remember them, were a glimmer in the Flemish dusk, under the Flemish moon, tremulous as her own heart was tremulous with love for Emile – fifteen years ago Emile had brought her here, his arm round her waist, and they had come through this arch that led to his father's brasserie.

They had gone through to the second inner yard where zinnias and nasturtiums were blooming all round the walls, plaques and clusters almost robbed of colour by the dusk, and it had seemed to her that through these prosaic business arches, where the smell of the dusk was pungent with the smell of malt, she was entering a new life.

And because she had always wanted to remember these things, she had through all these years kept the walls white and the zinnias and nasturtiums growing along the walls, and now that the brasserie was Emile's he laughed at her, called her romantic, and cursed any workman who trod on the flowers.

And thus the arch was dear and familiar, so that her heart felt as though it would break as she let go the children's hands and began to climb upon the flat cart.

It was not easy. She had become big and heavy, like Bossette. Incredible to think that once in England she had been able to swing about in trees, as agile as a monkey.

Trees in a hilly place, a place of climbing woods, beech trees on rocky spurs of chalk, a jolly tumble of country where you could never see far but always see something lovely: the hawthorn and bluebells in the spring and the lace of a bare wood woven in winter delicately along the edge of a hill that faced across a valley, the windows of Mrs Picton's drawing-room.

She had never been back, but the memory was clear and bright here amid the gravity of the wide Flemish plain.

She had often said she would go back, and now she was going. In all the confusion of her mind and body, that one thing became suddenly clear. That was what she would do: she would go back to Mrs Picton.

Throughout all these years they had written to one another. Mrs Picton knew about Jules and Louise: she had their photographs, and a photograph of Emile standing proudly in his shirt sleeves by the great casks in the inner yard of the brasserie.

It began to seem to Martha that no distance at all separated her from Mrs Picton, whom she had last seen when she was fifteen.

She was up at last, panting a little on the flat cart. She looked down at Louise, dark-eyed, serious, with straight black hair, combed down and hanging round her shoulders, and straight black brows beneath her smooth forehead.

People said Louise was her spit and image. That was how she must have looked when the long, agitated journey was over – that confusion of bleating goats and choking golden dust, and the strange terror of the sea, with hundreds of the homeless and woebegone wailing beside her on a stormy midnight deck black as pitch, and then the new incomprehensible, frightening land of people talking an unknown tongue, and officials arranging, sorting, indexing, and the awful knowledge that her mother was lost, and never more was found.

That was how she must have looked when out of that welter Mrs Picton's cool hand picked her up and Mrs Picton's cool voice soothed her torn nerves.

'She took me to an hotel,' Martha often said to Emile, recalling the moment; and Emile would say: 'An hotel, eh, cabbage?' grinning at her in a way to suggest that an hotel must have seemed a pretty expensive order for her in those days.

And so it was. Never had she imagined such a fashion of life as this.

She understood little that was said to her; but she understood this woman with the sweet face and the deep blue eyes and the gentle manners who held her hand as they got out of the taxi and led her to the hotel.

It seemed to little Martha from the labourer's cottage on the Flemish turnpike a delirium of luxury: the gilded lift, the quiet, carpeted corridor, the long lying in a hot bath with Mrs Picton sitting on the edge of it, smiling at her and saying nothing.

Then Mrs Picton carried her into the bedroom and tucked her into bed, and a young woman came with a tray on which a plate of soup steamed, and when she had eaten that, Mrs Picton sat by the side of the bed holding her hand till she fell asleep.

That was how it began, when she was as old as Louise was now, and Mrs Picton was thirty. Little Martha thought she had never seen a more beautiful woman, or a more beautiful house than the one they travelled to next day.

The woods rose from the back of it, and the valley fell away from the lawn in front of it, and the soft autumn weather was golden and drowsy under the faded blue of the sky.

It was not easy to forget the Flemish road, ruled into the landscape, with the tall, pointed poplars marching mathematically into the sunset, and maman with the work-worn hands leaning on her spade, scraping the clay from her clumsy boots upon the spade's edge, making bread in the kitchen, walking down the long road, wearing her white, starched coif, to church on Sundays.

But if these things could be forgotten anywhere, it was

surely at Cornerways, the low, white house with the red roof and the straw bee-hives, and the pond so choked with the flat leaves of water-lilies that here and there Mrs Picton cut them away so that Martha could see the goldfish.

Looking back at it, she could not remember a more dream-like autumn.

The stone figures round the pond were as golden and crumbling as cheese, and all their honey-combing was stored with sunshine.

Mrs Picton would sit on the grass with her back against one of them, looking at the child, with a smile as kind and dreamy as the weather, listening to the silence which was broken by nothing but the shrill whine of the gnats and the occasional glooping of a fish, snatching at some fallen infinitesimal prey.

And it was this that Martha had still in mind as she said to herself that she would take Jules and Louise to Mrs Picton: this vision of a beautiful woman, arrested in time, who would take her children by the hand and lead them over the green English grass to the fish-pond and help them to forget this frightful journey on which they must now embark.

Tregarrock sounded a nice name. She knew that it was in Cornwall, while Cornerways had been in Hertfordshire, but this did not mean much to her.

No doubt, everywhere in England there were fish-ponds and crumbling statues and peace – in the landscape and in the heart.

She tugged at the knots of the ropes that held the great casks in the flat cart.

She slashed at the ropes, pushed at the casks, sending them down one by one on to the cobbles. The last one burst asunder, filling the air with the smell of beer, splashing the legs of the old man and the children.

They gazed at her aghast, but she said nothing, vouch-safed no explanation, only called to the children: 'Up! Up!' and when they were beside her, shook the reins and sent Bossette at her heavy amble along the road to the house.

She did not take much. Emile had said: 'Take nothing. Fly!' but she was still her mother's daughter; she was still at heart a peasant.

Her mother, twenty-six years ago, she remembered, had snatched up a spade, and carried it as she ran.

Martha snatched up all the money that was in the house and a few clothes for herself and the children.

She belted Bossette till the poor beast achieved such pace as it had not known for years. When they reached the high-way, her heart again turned over.

It was all – all as she had known it. It was flight. It was terror. It was the eternal blind stumble of the humble before the crushing heel of power.

Jules began to cry. Louise demanded: 'Why are they all running, maman? Where are we going to?'

'To Mrs Picton,' said Martha shortly. 'I have told you of Mrs Picton, have I not?'

'Oh, yes!' Louise cried. 'And the lilies in the big round pond!'

Jules rubbed his cuff across his eyes. 'Shall we also see the goldfish?' he asked.

'You shall see all – all!' Martha promised, belabouring Bossette. 'If only your father had not taken the auto.'

But of course, they would not see all. They would not see Major Picton. It was years ago now since Mrs Picton had written: 'My husband is dead.'

Martha remembered him so well. That first English autumn was gone, and the winter too, with its leaping wood fires, its lamp-light falling already at tea-time, its long, quiet evenings in the drawing-room, with Mrs Picton showing her pictures in the book with big type and easy English words, and then from the bedroom a sight of the cold stars crackling over the leafless wood across the valley.

Major Picton came home from France in the spring. Martha had been left with Mrs Picton's one maid, and she could recall the ecstasy of expectation with which she awaited him.

Not that Mrs Picton had said much: she had merely announced his coming, and then, the next day, had gone up to London to meet him.

But surely, the infantile logic had run, the husband of this kind, beautiful lady, the master of this lovely place, the employer of this placid tolerant servant: he must be the sum of all these excellences.

It was dark when he arrived, and the first thing she heard was his voice in the hall, at once harsh and peevish.

All in the house till now had been soft and gentle: gentle voices, soft footfalls; and here were boots clanking, words rasping, and presently hard ironic eyes looking down into hers.

'He never did anything but hurt,' Martha thought, recalling his squat figure that the uniform made to look even harder and uglier than it was, the close-cropped hair, the stony face.

His French was not amusing, blundering, like Mrs Picton's; it was perfect. 'So you run, eh, little one?' he said, laughing. 'They do that well, the Belgians – eh? They run well!'

He looked at her without love, without even kindliness. 'Run again,' he said. 'Run up to bed.'

Mrs Picton was behind him in the doorway. She gestured mutely, and Martha went up to bed.

All the time he was at home she saw little of him, and every night she went to bed early. She did not see much of

Mrs Picton either, and what little she did see was not of the sweet smiling woman she had known.

Louise and Jules were overcome by the sights upon the roads; even more by the *sense* of all those sights; a terrifying sense of something vague, horrible, enigmatic, in pursuit.

It entered into their souls and held them beaten down and silent.

At last Louise said: 'Tell us about Mrs Picton's baby. She had a baby, did she not, Maman?'

And Jules said: 'Yes. Maman has told us. His name was Roger and he became a soldier. Shall we see Mr Roger Picton, Maman, as well as the goldfish?'

To the children, they were all like people and properties from a fairy-tale: the lovely lady with the blue eyes, the sunny garden, the husband away at the war, the goldfish and the lily-leaves, 'All stained with purple as if wine had been spilled on them,' Maman said.

But there was another soldier in the story, and they had never heard of him.

He walked into the garden one summer day, when Mrs Picton was on the grass reading a book, and Martha, facing her, was reading too, getting on famously, so that she could now understand most things that were said to her. She looked up and saw him coming, a finger to his lips, warning her not to show by as much as a wink that she had seen him.

He suddenly clapped his hands round Mrs Picton's eyes, and she didn't need to say, 'Who is it?'

'Oh, Colin!' she cried, and struggled to her feet all in a pretty confusion, blushing and laughing, and then, with her hands on his shoulders, merely gazing spellbound into his eyes.

'I didn't know you were in England,' she said. 'I didn't even know you were coming.'

And Martha remembered how, from time to time all

through the war, these two soldiers would appear, and how, with the coming of one or the other, the season would be of gloom or gaiety.

There was more than gaiety when Captain Colin Cumberland came. Child though she was, Martha could sense the electric tension of snatched happiness.

Martha was fifteen when she returned to Belgium, and she had by then put many things together and reached her own conclusions.

The baby who was called Roger was born just a year before she left, just a month after the day when all the glory of Cornerways turned suddenly to dust: the day when they heard that Captain Cumberland was killed.

And so, though the children had heard of Roger and of Major Picton, and of so much else, they had never heard of Captain Cumberland or of the gloom and neglect in which her last year in England was spent.

Tregarrock was just a shack. Wooden walls, roof of red corrugated iron. And on the roof the announcement in immense white letters: 'Teas.'

You could get more than teas at Tregarrock: you could put up there for your holidays if you were content to accept the inconveniences of the place.

The bedrooms were poky little cubicles partitioned off the main building; there was no bathroom; the cooking was erratic, because it had to be done on oil stoves, and water was scarce, because it had to be pumped by hand.

But till this year Mrs Picton had made a go of it. It was situated in a place of such beauty, so far removed from all that was meant by a 'holiday place' in the crowded, garish sense of the word.

A regular clientèle filled her few rooms from May till September, attracted by the loveliness of the creek at the foot of the garden and the wide pastoral country at the back, and the sense that one was lost to all stress and fever of competition, and that Mrs Picton's prices were extraordinarily reasonable.

It was so nice, too, to feel that one was staying with a perfect lady.

She had just kept her head above water. There was never a surplus; and when all the visitors were gone and she dismissed the small summer staff and withdrew to look after her own simple wants in her own neat tidy room, she was always troubled by the thought that the exhausting labours of the summer had been for so small a recompense.

A little more tired, a little more faded, with the long, lonely winter before her: mist drenching the trees, rain like buckshot on the tin roof.

There might have been a small surplus if it hadn't been for Roger. From the beginning Roger had been her shackle and her joy. She had given up wondering long ago what her husband had known or guessed about Roger. Whatever it may have been, he said nothing.

His voice was perhaps even bleaker and harsher, his manners were more hurtful, more inconsiderate, for her and for everyone else; and certainly he had never even pretended to take an interest in the boy.

When the war ended, he returned to his business on the Stock Exchange; and there was the slump, and some tricky work, which she never understood, in an effort to make ends meet; and then he was 'hammered on 'Change' – again something which she didn't understand, except, vaguely, that there was disgrace in it; and after that everything did not so much crumble as collapse with an awful and terrifying finality.

She almost loved him when he would come home, his rotten shoes soaked with rain, his strength gone from hours of tramping the streets trying to sell little gadgets that no one wanted.

He didn't last long; and then she had set about, in her own untutored and ineffective way, to make a living for herself and the boy.

She had sent him to a good school and to Sandhurst; and now, like his father, he was a captain – Captain Roger Picton – and, like his father, he was fighting in Belgium.

Mrs Picton, wandering through the big empty main room of the shack, was haunted by all the summers she had known there, all the visitors who had come and gone, who had first come as children and now came, when they came at all, as lusty young men and women.

Wandering there, a tall thin woman approaching sixty, with the ravages of an old beauty patching her face like yesterday's make-up, Mrs Picton thought of generation after generation battling, dying, and nothing coming of it all; and like Martha's heart across the water, her's was crying: Why?

If she had managed till now to keep her head above water, it seemed as though at last she would go under. In each of the little bedrooms the beds were made, but there was no one to sleep in them.

In the big general room the tea-tables were ready, and there were more of them out on the lawn, which sloped down to the creek, shining under as glorious a summer as she had known at Tregarrock.

But few people came even to drink a cup of tea; and as for those who had booked rooms for the holidays, they had all long ago written cancelling the arrangement.

No one wanted to leave home in this dreadful year of war. You didn't know what to do.

You got in food in the hope that someone would come along and eat it, and no one came, and it had to be thrown to the birds, who were her only companions for days on end; or you didn't get food in, and then a stray party of

hikers would turn up, find things unsatisfactory, and give
Tregarrock a bad mark.

Well, she had kept her pride. If she went under, it would
be no abatement, not by a jot, of the dignity, the quiet
acceptance of all that could happen to her, which caused
her visitors to say to one another that after all there was
something in staying with a perfect lady.

She had never given herself away, never breathed a word
of her altered fortune to anyone whom it didn't concern.

Lying in a deck-chair in the shade of the big sycamore at
the edge of the lawn, she put on her spectacles and read
again the letter from Martha Laporte.

She remembered the girl well. How could she forget her,
mixed up as she was with the one great romantic moment of
her life?

A slip of a thing she had been when she came; and already
when she went a first suggestion was appearing of heavy
Flemish hips, stolid Flemish face.

She had never guessed, this Martha Laporte, who had
married so well, that 'dear Mrs Picton', to whom she wrote
each Christmastime, had long since ceased to be the leisured
lady of Cornerways.

Always Mrs Picton had written to her on the special
notepaper. For business purposes, she used paper with the
printed heading 'Tregarrock Guest House', and for other
purposes she used paper embossed in a blue die with the
simple word 'Tregarrock'.

So Martha Laporte, for one, had never guessed; as her
letter so clearly showed.

'Dear Mrs Picton. – In my terrible distress, I turn to you.
Once again my beloved country is ravished' – now that is
the sort of thing I could *never* write, Mrs Picton thought
mildly – 'and again I fly, this time with my little girl and
boy.

'We were doing so well, my Emile and I, and now again I see all in ruins. We are here in London, and I appeal to you, dear Mrs Picton, to let us come to you till these terrible tribulations are over.

'Never shall I forget the lovely years I spent with you; and now I pray the good God that my little Louise and Jules shall know also what I knew then.

'They know you already, because always I tell them of your goodness and of your lovely English home, and Jules knows even the goldfish as if they all had names for him.

'So write and say we can come. The brave English and the brave Belgians fight side by side once more, and under our noble king we will never surrender.

'Perhaps your son, Captain Picton, is fighting in my country, while my children are in your country. God bless him, and let us be together again, dear Mrs Picton.'

Yes, thought Mrs Picton, letting the page flutter to the ground. Roger is fighting in Belgium and, thank God, the Belgians and the French are fighting with him.

As it was, she thought sometimes that her heart would break; if it were not for the staunchness of the old allies, she just could not go on; she could not face it.

Her father had been killed in the Boer War, Colin in the last war, and now her son.

The letter had come a few days ago, and she had written to Martha Laporte, saying: 'Yes; come along here, and bring the children with you.' They would be here late tonight. She had arranged for a car to meet them at Truro.

She looked out over the sun-dazzled water, across the lawn which always at this time of year she had known vibrant with the laughter of young sun-browned people. At least, these three would be company. And Martha Laporte seemed to be comfortably off.

Perhaps, Mrs Picton permitted herself to think, she would

offer to pay. It would be something. Not that she could ask her.

Everything was ready. She had made up a bed for Martha in the room next to her own. Jules and Louise could sleep in the room that had two beds.

She walked from room to room, smoothing the counter-panes, giving a last touch to the flowers that she had brought in from the garden. The poor mites! They would need them.

They would be exhausted, like little Martha, whom she had met twenty-six years ago. She thought of Jules, who knew the goldfish by name.

The children evidently expected so much, and would find so little. But Jules should not be altogether disappointed. She found a big bowl, filled it with water, and put it on the table by his bed. There was time for her to take the mile walk to the rectory and beg a goldfish from the pond there.

'See, Jules,' she would say, 'this is one of the very fish your mother knew. Alas! we haven't a pond any more, but we've kept this fellow in a bowl ever since we left Corner-ways.'

Yes; that was a good idea. She put on her shady, faded old straw hat and set out for the rectory, rehearsing her little speech in French. She had never been good at it.

'*Hélas! Nous n'avons plus un étang.*' Was that all right? Did one pronounce the 'h' in '*Hélas*'? Perhaps she had better say it in English to Martha and ask her to translate.

She always liked the rectory, with the figs bursting on the warm wall, and the great cedar sweeping its grave pinions down to the lawn.

And there was the rector, his hair white in the evening dusk, in the deeper dusk of the trees, pacing alone, the blue smoke going up in little puffs from his pipe.

He looked up, startled, on hearing her footsteps on the gravel, and she advanced, holding out the milkcan she had brought, and saying gaily: 'I want to beg a goldfish for a Belgian refugee.'

They had been friends for years. The old bachelor looked at her sadly. 'You haven't got a wireless, have you?' he asked.

She laughed the thin silver laugh that went so well with her sun-faded silk and straw. 'You always ask me that. Wretched invention. I refuse to allow all the Toms, Dicks and Harrys to intrude into my life.'

He went on puffing. It was some moments before he spoke. 'The Belgians are out of the war. The king has thrown his hand in.'

He took out his pipe and looked steadily at the burning bowl. 'I suppose we'll have to get our men out of there somehow. God knows how we'll do it. They've been handed over to slaughter.'

Handed over to slaughter. Our men! My Roger!

She had dropped the can and was hurrying home in the dusk, her mind a boiling of emotion. She ran blindly into the big hall of the shack, just pushing open the door that was never locked.

The room was dim in the warm summer dusk, and for a moment she was not aware of the three figures standing by the fireplace.

Then Martha Laporte came forward, voluble, pouring out explanations. 'I am so sorry. We are early. We are before we expected. The taxi ran – but it ran! And the man would not wait. He put us here and say "She will soon – " '

She paused, tongue-tied by the sight of this tall, haggard woman, looking at her with burning eyes. 'You are Mrs Picton?' she faltered.

Mrs Picton looked at the group before her, the boxes, the children, dressed with the slightly foreign touch that made them unsympathetic.

The middle-aged woman with the harsh business face,

the calculating eyes, the build of a Flemish mare. A sudden blaze of hatred for them all burned up in her.

She strode towards Martha and almost hissed, so bitter was her venom: 'What do you want here? I hate the sight of you. Go – and take your children with you. Go! Go!'

Martha clutched the hands of her children and backed towards the door, staring in wonder at this incarnate white wrath that was once the beautiful tender woman who had helped and healed her infancy.

Then as suddenly as the flame had leapt in Mrs Picton it died, like a lamp blown out. Her face went old and haggard and tired.

She began to sob. 'Oh, Martha, Martha! The things life does to us! The beasts it makes of us.'

Martha let go the children's hands and pulled Mrs Picton's head down on to her fat, comfortable chest. They clung together. They both cried.

Louise and Jules looked at the two women, overcome with shyness at the sight of adult grief, breaking out without restraint there in the darkening, shabby room. Then Jules grasped his mother's skirt and began tugging. 'Maman,' he demanded. 'Where are the goldfish? And why does the tall lady cry? And where is Mrs Picton?'

SEAMAN ARNOLD BAKER

MERCHANT NAVY

(This is a true story of heroism which appeared in *Went the Day Well . . .* edited by Derek Tangye in 1942.)

> *Went the day well? We died and never knew*
> *But, well or ill, Freedom, we died for you.* Anon.

When the war came Arnold Baker knew that his testing time had come with it. He loved all men; he would kill no man, whether friend or foe; and this he would probably declare. It would not be pleasant, but that was a side of the matter that must not be allowed to influence him. It was right, as he saw it, and the war, after all, was being fought, so it was said, to give men freedom to follow right as they saw it, not as other people saw it. But these other people were numerous and, by their weight of numbers, powerful. They could, and he had no doubt they would, bring great unpleasantness into a life which hitherto had been happy in service. There might even be persecution: not the barbarous persecution of the rack and the thumbscrew – though even that had been brought back by the modern barbarians – but the civilised persecution of the cold shoulder and the lost job. Very well. Something had been said about that in the Book which the supreme religious authorities of the realm had decreed to be the guide of life; and in this Arnold agreed with them. *Blessed are ye when men shall reproach you, and persecute you, and say all manner of evil against you falsely, for my sake. Rejoice and be exceeding glad, for great is your reward in heaven, for so persecuted they the prophets that were before you.*

For himself, thought Arnold Baker, going to his work

through the grey industrial Lancashire streets, he would persecute no man; but if men chose to persecute him – well, he must put up with it. He squared his broad shoulders, drew himself up to his full five feet ten, and the bright blue eyes under the fair hair were full of resolution as he marched on to his humble job – clerk in a paint works.

There was nothing about him of the pallid, squeamish intellectual. His cheeks were rosy, and he had just turned twenty in this September when England was again at war. All his young life had been lived in the nightmare interregnum between one war and another. He had never known peace, as some generations had been privileged to know it. He had known only the dragging consequences of one war merging imperceptibly into the dawning apprehension of another. Life was a disturbing and uncertain experience, with little that was solid on which a man's foot might come to rest. But there was one rock among the quicksands. He had read: 'A new commandment give I unto you: that ye love one another; even as I have loved you, that ye also love one another.' That was firm, that was unshakeable; and, thinking it over in his grave, puzzled way, seeking always for the truth, he saw that it had tremendous implications. 'The love our Lord revealed in face of Calvary,' he once said. *As I have loved you.* That was not easy; that was a love that involved a cross, a way of life that carried with it a way of death.

These things had been much in his heart before the war came. The truths of the Christian faith moved him in the deepest and manliest part of his being. He was no sectarian. Wherever the truth as he saw it could be proclaimed he was willing to proclaim it. He spoke in Methodist chapels; he taught in an Anglican Sunday school; he was drawn in friendliness to members of the Society of Friends. That title, perhaps, pleased him better than any other. It said what he wanted to say about life as he thought it should be lived.

What a happy day that would be for mankind when it was nothing but a great world-wide society of friends! This led him to make his declaration in a Bolton newspaper: 'I believe it is only when men experience the love of Christ in their own hearts that we have the true foundation of real peace.'

All these matters Arnold Baker pondered before the war came, and he made up his mind what his course would be. If he had to be killed, then let him be killed. He was ready for that. But that he should kill any one of the great society of those he loved – that was unthinkable, ruled out absolutely.

He was the youngest of a large family. There were seven brothers and two sisters. He lived at 13 Raimond Street, Bolton, and it was here in his own home that he made his first stand for his beliefs when the war came. One of his brothers joined the army, and Arnold tried to dissuade him. 'I think,' he explained later, 'that he had rejected the Christian way of living.'

A few months later he was called upon to declare his faith in public. He was summoned to Manchester to appear before the Conscientious Objectors' Tribunal, and there his sincerity was recognised by the grant of complete exemption from military service. Judge E. C. Burgis, the chairman of the tribunal, said he and his colleagues were satisfied that Arnold Baker's objection to taking part in warfare was rooted in conscience, and had been so rooted for a long time. He added, 'We are going to rely on you to pull your weight as a citizen. We think you have a sense of responsibility, and we are going to rely on it.'

I do not know whether the judge and the fair blue-eyed youth ever met again; but eighteen months later the judge, in that same court, announced the death of Arnold Baker in circumstances of what he called 'sublime heroism'.

We are going to rely on you. Those were the words that remained in Arnold Baker's mind as he went back from Manchester

E.S.B.   N

to Bolton. Well, he was a reliable person, because he himself
had something to rely on. He had, for one thing, all those
friends who believed with him in the commandment 'Thou
shalt not kill'. The world was not yet a society of friends,
but within the brawling, quarrelling, suicidal mass there
was a core of fellowship, a point of rest at the heart of the
cyclone; and here, whatever happened, he could find the
peace which, in this sad world, seemed to exist nowhere else.
But Arnold was to learn what some people never learn:
that this core of peace cannot be derived from others. It is in
a man's own heart or nowhere. His friends began to meet
him with embarrassment; some avoided meeting him; some,
when they met him, were subtly different in their treatment
of him; and some looked right through him. And this was
true even of some of his church friends. They had sons, they
had friends, they had brothers, lovers, husbands, who were
gone from the old haunts. Their lives were filled with new
fears, new apprehensions, new realisation of the uncertainty
of all human hoping and planning. There were simple homes
that had been built up by love and sacrifice and that now
were like paper houses before this cold wind that was blowing
through the world. There were other homes that had, so far,
existed only in the romantic schemes and promises of young
lovers, and these perhaps would now never have a foundation
on this earth. There was all this human sense of peril and
uncertainty and frustration. There was the deep human cry,
'Can't someone *do* something about it?' and so many young
men were missing from their places in Bolton, doing what
they could. But Arnold Baker still walked the Bolton streets,
an ever-present reminder of those who walked there no
longer, and it was no wonder that men and women began
to pass by on the other side.

No wonder to Arnold, at any rate. He understood the deep
wells of feeling from which resentment rose because his own
feelings were so deep; and he knew that to succumb to the

assault of a general emotion would be easy and, in a way, satisfying. It would 'let him out'. It would end his spiritual dilemma. But it would end it by a betrayal; and that was why it was the one thing which he could not do. The way of a transgressor might be hard, but the way of a man who trod what seemed to him the straight and narrow path was harder yet. He went on treading it.

So the first winter of the war dragged out its weary, uninspiring length, and nothing much happened, for as yet it was a war unlighted by faith, untouched by destiny, not heightened by heroism or depressed too much by the death of heroes. And then, as spring quickened even the drear industrial streets of Bolton, the tempo swung into its swift, dramatic acceleration. Norway, Denmark, Belgium, Holland, France. Countries were consumed like mouthfuls, and a new word was added to the litany of the nations: Dunkirk.

The world was stirred; Bolton was stirred; Arnold Baker was stirred. Men were dying, and he could die. He would not kill, but willingly he would die. He wrote to the Admiralty and asked to be employed on a minesweeper, but nothing came of it. But the thought of the sea remained in his mind. Landlocked at the heart of industrial Lancashire, he yet heard the surge and beat of waters. *If I take the wings of the morning and dwell in the uttermost parts of the sea, even there shall thy hand lead me.*

It was a terrible summer for Arnold Baker. Terrible to love mankind and to walk through one's own familiar streets, to catch the sad eyes of lifelong friends, with this cloud of hostility at worst, misunderstanding at best, growing and deepening about him. To love mankind, and to be increasingly looked upon as one who would lift no hand to help mankind in its direst need. To seem as though it mattered nothing to him that evil was cleaving its iron way through nations whose fault was that they had too much followed his own peaceful counsels, were too ready not to defend themselves. Was he wrong? Was force, after all, the only answer to force? No, he could not believe it. He had no doubt that this was an evil thing abroad in the world; but all that till now he had believed in and lived by would have no meaning unless he could still give a cheek to the kiss of the betrayer – even to this iron kiss of Hitler's Judas hordes. He held to what he had said before: 'Love revealed in the face of Calvary.' He began to think that his own life was demanded. To give one's life in sacrifice; to take no lives in bitterness: perhaps that was the way.

Now he was workless. He accepted that. It was not that work was not to be had, but that there were men who did not want *his* work. Well, that was a small part of the sacrifice. He was prepared to give up more than that. He found another job, and the year crept on, punctuated by war's deepening alarms. The bombs rained on London, and London stood. They fell on inland towns, almost razing some of them from the earth, and out of the smoking débris men and women crawled and began with bruised hands to build things up again. The pulse of the nation's life was quick. Gone now was the grey lethargy of last winter. The air was bright with anonymous heroism; men and women were doing everywhere what he felt he had it in himself to do. Striking no blow they were dying for the right.

So in September he came to his twenty-first birthday, and he did not forget two things: the words that were still in his ears, *We are going to rely on you*, and the sound of the sea. At times they seemed to merge, and he was visited with premonitions of what the end would be.

The autumn faded. A year of the war was over and winter deepened again upon the Lancashire plain, a winter with no lights blazing in the great glass-filled oblongs of the mills; not even the shops warmed to their Christmas gaiety; not even a street-lamp shed its gleam as he walked back to his home through the thickening dusk, with the war creeping nearer and nearer, for now Manchester, a few miles away, had felt the blow, had counted its dead and looked upon the ruins of historic buildings pounded to dust.

In that December Arnold Baker was walking with a lighter tread, for now his affairs were in train, and soon they were concluded. He was to go to sea. 1941 dawned, and this, though he did not know it, was the last New Year's Day he was to see, and of that year he was not to see much. For now he was stepping into the last act of his drama, and before the month was ended the curtain would fall on a climax of blood and fire.

On the 14th of January he made the short journey to Liverpool, looking his last, as the train sped through the dun Lancashire flats, upon scenes that were dear and familiar. He went on board Alfred Holt and Company's ship *Eurylochus* to take up his duties as a writer in the purser's office. The next day the ship sailed for Glasgow, and from Glasgow she set out on the first and last voyage that Arnold Baker was to know.

Now his mind was free and happy. He was serving his country in circumstances in which he might be killed but could not kill. He made no false pretences. He was one of those persons spoken of with contempt as 'conchies'. He had been granted 'unconditional exemption'. But this did not affect his position in the ship. His personality won respect, to which Mr J. A. C. MacGregor, the first mate, was later to pay a notable tribute.

The *Eurylochus* pitched her way southward through the cold English winter seas, and towards the end of the month she was a hundred miles off the Sierra Leone coast. The night of the 29th January came down as black as pitch. Anxious eyes were scanning the water. Upon the bridge were two men: Mr MacGregor and Arnold Baker, who, as soon as the voyage began, expressed a wish to do his share of the look-out. Suddenly the silence and darkness of the night were shattered. From close range guns of heavy calibre were pouring a salvo into the *Eurylochus*. A German commerce-raider had found them.

'Words will never describe the savagery we faced that night.' So MacGregor wrote afterwards. And as the savagery burst about them, as the shells exploded, and men died, and the steel débris of the *Eurylochus* sang and hurtled through the air, Arnold Baker stood on the bridge smiling. It is to Mr MacGregor that we owe all we know of his death. 'In the midst of the fire and bursting shells I remember so vividly seeing young Arnold standing straight and smiling, a picture of real goodness and godliness whilst the evening's brutality fell at our feet.'

But to stand and smile was not enough. A shell struck the bridge, and Arnold noticed that in the terror and confusion of the moment the wheel had been left unattended. He was a landsman. He knew nothing about the steering of ships, but he said quickly to Mr MacGregor: 'Show me what to do and I will do it.'

So they went into the wheelhouse, and Arnold Baker was shown what to do, and there he stood at the wheel while the pandemonium continued to rage. At last he found that the ship was not answering. A shot had wrecked her steering-gear. Only then did he leave the wheelhouse and seek out Mr MacGregor again on the bridge. 'What shall I do now?' he asked.

The night was going ill with the *Eurylochus*. There was not much now that anyone could do. The boats were being lowered into the dark, shark-infested water. 'Make for your boat,' said MacGregor. 'The bridge is being too heavily shelled.' As he spoke MacGregor himself was wounded, and he saw no more of Arnold. But others saw him. They saw the flash, and the staggering body that was now done with all the perplexing arguments of right and wrong. He had found the 'lesser Calvary', which he had perhaps unconsciously been seeking ever since the storm broke that was to put his faith to the test.

'He certainly fulfilled his promise to pull his weight,' Mr MacGregor wrote, 'and he died a wonderful example of British courage and bravery.'

It was not till months later that the facts were made known. Then on a summer day in 1941 Judge Burgis spoke in the court where, one drear day of two Decembers ago, he had recognised that there are men who must be allowed to live according to the light that is in them. He spoke of the manner of Arnold Baker's death. 'We can only contemplate his conduct,' he said, 'with humble reverence.'

I know where linnets make their nests,
  And broomy heaths where rabbits burrow;
I know, before a blade is seen,
  Where corn will greenly fledge the furrow.

I know old moles with bodies shiny
  As any grocer's Sunday hat
And pools where ancient pikes swim gravely
  That may have swum round Ararat.

There's not a man in all the county
  That hears a cuckoo call so soon
Or sees, before I do, a swallow,
  Or lives so lazily in June.

I can make Oxford chairs from osiers
  That grow along the swampy flats;
Perhaps 'twas parson's life in Oxford
  That made his eyes as blind as bats.

Parson says I'm an idle rascal,
  Ripe for the place where bad 'uns go;
But to us bad 'uns sometimes happen
  Things that the parsons never know.

Once, when the sky was blood and water,
  A thrush between two showers called clear;
I felt in me as sharp as passion
  The vinegar, the nail, the spear.

                                        Howard Spring

THE LITTLE VICTIMS PLAY

The beginning of the novel which
Howard Spring was working on when he died.

Chapter One

A very precise book tells us that Robert Lowe, Viscount Sherbrooke, said in the House of Commons on 15th July, 1867: 'I believe it will be absolutely necessary that you should prevail on our future masters to learn their letters.' This, the same precise and invaluable book tells us, has been popularised as 'We must educate our masters.'

Have it either way. One of the consequences was our school, which was solidly built of stone, with echoing stone stairways inside, a trim garden running along the front, high iron railings shutting this from intrusion; and, over all, an architrave incised with the words: 'Pro Bono Publico.' On the left was the entrance for girls; on the right the entrance for boys, behind which was an enclosure known as the playground. Therein, once every week, the 'drill sergeant' appeared, formed us up in ranks, taught us to touch our toes without bending our knees, to flex our arms so that the muscles, with which we were not abundantly furnished, should be developed, marched us hither and thither, in single ranks, in twos, in fours, and generally took a hand in the grim business of educating us *pro bono publico*. However, we liked the drill sergeant with his mock ferocity, his very real moustache, waxed and spiked. He was a relief from the ardours and endurances we suffered indoors when we had mounted the stone staircases, with a loud clatter of hob-nailed boots, and taken our places in the classrooms.

This was a long time after Mr Lowe had uttered his memorable words, but our education had not yet advanced far towards being for the *bono publico*.

Mr Candleford, for one, didn't think we were likely to contribute greatly to that admirable cause. He was himself little more than a youth, with faint beginnings of a moustache furnishing his upper lip. When school reassembled after the summer holidays and he faced a new set of boys – about sixty of us there would be in each class – he did so with ferocity. We had been told what his first action would be, and it was in accordance with rumour. He regarded us from a raised platform on which was a blackboard and, at the back, a cupboard. Leaning down lithely, he would produce from behind the cupboard a cane which he swished through the air. It made a sound like a hissing of serpents. Armed with this symbol of power, he would advance slowly to the front of his platform, glare upon us, and say: 'I am about to throw this cane to the back of the cupboard.' This he would then ritually do. 'And now,' he would say, 'God help the boy who causes me to bring it out again.'

After a pause to allow his words to sink into our minds, as the cane, often enough, sank into our flesh, he would begin to teach us to toil *pro bono publico*. 'Come on, you lot,' he would exclaim. 'You were born to be carpenters and brick carriers, plasterers and labourers, to do one sort or another of useful work. Now we must turn you into snotty-nosed little pen-pushers, a credit to your country.'

So it will be seen that Mr Candleford's conception of what the Viscount Sherbrooke had been talking about was not a very high one, though I think he was an exception rather than a rule. When the break came at eleven o'clock we would clatter down the stony reverberating stairs and in the harsh playground gather in groups to discuss what counter-measures would be necessary against canes that hissed like serpents. The general opinion was that resin, rubbed on the palms, was the best stuff, and some had taken the precaution of coming to school well-provisioned with this, as it proved, ineffective antidote. There was also a spit-faction, though it was generally admitted that nothing that really worked had yet been found. This conclusion, as time went on, was con-

firmed by experience, though I must say that I escaped being
called on to give evidence. Yet Candleford was a popular
master. This was because he was no more concerned than
we were to contribute to the public good by learning or by
anything else. He appointed monitors. So far as I could see,
their function was confined to two things: to clean the blackboard and to look out for Mr Ewing who was headmaster
of the school. It was Mr Ewing's habit to descend at unspecified times upon this class or that, to confer with the
master in charge, and to conduct a brief examination into
our progress. This did not please Candleford. It was his
intention that Ewing's unspecified times should not be so
unspecified as all that. He was a great hand at dodging the
column which should be, according to theory, heading
resolutely in the direction of the *bono publico*. For one thing,
he had some idea of himself as a poet. We had a school
soccer team, and it was his boast that, quicker than most
men, he could compose what he called a poem, bringing in
the name of every boy who was in the team. I remember in
particular one ringing line: 'That flying little forward
Tommy Erskine.'

When the afflatus was on him, and Candleford was entrancing us as he stood on his platform improvising verse, it
was necessary that Ewing should not descend unheralded
upon the classroom. Hence one use of the monitors. Boys
who were not giving due attention to their lessons, or who
were otherwise defeating Lord Sherbrooke's intention, were
sent from the room. They were commanded to stand outside
the door for the duration of the lesson, thus absorbing
knowledge, one must assume, from the chalky atmosphere
of the corridor. When that flying little forward Tommy
Erskine was being celebrated, or Candleford was otherwise
hell bent for the Poet Laureateship, to the delight of us all,
there, in place of dunces, the monitors would be, in their
true function of uttering monition. A long corridor led

from Ewing's room to ours, and when it became evident that Ewing was bearing down upon us, subdued kicks and knocks upon the door would amply presage his intention, so that he never came upon anything but a decorous class, all bent like beavers in maintaining and advancing the general good. So we were taught, if nothing else, that authority can be outwitted.

Of poetry as I have come to understand it, nothing was taught us. Anything that rhymed was 'poetry' and took its place in the poetry lesson. I remember, even to this day, the opening of some verses that were taught to us and that we were commanded to learn 'by heart'.

> *Only a story of boyish pluck,*
> *Of love that was brave and true;*
> *Only a lad with a hero's heart,*
> *Who did what few men would do.*
>
> *It was out in the Indian mutiny,*
> *In the midst of stress and strife,*
> *A boy stood guard o'er his father's house,*
> *Guard o'er his father's life.*

And we were given that heroic boy, who stood with a loaded cannon before him, trained upon a mob of mutineers.

> *Stand back, they shouted, back from the gun,*
> *You'll die if you dare refuse.*
> *But show us the place where your father hides*
> *And your life shall be spared – now choose.*

So we were taught how a boy might act *pro bono publico*, but we were never taught about India, or the Indian mutiny, or anything to which this heroic episode might have been an opening and a guide.

Anyway, this 'poetry class' having been sufficiently arduous, Candleford would allow us a little relaxation. 'Monitors to the door,' he would command. And the monitors, who knew their job by this time, would take their stations on the lookout for Ewing. Candleford would rattle a pocket full of marbles, roll back a bit of matting that concealed a circle chalked on the floor, and call out those who were to join him in a game. He always won. His pockets bulged with marbles.

Towards the end of the morning, there would come half a dozen or so of damsels who had been learning 'cookery' in classes recently begun in the girls' part of the school. They would be bearing baskets loaded with the results of their morning's efforts – small cakes and buns that were on sale for a copper or two. 'Any Good Samaritans to-day?' Candleford would cry; and, little toadies that we were, there were always some with the necessary pennies to take the edge off his appetite.

Candleford was perhaps not the best kind of master, and ours was not the best kind of school: not a bit like the schools of to-day where the pupils are enclosed within vast sheets of glass, like plants 'brought on' beneath cloches. But we had to do as well as we could unless we had the constructive genius of Charlie Stapledon. Stapledon had tried everything from resin to spit, and he knew better than most of us that these were puny aids against hissing serpents. He was a small boy, small because ill-fed, and he had an engaging impudence. He made a classic retort to Candleford when we stood in ranks in the school ground. There were seven classes for boys, and there we were, drawn up, as near as we could manage it, like soldiers in formation, while a master walked before each rank, an officer assuring himself that the troops were properly dressed. Thus Candleford came one day upon Charlie Stapledon, dressed, shall we say, somewhat casually. Boots were always Candleford's chief

object of scrutiny, and Stapledon never distinguished himself
in the matter of footwear. 'You haven't cleaned your boots
this morning,' Candleford said; to which Stapledon replied:
'Can't afford blacking, sir.'

'Can't you spit on your boots and rub them up with an
old stocking?'

'I keep my spit for another purpose,' said Stapledon;
grinning as always, spitting upon his hands, and giving them
a rub on his trouser-seat.

This, producing a laugh along our file, was insubordina-
tion. Stapledon was led before supreme authority, and Mr
Ewing, who had encountered him before for various lacks
of reverence, was in despair of this boy ever contributing
much to the *bono publico*. 'Send him to work in the
garden,' he commanded, which suited Stapledon literally
down to the ground.

And so, upon that plot of land which stretched between
the tall iron railings and the front of the school, Stapledon
was set to work. What he made of it I do not know, but there,
henceforth, he was often to be seen, with boots as dirty as he
cared to have them and beautifully free from authority – an
Adam Junior in Paradise before the Fall.

There were reasons of this sort and that why boys should
leave school half an hour or so before the customary time.
There were, for example, during the winter months, those
heroes of the soccer team whom Candleford's epic celebrated. No playing-field was attached to our school –
nothing but the gritty yard; and so our young athletes were
turned out in order to use one of the public parks. Or the
more unfortunate were released from their durance in order
to be on the spot whence our evening newspaper was issued
to its sellers in the streets. Thence they would emerge crying
the news of the day – 'all the winners', or, in more profitable
times, ' 'orrible murder' in this, that or the other place. They
made, when winter came on, our dark back streets direful

with intimations of the sins of the world. I often wonder, even now, why we have not a Sunday newspaper called *Sins of the World*. It would have a profitable sale among those whom Mr Lowe, some generations ago, was anxious to teach their reading. And that a thing should be profitable is surely a criterion of success, one guarantee of yet another knight-hood or barony.

2.

I suppose I was five years old when I went to the 'babies' class' in our school. The teachers in the babies' class were women. And why shouldn't they be? We had been taught for a long time that there was no reason why women should not do their share of the world's work. Or children for that matter. If our lordly 'capitalists' – the backbone of the nation – saw the advantage of sending them down the coal-pits, half-clad, half-starved, to crawl about in dark tunnels from morn to night, or to work amid the whirring noisy machines of mills, why shouldn't women have a hand in teaching children to read and write *pro bono publico*? Admittedly, the women and children no longer crawled, ghastly sub-human, in the dark places under the earth, but the time was coming when, whether they wanted it or not, they would be promoted to service with men in the dark places over the earth, in armies and navies and air forces. So there they were, in our school and in many another school. They were still too feeble-minded to be doctors or lawyers or Cabinet ministers or parsons, but their time would come.

I do not remember how long I remained in the babies' class, little boys and little girls all huddled together, but I remember clearly being taught to recite a poem about a robin who went hop, hop, hop, and shook his little tail and said 'How do you do?' before 'away he flew', and the flutter-ing gesture of the teacher's hands as she dramatised this homeward flight of master robin. Indeed, I never felt that the poem was complete without this fluttering of hands.

Only that, and three other things, I remember from the babies' class. One was a day of great cold, when the fire that blazed in the schoolroom grate was unusually bright, and our teacher, a good homely soul, encouraged us to come out in twos and threes to warm our perished fingers and diminutive toes. And there was, remembered perhaps because of contrast, a day when the sun seemed swooning with his own heat in the sky and our classroom was close and stuffy. A shuffling and an easing of sticky shirts over small backs forbade much attention to lessons, and we were admonished that the stiller we kept the cooler we would be.

These, and one third happening in the babies' class, remain in my mind. There was a 'block building lesson' that was the terror of my life. Each of us was given a long box containing the wooden blocks with which we were invited to build what we would. No building of mine was ever distinguished either by imagination or skill, though perhaps a modern architect might have thought it not without promise, seeing that it lacked both these qualities. Our 'building' done, we were commanded to pile our blocks into a symmetrical shape over which the box was then clamped upside down. Now the lid of the box was used as an extension of the desk and, holding this firmly, we were commanded to draw our boxes gently upon the lids, up-end the lot, and there it was – a box full of wooden bricks, ready for the next lesson. But never could I achieve this simple operation, and confidence in failure made the matter worse. Down would come my blocks upon the floor, while I was surrounded by triumphant competitors, smugly regarding their success. There was no punishment in the babies' class, and so the matter was more hard to bear. Commiserating looks and helpful hands made me realise all too clearly what a hopeless builder I was, unable to succeed with any mechanical thing.

3.

Standard I was our first class and, theoretically, the little victims advanced class by class to Standard VII, being then equipped to face the world. I never got as far, though I cannot, at this distance of time, remember in which standard I was when I left our school for ever.

I recall going home for dinner and being met on the threshold by my Aunt Shellabeer. Mrs Shellabeer was my mother's sister. She had 'got on' in the world, had married Mr Shellabeer, a builder. He had made a little money and had spent it, from time to time, on buying small houses in slums. What with the rents of these and with what he made as a builder, he was on the edge of being a prosperous man, but never more. Enough, though, to allow Mrs Shellabeer, my Aunt Jane, to give herself airs and to look down on my mother. They were the only children of a labourer, and my mother herself had married a labourer, whom Mrs Shellabeer never met. She did not consort with that sort of people, especially as her husband was now not only a builder but a house-owner. However, when my father died, in the year before this time of which I write, she did condescend to look my mother up once or twice, and I remember how she made one of these calls on a day which chanced to be my birthday. She had still not come round to so audacious an idea as taking my mother to see her husband; but when she learned that it was my birthday, she thought she might take me; and Mother, who had plenty on her hands and was probably glad to have me out of the house for a while, agreed to let me go.

It was a broiling summer day; I was a very small boy; and I trotted through the streets holding Aunt Shellabeer by the hand. She wore an immense flowery hat perched on a head that had a lot of fair hair, and carried an open parasol.

'You haven't got much to say for yourself,' she said; and I, who feared the grandeur walking at my side, tall and thin, unlike my mother who was small and chubby, closed my mouth tight. I felt like a bum-boat being taken in tow by a galleon.

I didn't know where the Shellabeers lived, but from my rambles abroad I knew all the streets thereabouts, and when we turned into one of them and Mrs Shellabeer said grandly, 'We live here,' I knew it well enough and was impressed, and nervous, too, at such splendour being our destination.

I don't suppose I should be either nervous or impressed to-day. Lilac Avenue, like Guelder Avenue and Mimosa Avenue, and other floral and shrubby destinations, opened their little veins off the artery of Floral Parade, and, as I see them now, they were all drearily alike, the sort of houses that Aunt Shellabeer's husband might himself have built. What occurred to me at the time was that Aunt Shellabeer had done very well for herself and was living in a region that justified the floral hat she wore and the beautiful parasol she carried. We stopped half-way down Lilac Avenue, and she said: 'Wipe your boots on the mat before you go in. Mr Shellabeer loathes – positively loathes – dirt about the house.'

We paused while I scrubbed and scrubbed my boots upon the mat outside a door boasting a glass panel of many colours. Little bits of blue, red and green glass were caught in a leaden mesh.

'The house is in a State as it is,' said Aunt Shellabeer, referring again to Mr Shellabeer's loathing of dirt. 'We're having the Gas Laid On.'

You must pardon these capital letters. They belonged to the way in which my aunt pronounced certain words. Anyone, I understood, might have the gas taken into the house. The Shellabeers had it, as a special concession to their status, Laid On.

The passage, when we entered it, after I had scrubbed my

boots as thoroughly as a sailor holystoning a deck, was a narrow corridor hung with varnished wallpaper. The gas, which had been Laid On, was imprisoned here in a hanging contraption made, like the door-panel, of bits of coloured glass. My aunt, accustomed to high living, gave it merely a passing glance, and said: 'We got the Gas Men out yesterday. We shall still have some Cleaning Up to do. But that can wait till to-morrow when the Woman comes. You'd better see my husband. Hang your cap on the Hall Stand.'

The hat stand was made of bamboo. She had already placed her parasol in a niche therein reserved for it, and I obediently hung my cap upon one of the hooks. Aunt Shellabeer looked, I thought, with disapproval at that tattered rag which had had many a rough passage, propelled by hob-nailed boots, about the school playground. 'Henry's Cap,' she said, 'has Blue Rings.'

My mother had mentioned Henry, so I knew that Mrs Shellabeer was speaking of her only son whom I had never met. I knew, however, that he was attending some select academy which charged a small fee. Mrs Shellabeer turned to the hook on which Henry was accustomed to hang his cap with the Blue Rings. 'It is doubtful,' she said, 'whether Henry will enter the Business. We have Other Plans for him.'

My mother, as I have said, had never met Mr Shellabeer, or she would have given me some idea of what to expect when I was presented to that gentleman. As it was, I should not have been at all surprised if I had found a satrap sitting on a couch, surrounded by houris and puffing at a hookah. While my aunt's hand was upon the knob of a door which led, she explained, to the Drawing-Room, it was, to say the least, a figure of magnificence that I expected to encounter. What met my gaze was, in fact, a very small man, bald as they come, with his coat thrown on the floor at his feet, his shirt sleeves rolled up, and a clay pipe in his mouth. The pipe, fortunately, was out, or he might have set himself alight, for it was trembling on the very verge of a fall and seemed held in by automatic suction. The heat of the day, I suppose, accounted for his dishevelled appearance. He looked as though he would, for two pins, have taken his shirt off while he was about it.

The opening of the door startled him into wakefulness, but he did not get up. His lids rose; two small watery eyes looked at me. Mrs Shellabeer was not at all disconcerted and said: 'This is Emma's boy.'

'What's he want?' Mr Shellabeer asked.

'It is his birthday.'

'Well, give him a shilling – no, sixpence,' said Mr Shellabeer, composing himself to sleep. 'I was having a bit of a nap. Show him Henry's room.'

Mrs Shellabeer opened the door and led me out. 'Mr Shellabeer is having a Bit of a Nap,' she explained, as though translating from a foreign tongue. 'I will show you Henry's Room.'

She said nothing about the shilling, or even the sixpence, but led me quickly upstairs lest my thoughts should hang too closely round that, to me, entrancing matter. I had never handled a shilling or a sixpence in my life except when sent out to do a bit of shopping. And I had to be content, so far as Mrs Shellabeer was concerned, with the memory.

I was shown Henry's room, which looked like any other room, except that it had a rickety easy-chair and a bookcase with a photograph over it. This showed a school-class, all wearing caps with their blue rings well defined. 'That is Henry,' said Mrs Shellabeer, pointing out one boy who seemed very much like the other boys. But not to his mother, I gathered. She gave him a fond look, and said: 'When we had the gas Laid On we took care that a good light should fall on his writing-table. This is where he Pursues his Studies.'

I was hoping that even at this late stage she might remember that it was my birthday and perhaps, though she withheld the shilling, ask me to stay to tea. But nothing of the sort happened. I was led down into the Front Hall and warned to go quietly past the Drawing-Room door because Mr Shellabeer might still be having his Bit of a Nap. Shilling-less, and even sixpence-less, I was turned into Lilac Avenue, wondering why I had been asked at all.

I was rounding a corner when a boy came towards me, with a satchel of books slung over his shoulder and wearing a cap embellished with blue rings. He collided with me so suddenly and forcibly that he went over, as I should then regrettably have said, smack on to his backside. His cap fell off, and I had been so well instructed in my own school-yard as to what caps were for, and was, though perhaps I hardly realised it then, so fed up with blue rings, through Mrs Shellabeer's chatter, that I put my boot behind it and sent it over the railings into a neighbour's front garden.

We did not stop to parley, but I went homeward unaware that I had made my first acquaintance with my cousin, Henry Shellabeer.

4.

I cannot at this distance of time remember dates very clearly. It is enough to say that some time after this – it may have been a year – I had left our school for ever. I had not in the meantime renewed my acquaintance with the Shellabeers. There had been so marked an absence of enthusiasm on Mr Shellabeer's part during my only meeting with him, so obvious an intention to get rid of me even at the cost of sixpence, that my aunt never again called on us. As for ourselves – my mother and me – we got on as well as we could, which was not very well. We lived in a ramshackle house in a ramshackle *cul de sac*, and as often as not my mother was out when I returned after a day at school. However, the key was under the mat; I let myself in, and I dutifully awaited her return in order that we might eat together. The rations were poor enough, but we were happy in our way, and I cannot remember that I ever wanted the way to be any different from what it was.

I can well imagine now, however, that my mother would have liked it to be different. There were so many careworn faces about us that I did not notice hers to be particularly careworn. I knew that she was out most days on some job of charring; and she occasionally announced that she was off to see the 'Guardians'. I was given to understand that these were august and powerful people whose business was to guard the poor. Sometimes, after a visit to the 'Guardians', a couple of shillings a week made life a bit easier; but a crisis would arise now and then, Guardians or no Guardians. As I see it now, one crisis after another had been, more or less, my mother's life-story, and she was always one to meet a crisis, not to sit down and weep under it.

There was, for example, that very day when I returned shilling-less from the Shellabeers. I had been in the house for some time when my mother appeared with a bundle under her arm. She had been, as usual, giving someone's house a 'run through', as she called it. She had come home tired but triumphant, for this bundle was nothing less than an overcoat in pretty good repair. 'This,' she said with satisfaction, 'is one of Master Thomas's overcoats.'

Master Thomas was the son of the house which she had been giving a 'run through'. 'He's grown out of it,' she explained, 'and Mrs Roberts thought it would do for you.'

She examined the garment this way and that. 'So it will,' she said at last. 'Just a bit of patching here and there. But with all the summer in front of us, you won't want an over-coat for a bit. You can take it to Solly's this evening. I'll get it out somehow by the time colder days come on.'

Solly's was our local pawn-shop.

'You needn't let anyone see you going in or coming out,' she said. 'Take a good look round you.'

She knew this was a job I hated, but now and then it fell upon me. I was not very good at the slipping in and out business, and 'Brass Balls' was not a welcome cry in the streets, though sometimes it followed me. I was, indeed, terrified of the pawn-shop; but Solly was a good-natured fellow who knew very well what tremors I endured. Indeed, more than once he had smuggled me through a back door into a narrow lane. 'Now run for it,' he would say, as though we were both engaged in a nefarious business.

But this sort of thing ended when two events tumbled on top of each other. The winter had come, Master Thomas's overcoat had been somehow redeemed, and warm and comfortable I felt in it as I made my way home one afternoon when a snow-shower was falling. My mother was for once in, and was making a cup of tea which was placed on the table with its accompaniment of 'soakers'. If you don't know what 'soakers' are, I can tell you that they were slices of bread which were placed in a saucer. They were then immersed in tea from the pot, a sprinkling of sugar was added, and that was a 'soaker'. You spooned it up in bits and washed it down with tea from the cup.

While we were engaged upon this exercise in gluttony with the lamp lit, for it was dark by that time of a winter's day, my mother said: 'You'll soon be having a better tea than this. I've been to see Mr Ewing this afternoon, and you are to see him to-morrow.'

It was a surprising announcement. That my mother had been to see so august a person as Mr Ewing in itself shook me, but what she said next was even more exciting. 'You are to leave school and go out to work. Schooling is all right, but a bit more in the belly is better still.'

The next day I gave particular attention to my toilet.

My face was scrubbed, my hair was plastered upon my skull with water, my boots were cleaned, and my clothes were brushed. For the last time, I took my place in the files in the school-yard. For the last time I marched with the others to my place in the class. I even began my lesson, which was concerned with prepositions. They were taught us by the simple method of repeating them as if they were a song. 'The prepositions are: About, Around, Against, Before, Beneath, Behind,' we intoned, and no one ever taught us what a preposition was, or what it did, or anything about it. However, it was all *pro bono publico*, and the little masters were learning their letters.

However, I told off this rosary more dully than usual that morning, for my mind was full of the coming interview with Mr Ewing. Should I hold up my hand, which was the signal that a boy wished to address a master? Should I then announce boldly that Mr Ewing wished to see me? Or what was the correct way of opening so serious a matter? My dithering was cut short by the arrival of a monitor – an august monitor who had attained the top class in the school. He was now no less than an *aide-de-camp* of Ewing himself, employed to run on his errands, and generally to make himself one of those who 'at his bidding speed and post o'er land and ocean without rest'. He boldly approached Mr Candleford, as one having authority, and whispered his message. 'Guy Marson to the front,' Candleford announced, breaking into the prepositions, and a hush came over us all. Anything would do to stop a lesson, and in the silence that had fallen I advanced to the front of the class. For my name – unfortunately I always thought – was Guy Marson.

'Go with this monitor to see Mr Ewing,' said Candleford briefly; and thus my schooldays, in that school at any rate, were done with.

Mr Ewing's room was at the end of the passage, and the monitor, having announced 'Marson, sir', left me to my fate.

Mr Ewing, a small, dark, whiskered man, with pince-nez on his nose, was sitting at a roll-top desk. He left me standing there while he went on with some writing on which he was engaged. I felt as though the wish to leave school were some peculiarly appalling crime of which I had been found guilty and that now, sentenced, I was summoned from the cells to meet the governor of the prison. The wait seemed endless, but at last Mr Ewing brought his fist down with a bang on to a blotting sheet, swung round on the swivel of his chair, and said: 'So you are Marson?'

I admitted the charge in a trembling voice, and Mr Ewing asked: 'Why do you want to leave school?'

'Because my mother wants me to, sir.'

'Why does your mother want you to?'

'To go out and work, sir. We haven't got enough in the house.'

'Don't you know that if you stay in school, and take advantage of what is taught in the school, you will be able to go out some day and bring far more into the house?'

'Yes, sir. I expect my mother was thinking of the meantime, sir.'

For the first time I thought there was something like compassion in Mr Ewing's face. He scratched his balding head and pulled his beard, and looked at me without speaking. Then he said: 'Very well. I will see that the necessary steps are taken.'

Pondering on this interview, I have often thought that Ewing might have patted my small head, or wished me luck, or pointed out that there were night-schools, or even private study; but he did none of these things. He merely swung round again in his swivel chair and took up some papers lying on his desk. He said over his shoulder: 'Very well, then,' and that was that.

I suppose I should have felt wildly pleased that an interview I had been fearing was over, but I went slowly back to

my classroom, depressed and unhappy. Candleford asked
nothing about my adventure with the headmaster. He was
busy enough, for a game of marbles was in full swing. I got
through the morning somehow, said nothing to anyone, and
spent the afternoon in a public park. I was just going to get
up from a seat overlooking a pond where swans were spreading their great white wings when I saw a boy coming towards
me with his nose in a book, reading as he walked. There were
blue rings round his cap. I was so insignificant a creature
that he would have passed me by unnoticed, but he tripped
over my feet that were stretched out on the gravel path
before me, and, recovering, he looked at me. Then, shutting
his book, he said: 'You're the boy who kicked my cap over
the hedge.'

'And you're the boy,' I answered, 'who thanked me for
doing it.'

He smiled, and there were few who could resist Harry
Shellabeer's smile. 'The fact is,' he said, 'that I was fed up
with the cap. I was glad someone had done what I always
wanted to do myself.'

He seated himself beside me, threw his cap on to the path,
and said: 'There it is. You can kick it into the pond if you
like.'

I looked at him – the first time of many to come that we
frankly looked at one another and took stock of what we saw.
He was a fair slender boy, with blue eyes and a way of
holding himself that was manly, assured, as though what he
said went, and he knew it. He was, I judged, a few years
older than I. What he looked at was a small thin boy, dark,
hungry, fearful of any authority, especially, at this moment,
of his.

'Go on,' he said, 'kick it.'

I kicked, without much conviction, and the blue rings fell
upon the water not far from the edge.

'Now I'll have to get it out again,' he said. 'I'm sick of it.

My mother brushes it every morning. She'll have a job to-morrow.'

The cap was just beyond his reach, but at that moment a gardener came up with a rake that he had been using on the paths. Henry addressed him. 'Will you please rake out that cap? I foolishly allowed it to fall into the pond.'

The gardener raked out the cap. 'There you are, sir. I'm afraid you'll have a job to dry that.'

'The more job the better,' said Henry. 'But thank you all the same.'

I was very impressed with the whole performance – Harry's way of addressing the man from whom I should have fled as from authority, the man's willingness to obey what I could only regard as orders.

The book lay on the seat between us. It was *Micah Clarke* by A. Conan Doyle. Seeing that I was furtively studying the title, Henry asked: 'Have you read that?'

I said that I hadn't, and he explained that it was about the Civil War. 'My teacher gave it to me to read. We're doing the Civil War, and so, I suppose, he thought this might be of some use. Take it home and read it if you like. I've done with it. I'll tell you what. You meet me here this day week and then you can give it back to me.'

He didn't wait for an answer, but took up his sopping cap, looked at it with distaste, and went his way.

5.

I hadn't any idea who this boy was who had now twice fallen in my way. Nor had I any idea what the Civil War was. History for us had been a list of dates which we were expected to learn off by heart, mainly the dates when kings and queens came to the throne and when they got out of it or were forcibly removed. That it had anything to do with boys like me, or that it was a matter for tales, such as this appeared to be which I held in my hands, was something that had never entered my head. I knew a few things as well as dates. There was a king called Canute who had sat on the sea-shore telling the waves to come no farther, and there was one named Alfred who had allowed some cakes to burn. These and such-like anecdotes were drilled into my head, when we were doing a history lesson. Still, I learned later from Froude that a legend may be good history.

The winter afternoon was now drawing to a close and with *Micah Clarke* stuffed into my pocket I dawdled home. I had been told when I had set off for school and for my momentous interview with Mr Ewing that my mother would not be back at midday, and so I had been provided with my dinner wrapped in a paper bag and slipped into my pocket. It consisted of brawn sandwiches – a comestible which, as they say, turned my stomach. But I had learned to keep silent about that, had been foodless since breakfast-time. Now, as a sufficient gesture that summed up all my thoughts of brawn, I rubbed it with its bread casing into crumbs and threw it to the swans. Then, as boys will, I dawdled towards home.

My mother was there. She had just arrived and was making up the kitchen fire. A fire was indeed necessary, for the house was as cold as death. 'You'd better keep that overcoat on for a bit,' my mother said; so I sat upon a kitchen chair and watched her as she coaxed the fire into a blaze. That she had some news to impart was obvious, for she asked me nothing about my interview with Mr Ewing and was silent about what she had been doing all day. She was always like that: she would come out with a burst when we sat at the table.

There were no means in that house of producing hot water except by putting a kettle on to the kitchen fire, and when this was at last achieved my mother said: 'You can lay the table now.'

'What for?' I asked.

'Fried bacon,' she replied. 'I've had a good day to-day.'

She had indeed. The mistress of the house in which she had worked had handed to her, on leaving, a food parcel. This contained a rasher or two of bacon and half a loaf. 'You cut up that bread,' she said. 'I'll fry it in the bacon fat.'

And that was what she did. When the kettle had boiled and the tea was made, she produced the frying-pan, and soon, with the oil-lamp lit, hanging from the ceiling, we sat at the table and fell upon our feast: fried bacon and bread, washed down by tea. It was good. There we sat, before the table that had no cloth, the lamp burning, the fire burning, a picture of The Thin Red Line hanging over the fireplace. The floor was made of stone, very cold, and there was a rag mat in front of the fire. It was all very cosy to me. I don't suppose there was a poorer room in our town, but I had no fault to find with it.

That was because of my mother. She was a small woman with nothing much to say for herself. But when she had to say it, she could say it effectively, as she would do to the Guardians and as she had done it lately to Mr Ewing. I felt a great comfort when she was about. If there had been a large family it would have been different, but all her love, as I see it now, was concentrated on me, and I was spared the squabbling and quarrelling that I saw and heard in so many houses round about us. We kept very much to ourselves, and if her work in larger houses gave her some knowledge of a different way of life from ours, I had no such knowledge, or only such as I gathered from her, and I was well content. The Thin Red Line on the wall, the fire burning, something good to eat, and my mother to eat it with – that was home, that was my greatest joy.

'Well,' she said now. 'I'll wash up these few things, and then you can tell me what old Ewing said.'

'Old' with her had no relation to age. It was just a word.

'What's old Candleford been up to to-day?' 'What did that old drill sergeant have to say to you?'

Opening off the kitchen was the scullery or, as we always called it, the back kitchen. There was a cold-water tap in it – the only water-supply in the house. No such luxury as water in the bedrooms. No bathroom. Indeed, apart from this room in which we sat and two small bedrooms, there was no other room in the house except what we called 'the front room', and that was never used. Its window looked on to our *cul de sac*; it was stone-paved like the other rooms of this ground floor, it was very cold and never had a fire.

So my mother, who had filled the kettle and put it on the kitchen fire before we began to eat, now took the kettle off, filled a tin bowl in the back kitchen, and washed up our few things. I dried them and put them away, and then we drew up her wooden armchair to the kitchen fire. She sat upon the cushion we had made for it out of old newspapers bundled together with string. I was on a stool at her feet. 'Now then,' she said. 'Tell us what old Ewing said to-day.'

It didn't take much telling, and when it was told she said: 'I'm glad of that anyway. It's just as well to ask for what you want. If you don't get it – well, you've done what you could and then you can take it just the same. I'd have had you out of that old school, Ewing or no Ewing.'

It was comfortable as a philosophy, but like most philosophies it didn't work out in practice. There was plenty that she wanted and asked for and didn't get, but, though putting a brave face on it, as she did now, she didn't get it and didn't take it. There was plenty that she would have liked to take and never took, though it was little enough, any reasonable being would have thought. But she indomitably went on with what she had, and I never heard her grumble that it was not enough.

Now she came out with her great news. I was to go to work on the next Monday morning.

She had spent the day in a place where she liked to be. There was no regular place. One day it was one house, the next another. But this house was her favourite. 'She talks to me just as if I was a human being,' she said.

There's something to be thankful for if you like! But I was a lot older before I realised that it was a rare thing indeed.

'We got talking to-day about you,' she said. 'I told her that you were seeing old Ewing this morning and that you were leaving school. And what d'you think she said?'

She said, in effect, that if I really wanted a job, she thought she could get one for me. Her brother, who had not done so well as her husband, was a corn chandler with a shop on that road which ran right through our town. I knew the shop. It was small, with only one window. I used often to gaze into that window because it was banked up with seed in a fascinating way. There was a layer of maize that made a golden base, and upon that was a layer of some black corn whose name I didn't know, and upon that was another layer of a different colour. And so it went on, a wonderful picture to me. Within was a collection of song-birds in little cages. At any rate, I assumed that they were song-birds although they didn't sing; and there were mice and white rats that went frantically round on treadmills, and goldfish that sluggishly ambled through water. Leaning against the wall were sacks flowing over with one kind of corn or another, and dog biscuits and a few gardening tools. I thought it a most desirable shop, and to work there seemed to me a far better thing than to be reciting lists of prepositions or watching Mr Candleford showing his skill at marbles. Five minutes' talk with Mr Ewing had made this paradise accessible, and when my mother's employer had talked to her brother about it, it was mine.

My mother and I talked it over that night, when we had regaled ourselves with bacon and fried bread, as though El Dorado was at my feet. 'There was a boy before you,' she said. 'He was getting three shillings a week. And, more than that, he was getting his dinner.' The midday meal was always dinner to us. 'And what do you think? The silly little fool went and stole one of those birds, cage and all. So out he went. Don't let me catch you up to them tricks.'

I got to know the boy later, and he told me that he had stolen the bird only to let it free. It was winter-time, and he took it out into the country, set it down with plenty of bread to eat, and watched it feebly fluttering about, eating nothing, a foredoomed prey to larger, stronger, hungry creatures who came to eat the bread.

But what occupied our thoughts that night was the delightful prospect of the midday dinner.

'Fancy something hot in your belly *every* day,' my mother said. That, and three shillings a week, seemed joy beyond endurance.

It had all been arranged by the following Monday. I presented myself at eight o'clock, so that the shop might be swept out before opening-time at nine. We must have been a queer-looking pair: my mother dressed up for one of her eternal 'jobs', I wearing Master Thomas's done-with overcoat; she, so small herself, walking with me to the very door of the shop, inducting me into the status of wage-earner, throwing me upon the first step of the ladder of commerce.

6.

I liked Mr Price, my employer. His business was small enough but he didn't seem to want it to be larger, and he made up for the muteness of his caged birds by doing his own whistling. Whenever he was in the shop it rang like a spring-time spinney. 'Imitate any bird, I can,' he would say, and up and down the rows of cages he would wander, giving to every bird its appropriate music. They would watch him mutely with heads on one side, or with fluttering wings, seeming as though life could offer nothing better than to be competing with him from some budding branch, green under a blue sky. He was very kind and friendly to his young customers, boys mostly, clutching a penny in hot palms. 'A pennorth of bran-and-oats,' they would demand, and Mr Price always added: 'For the rabbits,' and off they would go with what seemed to me a generous pennorth indeed. Sometimes Mr Price would heave a sack or two of oats or some other corn on to a small hand-truck, and set off to supply the needs of someone who kept a horse or a coster's donkey.

There was nothing much for me to do except sweep out the shop every morning and eat my midday dinner. I could be counted on to do it with gusto, and this was almost the only time of the day when I saw Mrs Price. There was a sitting-room behind the shop and a kitchen-scullery behind the sitting-room. Towards midday agreeable smells drifted from this scullery into the sitting-room, and at one o'clock on the dot Mrs Price would appear in the shop and announce that dinner was ready. For half an hour thereafter Mr Price would disappear with his wife, leaving me in sole over-lordship of the shop, and I would watch the mice running like mad on their treadmills or endeavour to entertain the birds with a whistled chorus which I hoped was not too bad an imitation of Mr Price's.

At half-past one Mr Price would appear, succulently exploring his teeth and moustache with his tongue. 'When you marry, my boy,' he would say, 'marry a good cook.' He would get through the day on a few clichés, like 'For the rabbits', 'Marry a good cook', and, as he set off for some donkey's stable with corn on his hand-cart, 'This'll make him bray'. He was not a born conversationalist as his wife was a born cook.

At any rate, I thought she was, sitting behind my plate in the scullery. I was not permitted to eat in the sitting-room.

The social niceties had to be observed. After all, I was only 'the boy'. But I didn't worry about that. A plate of Irish stew was full compensation, especially if it were cargoed with little herbal dumplings that Mrs Price usually knocked up. She was always 'knocking up' something. Her head would appear in the morning, looking into the shop round the door that led to the sitting-room. 'I'll be knocking you up a bit of mutton to-day,' she would say; or, 'I'll be knocking up a few chops.' It was all one to Mr Price. He would go on whistling to his imprisoned birds or setting his mice awhirl on their treadmills, and he would say, 'All right, old girl,' and proceed with his own affairs. I listened far more keenly than he did for news of the day's banquet. But there was nothing I listened for more keenly than an announcement of dumplings. There, I thought, Mrs Price's culinary skill reached its apotheosis.

Altogether, I was happy in the six months that I spent with Mr Price. I sometimes wondered whether he did not run the shop for his own pleasure. Customers were few enough, but that didn't seem to worry him. He would moon about, smoking a pipe, holding long conversations and whistling sessions with his birds, admiring a few tortoises that lived on lettuce leaves, and speculating aloud on a scheme for introducing snakes. On the whole, he seemed to think they would terrify Mrs Price. 'Well, young feller,' he would sometimes say to me, 'there's a few bones you can take home to-night in a dish,' and, homeward bound, I would carry something that Mrs Price had been knocking up that day. In our dim little house these would be transferred from the dish to a saucepan, boiled anew, and make a meal that was rather better than many a meal we had eaten.

For myself, this life would have satisfied me. There was nothing I liked better than turning out my meagre wage at the week's end and feeling that thus my occasional visits to Solly were no longer necessary. No ambition stirred me. I have often read since then of famous men who began their lives in very poor circumstances indeed, and were plagued all the time by ambitious stings and stirrings. I can only say that nothing of the sort ever came my way. To take home a few shillings a week and an occasional dish of bones was all I then asked, and I would happily have remained for ever with Mr Price, his corn, his mice and his birds. But when the springtime had come and was turning into summer the second of those things happened that I have already referred to. The first was my leaving school; the second was the death of Mr Shellabeer.

7.

I had forgotten Mr Shellabeer. I knew only that he had married my mother's sister Jane, that we were not socially welcome at his house, and that I had been there only once in my life. That was on my birthday about a year ago, when I had found him asleep and stertorous in his drawing-room. He had beaten my birthday shilling down to sixpence, which Mrs Shellabeer had conveniently forgotten to give me. Then she and I had explored the house, which had just had the gas 'Laid On', and I had been shown her son's room, and was told that he had a cap with blue rings.

It had all seemed very wonderful to me at the time, but, as boys will, I had forgotten all about it. What with Mr Ewing, and leaving school, and working for Mr Price, and becoming a wage-earner, and seeing my mother brighter than I had seen her for a long time, the world seemed to be changing quickly for the better, and I saw no need to think of any life but the one we were leading. And then Mr Shellabeer died. When I got home on an early summer evening, Mrs Shellabeer was filling our small house with lamentation. And, startling apparition, there was the boy whose cap had blue rings: the very cap that he had told me

to kick into the park pond on the day when he lent me
Micah Clarke. This cap was before my eyes, sitting on our
kitchen table. I had burst into the house, and there, alone,
was the boy, who now said: 'Hallo!' A voice which was his
mother's came from our scarcely-ever-used front room and
was filling the house, as I have said, with lamentation.
But I didn't know then that this was his mother, and neither
of us knew that we were cousins.

I said: 'What are you doing here? What's all the row?'

The row, at that moment, became incarnate in Mrs
Shellabeer. She entered the kitchen clinging limply to my
mother's arm, relinquished this in order to seize me in a
frantic sort of way, smother me in wet kisses and, laying
hold of her son, transferred the kisses to him. She then
exclaimed: 'I can't bear to look on your bliss, Emma,' and
ran with her son out through the front door.

My mother was very calm. 'Well,' she said, 'she's making
the most of it.'

For myself, I could never think of Mrs Shellabeer save as
the woman who had once done me out of sixpence. 'What's
the matter with her?' I asked.

'I'll tell you all in good time,' she answered. 'Let's have
something to eat.'

So I went into the scullery and washed under the cold-
water tap. When I came back she was laying the supper.
We fell to, and I waited for her to begin. 'I wasn't good
enough for him when he was alive,' she said, 'and I'm not
all that interested in her antics now he's dead.'

I did not answer this. It was her customary round-about
way of coming upon a topic. I gathered that, after lunch
that day, Mr Shellabeer had made his usual announcement
that he would take a little rest in the sitting-room before
going out again. Thinking that the little rest was prolonging
itself beyond its usual limits, my aunt had gone in to wake
him up, and found him beyond all waking. He was lying

on the floor with his mouth wide open, dead as a door nail, as my mother put it.

8.

Mrs Shellabeer, or as I was instructed to call her in future, Aunt Jane – had not been much liked by anybody. She had not been much liked even by Mr Shellabeer after the first moment of entrancement. She and my mother had been down and out when their father died. My mother had tackled the matter with her usual resolution by 'going into service'. She had later married my father, and this had been a matter of dispute between the sisters ever since. Jane, who had gone into a shop where she 'slept in', thought this to be living at a much higher standard either than that of a general servant or that of wife to a working man. (It is strange how 'working man' became a term almost of contempt, as though 'work' were done only by people who could do nothing else.) And so Jane, or 'Lady Jane' as her acquaintances called her, not without reference to her nose sticking always in the air, became shunned by all who knew her, including her sister; and when Jane herself married someone who was not a 'working man', but who lived on rents and by putting up jerry-built houses, the breach between them was absolute, save for rare occasions such as the one of which I have already written when she bore me off to be a wondering spectator of her grandeur.

My mother did not attend the funeral of a man she had never been permitted to meet, but I, more favoured as a person who had met him once, was given a place in the only cab which followed his hearse to the cemetery. Henry Shellabeer sat on one side of the cab, I on another, with Mrs Shellabeer weeping violently between us. It is perhaps a comment on the regard in which the Shellabeers were held that no one else attended the funeral or sent a wreath. But

Mrs Shellabeer made up for this by providing a wreath of surpassing splendour, with a card attached to it by a purple ribbon. On this card she had burst into verse, so that, until the sun of that splendid summer faded the letters into an indecipherable scrawl, one could read:

> *Thomas Shellabeer from the wife he loved so well,*
> *Passed hence, at sudden call with saints to dwell,*
> *Leaving a poorer place for us below,*
> *Who languish on, while heaven's joys overflow.*

Lest Heaven's overflowing joy should diminish, she intended, she assured my mother, to memorialise Mr Shellabeer in white marble with an angel for ever blowing a blast to let all Heaven know that it was now honoured by Thomas's arrival, while two small angels, one on either side, wept copiously and appropriately. But she never got round to this, for when certain mundane fellows looked into the late Mr Shellabeer's affairs, it was found that she had better be careful with her shillings. This was not difficult, because she always had been.

9.

Mrs Shellabeer cared no more for the departure of her husband than she would have cared for a pair of cast-off shoes; but she did very much care for herself and for the straitened way of living into which she was now suddenly thrown. Henry remained calm throughout. His mother, as was only to be expected, could suggest nothing. She could only weep when the true circumstances in which she now found herself were made clear to her.

My mother from the first 'took to' Henry. I think that, but for him, she would have left her sister to stew in her own juice, as she put it. But Henry, from the time we discovered

THE LITTLE VICTIMS PLAY

we were cousins, treated me well, and looked in now and then at our house, and called me Guy and insisted on my calling him Harry. He also called my mother Auntie Em, and our house was always livelier when he was about. We walked together in the evenings, and it did not take me long to discover that he was as lonely as I was myself. His mother's posturing as a grand lady, when he knew that she was nothing of the sort, had for some time become apparent to him, and Saturdays, when he was home from school, had been made burdensome by the rent-collecting round. 'You must learn to do this yourself,' his mother would say, as they plodded from house to house, and what they saw in the course of their perambulations fixed his determination that he would never do it himself. It was his mother's threat, often repeated, to 'put the bailiffs in' if the rent were not paid by this date or that; the timid offers of some half-starved child to 'pay the rent as soon as Father's in work again', and the general loathing his mother evoked, of which he became more and more aware, and in which he felt himself involved, that made the Saturday afternoon round something that he increasingly shrank from and detested.

Henry, for some time after his father's death, was still at the school which stylishly demanded blue rings round the cap, and I was still with Mr Price, carrying home now and then my basin of bones. It was towards the end of that summer that I returned, so laden, to find Henry and my mother in the house. With pride I displayed my basin of bones, and my mother was putting them in a saucepan to simmer, when Henry dramatically cried: 'Oh, my God! My God! I didn't know you were down to eating other people's bones!'

'There's a lot you don't know yet, Harry my boy,' my mother calmly informed him. 'You'll learn as you grow up that not everyone can live by knocking at the front doors and saying: "Rent, please."'

Harry did not answer. He took up his cap from where it lay tossed on to a chair and ran out of the house.

I did not expect that a basinful of bones, to which both my mother and I were well accustomed, would dramatically alter my way of living, but so it was. We sat there crunching like cannibals returned from a day on the warpath when Henry returned, wind-blown from running, and announced: 'My mother will be here in a moment. We're going to talk things over.'

'Oh, we are, are we?' said my mother. 'And what are we going to discuss now?'

Henry, who was, as they say now, very 'het up', took one of the bones from the dish, held it dramatically aloft, and said:

'Do you call this proper food for a human being, Auntie Em?'

'It's better than a lot I've eaten in my time,' said Mother. 'What's got into your noddle now?'

'What have you had to eat all day?' Henry asked.

'I don't see that that's much business of yours, my lad. But since you ask, nothing much. I've been out at one of those places that don't run to over-feeding the charwoman. A bit of bread and dripping and a cup of tea about sizes it up.'

How the strange discussion would have ended I don't know, but Mrs Shellabeer appeared at this moment, swathed in widow's weeds and folding, as she came into the room, a black parasol. A brooch was at her throat, depicting an angel weeping at a tomb beneath a willow-tree.

Henry, who was still hot with indignation, held aloft his bone, almost shook it in his mother's face. It was a moment of comedy, and as such I see it as I look back upon it. My mother alone was calm. Indeed, I think she was wondering when anything so funny had happened to her. There was Henry, with the bone held over the blue rings of the cap he had forgotten to remove. There was Mrs Shellabeer looking distastefully round this house which had not even gas Laid On, and trying hard to maintain the tragic sorrow of a widow who but lately had laid her husband in the grave; and there was I, wondering how my basin of bones had brought all this about, confused and bewildered.

'Put down that bone, Harry, for God's sake,' said my mother. 'Sit down – and you, Jane – and have a cup of tea. Then you can tell us what this all comes to.'

'Tea would choke me,' said Auntie Jane, sitting down and looking longingly at the teapot.

My mother poured her a cup of tea, concerning which Aunt Jane said 'Six lumps, please,' and she gave a cup to Henry. As for us, we had finished our quite satisfactory meal and sat there watching them. Henry laid his bone before his cup like a Lord Mayor's mace when the proceedings of the council are about to begin.

We gathered that our simple meal, coming, at that, as a gift from a corn-chandler, had horrified him, and he had rushed upon his mother with the news that her sister and nephew were starving. Our simple way of life had never appeared to us in such a way as that, though my mother had often said to me: 'I'd like to see a bit more flesh on you.' But we were now more or less contented, seeing that I was getting a midday meal from Mr Price, as well as an eleemosynary bone or two for stewing. We had for some time been congratulating ourselves that the worst was over and that we were on the way to peace and plenty. Indeed, the theme of my mother's conversation had recently been Auntie Jane's plight rather than our own. 'I'll bet,' she would say, 'that my Lady Jane's going to feel the pinch now that her Old Man's gone. We ought to go round soon and see how she's getting on.'

But Henry's view was different. The sight of us sitting there in a room without so much as a mat on the floor, at a table without a cloth, looking through an open door upon a scullery that contained nothing but a cold-water tap, was a sudden eye-opener to him who had always been accustomed to some trimmings of refinement. He had never been in such a cave as ours and seen the occupants at a meal. During his rent-perambulations with his mother, he had never got beyond a doorstep. His glimpse of what to us was a normal way of life had shaken him out of complacency.

All this was to Henry's credit, but my mother and I did not then realise how much he was moved by what he had seen, and how this had sent him, hot-foot, to the deep disturbance of his mother. What shocked her was not the thing itself but that Henry had seen it. Her own early days made her well enough aware of the conditions in which her sister was living, but Lady Jane had thought herself well beyond the touch of such matters. She was quite content, when she was abroad on her rent-collecting journeys, to be aware of them without going beyond the doorstep.

My mother and I were not aware that, while Henry was at school that day, Aunt Jane had been very uncomfortably occupied. She had been visited by a member of the firm which she had employed to go into the affairs of her dead husband's business. She had dreamed of herself as now an independent woman, for her husband's will had left all to her. It was her idea that, once matters had been straightened out, she would employ a manager to run the business, and that, when his salary was paid (and that in her calculation would not amount to much), she would settle down to a life of luxury, with this manager even collecting the rents. It had been a matter of grievance with her for some time that her husband had expected her to burden herself with this disagreeable task.

The interview of the afternoon had shattered her dreams as effectively as a brick thrown through one of the fancy panes on her front door. When Mr Shellabeer had so handsomely left her all that he possessed, he had, in fact, left her a mess of debts. He had left her nothing but the odious rents, and those, she had good reason to know, were an asset of dubious fluctuating value. Even her constant threats of 'putting the bailiffs in' could not make them look very rosy. But the young man who had called upon her seemed almost to treat her as though she were herself a partner in conspiracy. He was a frank young man. 'I've never seen such books,' he declared. 'If you can call them books. Half the liabilities haven't been entered at all. There's nothing much we can lay our hands on but a heap of unpaid bills. As for the assets, they come to precious little. A few piles of bricks and a couple of planks. Talk about a mess! We'll be lucky if we pull you out of it with a roof over your head.'

Mrs Shellabeer had been looking forward to a very pleasant day indeed. She had even got in a bottle of sherry with which she hoped at the right moment to regale the young man, all business ended, good friends together, and she a lady of leisure, thanks to the beneficent forethought of a husband in a million. There would be nothing to do but ask the young man to send in his firm's bill for what they had done, and perhaps suggest a good manager. Now she could only keep the sherry safely locked in its cupboard and tragically exclaim: 'Shellabeer has deceived me!'

The young man softened enough to say: 'Well, I wouldn't put it like that, Mrs Shellabeer. Perhaps he just thought, like a good many people, that he could get out of a mess and straighten things in time. But he couldn't, that's all. I expect,' he conceded magnanimously, 'that his intentions to you were quite honourable.'

Mrs Shellabeer looked as though she doubted it, and she spent the rest of the day, when the young man had gone, with a promise to 'report progress', as though she doubted it very much indeed. It was upon this woebegone mother that Henry burst, flourishing his stewed and symbolic bone.

I don't remember much of what followed, except that Henry and I left the two sisters to themselves in the now darkening house and walked together. We walked and walked, right away beyond the confines of our town, saying little; and yet there flowed into me a deep sense of being with someone who understood me and my need for friendship. We came back when it was quite dark. Mrs Shellabeer was gone. Harry shouted into the dim house: 'Good night, Auntie Em,' and ran off to his own home.

I found my mother sitting by herself in the kitchen, and she said: 'Get off to bed. I'll tell you all about it to-morrow.' So I climbed our narrow, echoing, carpetless stairs, and got into bed, wondering what had been happening and what 'all about it' might be. It was very late when my mother came up, which was unlike her. She popped her head round my door and asked: 'Are you asleep?' I pretended that I was, and heard her go to her own room on the other side of the landing. Then I fell asleep – the last sleep that I was to have in the only home that till then had been mine.

10.

My mother was usually up and about before me in the morning. By the time that I came down, she was, as a rule, girded for the day's work in whatever 'place' called for her ministrations. She would put my breakfast before me and be off, leaving me to eat alone, do the washing-up, and get out on my own concerns – until lately to school, more recently to Mr Price's shop.

But that morning she was not dressed for her daily battle, and I saw that places were laid not for two but for three.

'Your Aunt Jane is coming to breakfast,' she said. 'Sit down and I'll tell you all about it.'

I suppose she had been too tired by her long talk with Aunt Jane to tell me, when I came in so late, what had happened. Aunt Jane stayed after Harry and I had gone walking. This was surprising in itself, for she and my mother had fallen wide apart in recent years. But now a great deal came tumbling out, and especially there came out Jane's plight now that her husband was dead. She had been looking forward to a 'fine old beano', as my mother put it; but the visit she had received that afternoon from the young man who had been looking into her affairs put matters into a new and rather terrifying light. She realised that she hadn't a friend in the world, that all her 'rents' would go, for her slummy houses would have to be sold, and that she would be lucky if she kept over her head the house she lived in.

'And what's going to keep you in that?' my mother remorselessly asked. 'You'll have to eat.'

'I was thinking of keeping a lodger,' Aunt Jane answered, and the thought of doing anything so dreadful loosed a flood of tears, so that my poor mother could do nothing but pat her on the back and give her another cup of tea. 'And I haven't,' Aunt Jane blubbered, 'dared to say a word about all this to Henry.'

'He can go out to work as mine has had to do,' Mother informed her.

This 'put the lid on it', Mother said. 'The weak-minded nincompoop could do nothing but cry. She couldn't bear, she said, to see Henry going out like any common boy. That's you, my lad, for one. "I couldn't bear," she said, "to see him going off in the morning without his cap with the Blue Rings." Blue Rings! She'll have something more than Blue Rings to think of now. Anyway, she's coming to breakfast, and we'll talk it all over again. Though what's fresh to say I don't know, and why I should bother about her at all beats me.'

So we sat and waited for her, and all that we had to say was made easier because Henry came too. He kissed my mother, called me Guy, and said to Aunt Jane: 'Now you eat a bit of food, and then let me explain what I think we ought to do.'

Aunt Jane was inclined still to be tearful, and said as usual that she couldn't eat a mouthful, that her dear husband, who was watching her from a better world than this, would be horrified to see her eating like a wolf, and then settled down to what we had, which wasn't much, and wouldn't have satisfied many wolves.

'Now,' said Henry, 'you sit quiet, Mother, and let me speak.'

We all looked up at that, for it was the first time that any one had spoken with authority. 'As for Father looking down from a better world than this,' said Henry, 'it wouldn't be hard to find one; but he's left us to make what we can of this world as it is – left us in a pretty stew if what you've told me this morning is correct. Now I'm going to tell you what I propose to do about it.'

What Henry was going to do was quite simple. 'From now on,' he said, 'you'll leave it all to me and do what I tell you.'

Aunt Jane started up in a great stew. 'You wicked boy,' she exclaimed. 'Your dear father never talked like that to me. He talked to me with respect, and you'll do the same.'

'I'm speaking to you with perfect respect,' said Harry. 'And that's more than Father ever did. He didn't speak to you at all. When he was in the house, he was mostly asleep, and he's left us now in a mess. Do you want me, or don't you, to suggest a way of getting out of it?'

Both my mother and I were as surprised as Aunt Jane to hear Henry speaking like this. It was an altogether new Henry. He had got up from the table and was stalking about the room, with his mother in tears, declaring, as she often did, that another mouthful would choke her, which she avoided by quickly putting another mouthful down. 'Well,' she conceded at last, 'let's hear what you've got to say.'

'In the first place,' said Henry, 'I don't share your view of Father, and never did, though for the sake of peace and quiet I kept my mouth shut. But a pretty pickle he's left us all in, and what I'm doing now is trying to get us out of it. You'd better write a letter, which I'll take to this young man who saw you yesterday, and I'll go thoroughly into the matter with him. Say that I have your authority for anything I do.'

And that is what Henry did. I heard later from him of all that happened.

We had better henceforth call the young man by his proper name, which was George Chirk. Mr Chirk was a man in his early twenties, and as soon as he saw the blue rings on Henry's cap he said: 'Hallo! You go to old Garrity's place, do you?'

Garrity was the proprietor and headmaster of the school whose boys were privileged to wear blue rings round their caps. Mr Chirk said he had been to Garrity's himself, and Henry, who was no fool, realised that he need not at once plunge into his mother's affairs. He talked to Mr Chirk of Garrity's and such matters and was soon on a friendly footing with him. Chirk said: 'I wanted to go to Cambridge, you know, to study law; but Garrity's is a measly little place and there wasn't the ghost of a chance of a scholarship. So my father paid the fees. I've been down for just a year or so, and Father has articled me to this firm. However, I'm nothing but a dog's-body so far, looking after the most trivial things. There's this affair of your father's estate for example. If you can call it an estate. I'm afraid you're in the soup, old boy.'

Henry was very pleased to be called 'old boy', thought Mr Chirk a most agreeable fellow, and decided that this was the moment to produce his mother's letter. He did so, and George Chirk said: 'Sit down, old man. I'd better have a word with the boss.'

He did so, leaving Harry in a rather grimy outer office. He was away for half an hour, and then came back to announce cheerfully that Mr Leadbitter, who was the boss of Messrs Leadbitter and Frost, thought it one of those measly little affairs that Mr Chirk might well use to get his hand in. It didn't take long to convince Harry that the account which Mr Chirk had given to Mrs Shellabeer the day before was substantially correct, that the houses from which the rents had come would have to be sold to meet the debts, and that little was left except the house they now lived in.

It was eleven o'clock when they reached an end of the business; and then Mr Chirk proposed going over the road to a convenient coffee-house. Poor Harry – poor, now, in every sense of the word – floundering in very deep waters, with all that he had known of the world knocked from under him, accepted this invitation. He liked Chirk, a gay young spark, and clung to him like a drowning man to a life-belt; and Chirk, on his side, had taken a fancy to this boy who had so bravely shouldered what seemed to him a hopeless task. He talked to Harry, over their coffee, like an ancient man of the world. 'Now look here, old boy. Don't hesitate to come to me if there's anything I can do. I've put all the facts before you as honestly as I can, and so far as the past is concerned – well, that's all done with. What we have to do now is consider the future. What are you going to do? There's your mother's house to live in, and there's precious little else. For one thing, you'll have to hand in your checks to old Garrity. You'll have to find some work to do. Something with a wage attached to it. Not like me. I'm one of the lucky devils. My father is paying Leadbitter to have me articled. I'm a drone, but that won't do for you.'

It was getting on for lunchtime when Henry returned to our house. In the meantime I had learned that my mother, too, believed that here was a situation that needed instant action. She put a simple proposition to my Aunt Jane, which shook both me and Auntie. She came in from the scullery where she had been washing up our few breakfast things and found her sister sitting in a wooden chair, still occasionally squeezing out a residuary tear and obviously good for nothing. 'I've been thinking things out,' said Mother, wiping her hands on a cloth. 'We've lived together before this. Why shouldn't we do it again?'

The proposition startled Auntie Jane out of her tears. She looked aghast and, as for me, I suppose I was as astonished as she was. '*Me?*' she demanded. '*Me* live here, when I've only lately had the gas Laid On?'

My mother looked at her pityingly. 'I'm not talking about you living here,' she said. 'I'm talking about me living there. Money. There's rent to be paid here, little as it is. You've got at any rate a rent-free house, and I'm proposing to come and live with you. Take it or leave it. I can get along well enough as I've done for a long time now, but how you're to get on with only a house and nothing coming in to it beats me.'

Put starkly like that, embodying the fact of the matter in a phrase, it showed Auntie Jane just where she stood and revealed her as the weaker of the two sisters. She could say nothing, suggest nothing. She began to cry again. Mother was furious, as I had not seen her before, and she seized her sister by both shoulders and shook her as she would shake a naughty child. 'Well,' she exclaimed, 'I've heard of weeping willows, but for weeping widows I must say you take the cake. Well, that's my last word. I'll come in with you and we can make the best of it, or I'll stay where I am and you can go and do what you like.'

It was by now well on in the morning, and at that moment Henry returned. 'Where have you been all this time?' Auntie Jane demanded. 'You've been gallivanting about the town, leaving your poor mother to be set upon and insulted, and you not here to say a word in her defence.'

Henry surprised us all. He said nothing to his mother, his aunt or to me. He simply took off his cap with the blue rings and threw it up joyfully till it hit the ceiling and fell with a plop on to his mother's lap.

'From what Mr Chirk has told me,' he said, 'we'll have to do without most things now. So I'll do without that cap to begin with. I've been to see Mr Garrity and handed in my checks.'

His mother fondled the cap which lay upon her knees. Her tears fell upon it. When all is said and done, it represented what she had hoped to do for Henry. He appeared to be somewhat moved and put his arms about her, kneeling at her feet. She tried to put the cap back on his head, but he would not have it. 'Listen, Mother,' he said. 'I've had a busy morning. I've seen Mr Chirk and all that he had to say to you yesterday is correct. We're as good as ruined, and one thing I've got to do is find some work to help to keep you. I can't do that, can I, so long as I remain a schoolboy. So I've been to see Mr Garrity.'

'You've told Mr Garrity that we are ruined?' cried his mother. 'How shall I hold up my head again?'

'We'll hold up our heads all right,' Henry assured her. 'But the first thing is for me to get work. Mr Garrity was very kind. You know that if a boy at his school leaves in the middle of a term the parents have to pay part of his fees.'

'We can't do it,' Auntie Jane moaned.

'You don't have to,' Henry consoled her. 'Seeing the plight we're in, he has given up his right to that.'

'Who told him of the plight I'd like to know?' Aunt Jane demanded.

Henry held her more closely, and said: 'Now, now, Mother. Don't make things more difficult. Just leave all this to me. I'll look after you.'

II.

My memory of that day is of frantic activity. From the moment when Henry said: 'I'll look after you,' Mrs Shellabeer collapsed into a being ready to take orders and do what she was told. My Mother and Henry recognised one another as allies. They arranged everything, and I became a subaltern who carried out their orders. My mother explained her scheme to Henry, which was that we should all live together in Aunt Jane's house. There would be no rent to pay there, for it was her own, while for this shack of ours – it was little more – there were at any rate a few shillings a week to find. So Henry sat down at the table and wrote a letter to the landlord cancelling our tenancy and saying that we would be out in a week's time. I was sent out to post this at once, and when I returned I found the others ready to move off. Auntie Jane was flaccid but obedient. My mother, as though fearing that even now what was proposed had not quite entered her sister's head, asked: 'You're certain that you understand all this? Guy and I are coming to live with you and Harry.'

Aunt Jane nodded her head. 'But I wish you'd wear a different hat,' she said. 'You look like a charwoman. What'll all the neighbours think?'

'I *am* a charwoman,' Mother answered. 'If I'm not good enough for the neighbours, and for you, too, we can call the whole thing off. You haven't got a penny, and if I don't come in and help you, there's nothing for it but a lodger.'

'God forbid,' said Aunt Jane.

'Very well, then. Come on.'

'Yes, come on,' Henry said, and repeated, 'I'll look after you.'

He took his mother's arm and led her down the stony

passage into the street. My mother followed with me, and banged the door.

'Well, that's that,' she said.

12.

Henry and I the next morning hired a hand-cart for a couple of shillings and transferred a few of my mother's small possessions from the old, now abandoned, house to the new one. There was a bit of junk which we sold. Mother told us to do so, and there were plenty of buyers among the neighbours in our little street. Pots and pans, the kitchen table and all save the beds we had lain in and the picture of 'The Thin Red Line' went west. My mother, for some reason or other, was attached to that picture and insisted on its coming along. 'A pretty penny that will fetch one of these days,' she inaccurately prophesied.

I suppose it is a social comment of a sort that all we sold went for about a pound. With this treasure – one pound made up in odd shillings and pence – and with the beds and bedclothes on the hand-cart – we made our final journey. When we arrived at the new house my mother received us. Aunt Jane couldn't bear the thought of these dilapidated beds being seen by the neighbours. So she had decided to go to the cemetery and weep upon her husband's grave.

Aunt Jane's house contained three bedrooms and a pokey room called the attic. My mother and Aunt Jane were to have a bedroom each. The house itself was grand enough to have no number on the door. It had, instead, a name. It was called The Grove. When we had arrived at The Grove, Henry and I lost no time in setting things out as we had already decided. One of the beds was put into the room that was to be my mother's, and the other was put into Henry's bedroom, which we were to share. Henry had used it both as a bedroom and a study. It contained a few books, a table for writing at, a globe, and other odds and ends of his impedimenta. Hanging upon a hook over his bed was Henry's cap with the blue rings. We thought we had seen the last of that, and we knew who had put it there. Henry shrugged his shoulders and sighed. 'Well,' he said with resignation. 'If it pleases her . . . Come and see this other room.'

We went up to the attic which was little more than a box-room. It had a fan-light in the roof, contained nothing but odds and ends which Henry said could be burned, and, when the gas had been Laid On, this little room had not been thought worth the honour. Henry rustled through it, kicking up old packing-paper and dust. 'It's small,' he said, 'and doesn't look much, but I think we could make it do.'

'Do for what?' I asked.

'For a study, of course,' said Henry, as though life without a study were not to be thought of. 'Well, we'd better go down now and see if we can give your Mother a hand with anything. And consider yourself lucky to have such a mother. Blue rings! It's what's inside a cranium that matters, not what's perched on top of it.'

It was by now late afternoon, and nobody had eaten much that day. But while we had been busy upstairs my mother had been busy in the kitchen. Aunt Jane had returned from her communion with the ghosts and seemed refreshed. She was ready to take up again the battle of life, and began with my mother, whom she informed that she was not accustomed to eating in the kitchen. This was where my mother had laid out our meal, and very cosy it looked to me. There was a blue-and-white check cloth on the table, the gas was lit, and from four plates steamed soup that smelt good. My mother had raided the larder, found a few bones which she was an expert in turning into a meal, had added some tinned soup, and had toasted some bread which adorned the table in a toast-rack. To me it all looked palatial; to Henry, tired with

our exertions, it was not unwelcome; but Aunt Jane turned
up her nose. Henry, she declared, was not used to eating in
the kitchen.

'Henry, and you too,' said my mother, 'will have to get
used to a lot of new things. You were glad enough once on a
time to eat in the kitchen when there was any food to be
eaten; and as for me, I'm fagged out and I've just slapped
this food down in the place nearest to where it was cooked.
It's not as though servants fetched and carried for me.'

'A Woman,' declared Aunt Jane, with dignity, 'comes in
for a day a week and Turns Things Out.'

'*Used* to come in one day a week,' said Mother. 'That's
one of the things you'll be without in future. You'll have to
do with my horrible ways and no cap and apron.'

Henry, I could see, was getting very tired of this senseless
argument. 'Mother,' he said, 'let's eat, for goodness sake,
and be thankful to Aunt Emma for having something ready.
I'm starving.'

But we were not to eat that meal without interruption.
We had just pulled in our chairs when there was a loud knock
at the front door. Henry answered the call, and almost at
once returned with Mr Garrity. I had not seen Mr Garrity
before, nor had my mother. He was a tall blue-eyed man of
middle age, with fair hair not yet greying, and with what
seemed to me the sweetest smile I had ever seen. He was
carelessly dressed.

Mrs Shellabeer at once rose. 'Oh, sir,' she cried. 'Please
excuse Henry. I've told him again and again to ask Visitors
into the Parlour.'

Mr Garrity smiled and sniffed. 'Well,' he said, 'I'm glad
he has disobeyed orders this time. That soup smells good.'

It was Henry who introduced Mr Garrity to me and my
mother. He shook hands warmly and said: 'When Henry
came and told me he was giving me the cold shoulder he

mentioned both of you. But I didn't expect to find you here. I just dropped in to have a chat with Mrs Shellabeer.'

'We could talk much more comfortably in the Parlour, sir,' said Aunt Jane.

'We can talk comfortably enough where we are,' said Mr Garrity. 'If you could find another plate, I'd be glad. I've been at it all day, I've come on without a bite, and I must say this food tempts me.'

It was obvious that Mr Garrity was determined to be genial. Not, as I was to find later, that this was difficult for him. My mother at once bustled about and began to lay another place. 'You'll find some Spode china in a cupboard in the dining-room,' said Aunt Jane, but Mr Garrity took her firmly though kindly by the arm and sat her back in her chair. 'You must be very tired,' he said. 'You've had a trying time, Mrs Shellabeer. Please don't put yourself out for me. Any old crocks will do. Believe me, I often snatch a bite in the kitchen.'

Aunt Jane was very pleased to have attention thus directed to herself; and soon we were all seated, and Mr Garrity, I was pleased to observe, was as good a hand as I was myself at making a meal of stewed bones. When we had finished, he said: 'Now, Mrs Shellabeer, it's about this son of your's that I wanted to have a chat with you. We can, if you like, now adjourn to the parlour. If Henry will give us his company there, one or two things can be talked over.'

My mother and I did the washing up. It was not till Mr Garrity was gone that Henry and Aunt Jane joined us there and we learned what had happened.

'To-morrow,' announced Aunt Jane proudly, 'Henry's Career will begin.'

She looked upon him like the mother of a juvenile Dick Whittington to whom the future has been revealed.

'Sit down, Mother,' said Henry, 'and let's tell Aunt Emma exactly what's happened.'

It wasn't much. Indeed, in these days a man would probably be prosecuted for making such a suggestion. 'I've never had a better or more promising boy,' Mr Garrity said, and he proposed that, instead of paying a fee, Henry should himself be paid. Garrity's, as it was called, was a private affair between Mr Garrity and the parents of certain boys. It was not subject to inspection by people who had to report to Authority. It could do what it liked, and no parent was ever known to complain. Like most schools, it turned out plenty of average stuff and a little that was better than average. Of those who were above the average Henry had his place, and that is what Mr Garrity had now come to see Aunt Jane about, disturbed by Henry's withdrawal from the school and by his report of trouble at home. His proposal was, in short, that Henry should become what was later known as a pupil teacher, that he should go on with his learning but that he should, as opportunity arose, teach those who knew less than he did himself. In payment for this he would take his luncheon with Mr Garrity and his daughter Rosa, and would receive a salary of ten shillings a week.

I was at this time thirteen years old. Henry was about fifteen, I should think.

We settled down. Aunt Jane, who had done little since the happy day when she came to The Grove with a woman to 'do the rough', found that she now had to work as she had not done since before her marriage. Save the worth of the house itself, she hadn't a penny coming in. She stayed at home, did the housework in a slap-dash way, and cooked the meals. My mother – and to the dickens with what neighbours thought – went out daily to work; and to the bit that she was thus able to contribute to our income Henry added his few shillings and I added mine. For though I was now finished with Mr Price's cornshop, I was soon at work again. Through the good agency of Mr George Chirk.

George Chirk was a young man much given to amateur

dramatics. His father, who paid all his expenses, wanted nothing more than to see George's name profitably displayed on a solicitor's brass plate, George wanted nothing so much as to see it displayed on a show-bill, at the bottom of the caste if needs be. It would soon work its way to the top. At the moment he had to be content with the reputation of being the best amateur Falstaff in our town, which didn't help him much with his father or with Mr Leadbitter who employed him.

On a dark winter's night soon after Mother and I had moved to The Grove, I was with Henry in our attic study, the small dark room which had not been used except as a lumber room. With all its rubbish cleared away, a few shelves knocked up as a bookcase, and a table each to write at, we were now in there more often than not when we were at home. A candle in a blue-enamel candlestick was all we needed for light, and if we wished to relax and talk we did so by sitting on the floor with the wall behind our backs and a rug over our knees. However, we rarely did talk. Henry became my schoolmaster. He told me what to read and what to write, persuasive rather than peremptory, but firm enough in the long run.

While we were thus engaged on the winter's night that I am writing about, there was a loud knock at the front door. We were alone in the house, for my mother and Aunt Jane were gone to see a magic-lantern show at a chapel that Aunt Jane attended; so I left Henry where he was, correcting some papers by Mr Garrity's pupils, and went down to find that the caller was George Chirk who had called to see Aunt Jane. He had called, he said, to get Aunt Jane's signature to a few papers which finally wound up her affairs. She was now, he informed us cheerfully, as good as bankrupt.

I suppose we were little more than children to George, but he consented to sit on the floor between us, in a good humour, because, as he told us, he was just returning from a rehearsal of *The Merry Wives of Windsor*, in which, he gave us to understand, he had distinguished himself, being informed by the producer that he was as good as a pro. He took a packet of cigarettes from his pocket and handed them round, and as Henry and I had never smoked in our lives, we were soon coughing and choking companionably together.

Chirk was interested when he heard that Henry was doing work of a sort for Mr Garrity. He called himself and Henry 'Old Garritonians', and was so hilarious in general that, at this distance of time, I can imagine that the rehearsal from which he had come had ended in an adjournment to the nearest hostelry. 'Well, Henry my lad,' he said, using his Christian name for the first time, and lighting for himself another cigarette, 'I would call this a bit of the real *vie bohème*, with attic complete. All you want now is a Mimi or Fifi, and perhaps a truckle bed, and what more could you ask?' He looked around as though picturing himself free from all parental control, one of a happy-go-lucky band, mewing their mighty youth, confident that it was only a time before the dawn of a glorious morning.

'What about the young Garrity?' he asked. 'When I was at the place she was nothing but a child, but passing fair. A bud, my boy, but a bud promising a lovely flower.'

'Do you mean Miss Rosa?' Henry said.

'If you must have a name,' declared Chirk, 'call her Rosa. But a rose by any other name would smell as sweet.'

I had heard of Miss Rosa who helped her father, now that Mrs Garrity was dead.

'I'm afraid,' said Henry, 'you wouldn't find her a child now. She's taken a B.A. degree as an external student of London University.'

Chirk raised himself from the floor, a little rockily.

'Thanks for looking in with the papers,' Henry said practically, getting up too. 'I'll ask Mother to sign them and

I'll bring them back myself. Well, you see how we are here.'

'Call me George,' Chirk said magnanimously.

'What we're worrying about is young Guy here,' said Henry. 'We'll have to find work for him soon. We could do with a few more shillings a week in this house.'

Chirk seemed more and more unsteady. 'Don't mention it, dear boy,' he said. 'It shall be done. Now into the night.'

Henry kept a hand under his elbow. We watched him go, making a sweeping obeisance with a sombrero.

'I think,' said Henry when he came back to our attic, 'that he is a bit squiffy.'

13.

Very much later, when he had taken silk and I was not the small boy who had sat with him on the floor of our room, Mr George Chirk, K.C., was dining with me in a London restaurant. We hadn't met for years and he was reminiscent over his cigar. 'Do you remember,' he asked, 'that night when Henry Shellabeer and you and I sat on the floor?'

It took me some time to recall that moment. At last I did so, and I said: 'Yes, I remember it now. When Henry had seen you into the street he said you were a bit squiffy.'

'We hear a lot,' George said, 'about turning points. Well, that was a turning point in my life all right. In your's too, come to that.'

He had gone out that night very squiffy indeed. He had been, as they say, a pain in the neck to his father for some time. The old man, who had been a widower for many years, had spent a lot on this boy. Sending him to Cambridge had not been cheap and, when he had left there, it had not been cheap to get him articled to a good firm of solicitors. But old Chirk, thought to be a rich man, had gone ahead with it, lured always by the vision, not uncommon, of a son he would be proud of. Now that he was a widower, there was a housekeeper to be paid as well as George's allowance to be found, but there was always this vision of a son to be proud of.

It was about this time that Mrs Shellabeer's troubles had involved us with George. He had become, as he would have put it, 'one of the lads'. He began to fancy himself as an actor, which he never was, save, quite successfully, in a Court of Law, and he began to drink. Some of his fellow-amateurs were in the habit of adjourning to a hostelry, and George joined them, for he was the best of that bunch, and might even have been, some day, an actor if he had gone another way about it. As it was, he loved to hear his praises sung and took more and more to company that was no good to him.

Old Chirk was not unaware of this. He had heard the key turn uncertainly in the lock more than once, and on that evening, when George had called on Henry and me, had had a very disagreeable experience indeed. Mr Leadbitter, the solicitor to whom George was articled, had paid him a visit. There is no need to go into what passed between them, but it left Mr Chirk resolved to have it out with George once and for all. Reform, or I cut you off with a shilling, my boy. That sort of thing. But old Chirk was not that sort of man. It was going to be difficult.

When George had left me and Henry he was, as Henry had diagnosed, a bit squiffy. George was aware of this, aware, indeed, that he was a little more squiffy than he had ever been before, and that, this time, there might be some difficulty in meeting the old man. So much so that he was reluctant to go home at all. He decided that another drink might help him to face the ordeal, and swung into the bar which his fellow-thespians were accustomed to use. 'Time, gentlemen, time,' were the next words he heard with any clarity.

A few of the greatest amateur Falstaffs in our town decided that the best thing to do was to leave him at his own door, ring the bell, and depart. This they did, and his father found him sitting on the top step. The old man was tenderness itself. He saw that George was in no condition to put up with much talk, helped him up to bed, tucked him between the sheets, and said rather sadly: 'Good night, George,' then he left him.

George did not wake till morning. He felt much better and when he had drunk a glass of water, fortified by an addition that he had found useful on such occasions, he got back into bed and was soon well enough to regard himself in a not very favourable light.

Presently his father entered, carrying a breakfast tray. It contained only tea and dry toast. 'I thought you might like to have breakfast in bed,' he said.

George could do no more than nod his head penitently. Still speaking no word of last night's dramatic appearance on the doorstep, Mr Chirk smoothed the coverlet, placed the tray on his son's knees, and departed quietly, saying as he went: 'What about a good walk this morning – just you and me?'

Again George nodded. This was it, he thought. It was overdue to come out, and it would come out during the walk.

It was a Sunday morning. There would be no office for him or his father, and the housekeeper always took Sunday off to visit her relatives.

It was half-past ten when George, bathed, shaved and breakfasted, came down and found his father in the kitchen. He was awkwardly cutting up sandwiches. 'I hope you've got good stout boots on, George,' he said. 'We shall be out all day. It looks good weather for a stroll. Here, push some of these into your pocket.' He was wearing a Norfolk jacket, with knickerbocker trousers. A worn ash stick leaned against the wall. 'It's a long time since we did this,' he said. 'We used to walk a lot before you went to Cambridge.'

There was some good walking country around Cardiff in those days and they walked pretty well all day. It was about midday when Mr Chirk said: 'Dry work this, my boy. What about a drink?'

They went into a roadside pub and drank a pint together. 'Mind you,' said this grown-up George Chirk, K.C., 'not a word about the evils of drink. Not the sermon I was expecting at any moment. Just a walk and a friendly drink together. I began to see the old man in a new light. Began to see myself in a new light too. It may have been just a superb bit of acting on my father's part, but so far as I was concerned, it was just loving-kindness. Not that there's much reason to believe in that, as one looks around the world to-day. Anyway, it started me wondering. Because when all's said and done, there's such a thing as giving back as well as taking.'

Mr George Chirk, K.C., didn't say anything more about what evidently was to him a memorable day. But I know that from that time he took a new view of his father. He was out now to justify both himself and his father's expectations concerning him. He resolved to be a barrister, not a solicitor, and about a year later went into the chambers of Mr Foulkes, K.C., who had a reputation for bringing young men on. Once he had started, George didn't take much urging.

This ragged start of his career had the consequence of introducing me to Chirk senior, so that that night, when George was, as Henry had said, a bit squiffy, had notable consequences for me as well as for him.

14.

There was not much that George remembered of that night when he had sat on the floor between me and Henry. But one thing remained in his mind – that Henry had spoken of the need for me to be earning money. Through having been concerned in the disastrous end of my aunt's affairs, he was well acquainted with the situation at Aunt Jane's house, The Grove. The need that I should contribute to its income was there for anyone to see, and George saw it clearly enough. I saw it too. It would be a means of my getting out of the house and so escaping the perpetual company of Aunt Jane. Henry was away helping Mr Garrity. My mother was out on one of her jobs most days of the week, and that left me alone with my aunt.

Aunt Jane never saw that my mother's sudden resolution to come to The Grove had lifted her out of an awkward situation. All she could see was that her husband was dead, that she had no money, and that her sister had used this opportunity to Take up Residence at The Grove. That she herself was contributing nothing to the income of The Grove did not occur to her. So all day long I had to listen to her moans as I cleaned the cutlery and did the washing up and swept and polished. She could have let the place and tried living on the rent; but as Henry, in his quiet reasonable way, pointed out to her, the rent would go on renting another place to live in. So she was in a dilemma, and my mother, with her masterful ways, did not make things easier. She had, she said, come to her sister's rescue, and she made it plain that rescued she should be. I often sighed for the old days when she and I were together in our small house lacking all these things which Aunt Jane proudly called Modern Conveniences. Even the Gas, she said, was Laid On. And what had she got out of it, except that Henry was now working without even the privilege of being allowed to wear a cap with Blue Rings.

Henry and I were always very glad when the time came for us to go to our own room, stretch out our legs on the floor, or get down to some work at our tables.

We were thus engaged one night, about a week after George Chirk had called on us, when he came again. 'I'm not staying,' he said. 'I've just come to ask the pair of you to eat with me and my father to-morrow night. Say seven o'clock. If you're at liberty, that is.'

The idea of me and Henry *not* being at liberty once our day's chores were over was comic enough, but the idea of going out to eat with Mr Chirk was not comic. It was rather frightening. It will doubtless seem odd to many people that up to this moment neither Henry nor I had eaten away from our own houses. This is easy to explain in the case of me and my mother. You do not ask people to eat with you unless you expect to be asked back, and we certainly had neither the means nor the intention of asking anyone. Put briefly, the poor did not go out to one another's houses. Henry might just have mounted into the tea-giving ranks if his mother had not been the sort of woman from whom an invitation would not have been welcome and to whom it would certainly not have been returned.

So we were both turning over George's invitation in our minds, rather doubtfully, when George said with a laugh: 'Come on, you silly pair of young coots. All it amounts to is that Father wants to have a look at young Guy. I've been telling him that you're both stuck in a bit of a hole. You're on your way out of it, I should think, Henry, and there's a chance that he'll find a way for Guy too.'

15.

We turned up the next evening, looking a very respectable pair of boys: our hair sleeked down with water, our boots polished, our collars clean, and our 'best' suits upon our backs. We might, from the way my mother and Henry's fussed over us, have been ambassadors setting out for a foreign capital. But there was need neither for fuss nor anxiety. Mr Chirk was a simple good-natured man who literally allowed us no time to be nervous or anxious. 'Come on in,' he said. 'George is upstairs having a wash. He'll join us in the dining-room. Ha, George, it's you! These boys have come. Which is Henry and which is Guy?'

He put a hand on the shoulder of each of us and shepherded us into a plain unfrightening room. His housekeeper
came in and set a plain unfrightening meal before us. I
remember it as roast beef and Yorkshire pudding, with roast
potatoes and cabbage. Henry was quite at home with
cutlery. It was such a meal as his mother had often prepared
for him and his father. I had to be more careful, for our meals
at home had tended to be slap-dash affairs, which we got
through as best we might. Henry and George Chirk did their
best to make things easy. They talked of Garrity's, kept the
conversation going, and saved me much embarrassment.

As for Mr Chirk, he was not a difficult man. I knew his
shop well. It was in the main street of our town, a stylish
establishment, I thought it, with the name Chirk in golden
letters on a blue fascia. Our local newspaper, in those days
when advertising was not the boisterous pushing thing that
it is to-day, said simply on its back page from time to time:
'Get it at Chirk's', and what 'it' was all the town was
supposed to know, for you could get anything at Chirk's
from a bed to a bedroom suite, from a table to a dining-room
outfit, from a trowel to a lawn-mower. If you were out on a
real spending spree you could move into the 'silver department' where, I used to think, a sovereign didn't go far. For
Chirk's was one of those open shops where customers
wandered at will, and I had been through it more than
once, bedazzling myself with thoughts of what I should buy
for my mother if only I had the money. I would toil up the
carpeted stairs from one floor to another, for lifts had not yet
arrived, listening to the satisfying 'ping' as containers of
money arrived on overhead wires at cash-desks, and sleek
counter-jumpers, dressed in frock coats, moved silently over
the floors. And when a winter's day was drawing to a close,
on would go all the gas jets, and Chirk's would become a
fairy palace, with light showering down on inestimable
treasure. In a word, Chirk's was one of those 'emporiums'

that heralded, to those who cared to hear, the modern shops where you can buy anything from a packet of pins to a trousseau for a bride.

And here, now, was Chirk in person, sitting at this table in a dull and rather dreary little room; and here was his son George taking Henry by the arm and saying, 'Let's go up to my den and have a bit of a chin-wag.'

They went, and, with fear and trembling, I was left alone with Mr Chirk. 'Come into the other room,' he said; and he led me into a small room behind the dining-room, shouting to the housekeeper as he went: 'You can clear away now, Mary.'

Above the mantelpiece there were opaque white gas globes, and Mr Chirk lit these and put a match to the fire, unnecessarily for it was quite a warm night. He was a short, stout man, spectacled, with white hair and a kindly face, rather Pickwickian I should have thought it if, then, I had ever heard of Mr Pickwick.

'Well,' he said, after watching me through his twinkling spectacles for a while, 'George, you know, is going to be a solicitor.' He said it proudly, for being a solicitor was being a professional man, while the owner of Chirk's was only a tradesman, though I imagine that Mr Chirk could have bought up all the solicitors in our town.

'Solicitors,' he added, 'don't, as a rule, discuss their clients' affairs, but George has been telling me about your aunt's misfortunes, and how your mother has come to her rescue.'

'She wouldn't call it that, sir,' I said, for to my surprise I found Mr Chirk easy to talk to. 'Mrs Shellabeer thinks she is doing us all a favour. And it *is* a favour in a way to be living in the same house as Henry.'

'Yes,' said Mr Chirk. 'I've been hearing from George about Henry too. Happily, Mr Garrity has found him some work to do, helping in the school.'

I wondered where all this was leading to, and was glad that Mr Chirk seemed to know all about us.

'Yes, sir,' I said. 'Henry has to bring some money into the house now, instead of taking it out.'

'And I understand from George that it wouldn't be a bad idea if you were taking in a bit too. Well, I shouldn't be surprised if that were possible. Would you allow me to smoke?'

It was a rather startling request, but I magnanimously gave permission. Mr Chirk got up and took a cigar from a box on the mantelpiece. He said, lighting it: 'I allow myself one cigar a day, and this is the time when I usually take it. I find it is a very good thing to regularise my indulgences.'

He poked the fire into a glow and puffed at his cigar with satisfaction. It was only later that I learned how Mr Chirk had indeed been compelled to 'regularise his indulgences'. That belonged to the time when a rather ragged young man was going all out to make a corner shop a success – a corner shop out of which, step by step, Chirk's arose. Those times seemed to be in his memory as, that night, he gave himself that small luxury.

At last he turned to me and said, as though this had all been settled between us: 'Well, you'll call, then, at Chirk's to-morrow morning at nine sharp. Ask to see me. Mind you're not late.'

16.

You may be sure that the next morning I was indeed not late. I was hovering outside the shop at ten minutes to nine, waiting for it to open, and at nine sharp shutters were rolled up, the main door was flung wide, and I was the first person to enter Chirk's that day. At least, I thought I was; but to my surprise the shop was already full of people who had come in by a side door marked 'Employees' Entrance'. And there the employees were, busy as bees, displaying goods on counters, setting out price-tickets, giving a last wipe where a speck of dust might, unperceived, have taken a nefarious lodging, and generally making Chirk's a place where people with money to spend would find opportunity to spend it. Among them all, shop-walkers in morning clothes walked up and down, like so many hawks overlooking the operations of sparrows, and one of these, a dark little moustached man, his hair shining with hair-oil, and having, I was sure, a dusting of powder upon his cheeks, moved like a commanding officer among troops. I heard him addressed as Mr Carlino, and to my consternation Mr Carlino saw me hovering there and descended upon me, rubbing his plump little hands. It is true that I was wearing my best suit and had sleeked down my hair and, as a concession from Aunt Jane, was wearing Henry's cap with blue rings, which she thought would give entrée to any society and kept, brushed carefully every day, on a hook in the hall, like a battle-flag in a cathedral; but I doubted whether even such splendour would avail in the presence of this little well-dressed oily man who now bore down upon me.

'Good-a morning, sir,' he said; and so polite a greeting made me wonder whether the cap with blue rings had, after all, some magic power. 'Can I direct you,' he asked, 'to any particular department?'

Now all my pride in an appointment with Mr Chirk came to my aid. 'I am looking for Mr Chirk,' I said. 'I have an appointment with him at nine sharp.'

Mr Carlino, the manager, as I later came to call him, was an Italian, who had never learned to leave certain inflections of his native speech behind him. Happily, the use of Mr Chirk's name had an instant effect upon him. 'Come-a with me,' he commanded. 'The name, please?'

'Guy Marson,' I said, and, more boldly now, 'a friend of Mr George Chirk's.'

Mr Carlino gave a little bow, which I think had become habitual with him in that place where little bows seemed part of the stock-in-trade. He went before me up, I thought, interminable stairs, and named each department as we came to it, with a respectful bow at the floor indicated. 'Silver department,' he said. 'Beds and bedding. Gents' suitings. Ladies' undergarments.'

At length we were at the very top of the building, and here, in a long corridor, he said, with a finger to his lips: 'I will see. Guy Marson, eh?'

Mr Carlino, approaching on tiptoe, as if he were about suddenly to pounce upon some unsuspecting prey, knocked softly at a door and entered. A moment later he was back. 'You may go in,' he said, as though the gates of paradise were now open to me, and went back softly the way he had come. Not without trepidation I entered, and there was nothing more frightening than the Mr Chirk I had met last night. Somehow, after so much preliminary induction, I was a little disappointed, as a visitor might be to a shrine of relics who found himself at last confronted by nothing but a pile of old bones.

Mr Chirk had a heap of letters on his desk, and he went on turning these over and taking no notice of me. At last they were sorted into two heaps, one, I afterwards learned, for his own attention, and one – the greater by far – he put on one side. 'These,' he said, 'are for Mr Carlino's attention. Find him and bring him to me.'

'Yes, sir,' I said, and turned away rather disappointed. I had not expected this cold reception. I should not have been surprised if bells had rung out announcing my arrival at Chirk's, or at least if Mr Chirk had received me with a handshake. But I was soon to learn that Mr Chirk in the office was one person, and Mr Chirk enjoying his evening cigar was another. The office, I must say, disappointed me. What I had expected I don't quite know, but not this bleak chamber perched like a rather battered nest on top of the tree of many branches that was Chirk's.

I descended many stairs and at last found Mr Carlino's office, which seemed to me much more comfortable than Mr Chirk's. It was on the first floor, with a window looking out on to the main street of our town where horse-drawn trams, open at the top, rumbled to and fro. The room was carpeted, and Mr Carlino's desk was a stylish roll-top affair before which he sat in a comfortable chair. Other chairs, even more comfortable, were in the room, and everything there seemed burnished and polished, twinkling and gleaming. It was here, I learned later, that important callers were received. Only one in twenty was important enough to penetrate the rather grimy precincts of the office under the roof.

I handed the letters to Mr Carlino, who placed them on his green leather-topped table, beneath a paper-weight that shone internally with many fires. Mr Carlino was rather given to things that shone. In his tie at this moment was a pin that shone with rubies, and I noticed that his manicured fingernails shone as if with furniture polish. His hair shone; his boots shone; his watch-chain shone. He was altogether a most shiny little man; and there flashed upon his face now and then a shiny smile as though he had just sold a bedroom suite or a bride's trousseau costing heaven knows what money. He looked at me as if a shine here and there would do me no harm: and he was right enough about that.

We must have looked an oddly contrasted couple as we climbed the stairs once more to Mr Chirk's office; but the sight of Mr Chirk himself, grey, unshining, a bit bald on the top, restored the balance. He turned towards us on a swivel chair and said: 'Mr Carlino, this is Mr Marson.'

Mr Carlino turned to me with one of his best bows, and said, as though he had not met me before: 'Good-a morning, Mr Marson.'

'Mr Marson,' said Mr Chirk, 'is a friend of Mr George Chirk. We must do our best for him.'

Mr Carlino looked reverent at the name of Mr George Chirk. Perhaps he had heard of the best amateur Falstaff in our town; perhaps he was only concerned to please old Chirk.

'Mr Marson is going to join us,' said Mr Chirk. 'To begin with you will take him around the various departments and explain to him what is done in them and how they are run. In the meantime –' and he looked at me with sad speculation – 'you had better Fit him Out. Yes,' as though this were a solution he had long been making, 'you had better Fit him Out. At once. And then he can go home for the day. Report here, Mr Marson, at nine o'clock to-morrow.'

17.

I was at Chirk's for about five years, and these were happy times for me. We became quite affluent at The Grove! What was the happiest thing of all to me was that my mother did not go out to 'places'. There was no more calling on Guardians, no more visits to Solly's. Mother simply became our housekeeper and looked after us all.

Henry was getting on very well at Garrity's. His pay was increased and, like a good son who had been well trained by his mother, he turned in almost every cent to the support of the house. My own pay at Chirk's increased too. It was fortunate that Mr Carlino and Mr Chirk himself were fond of me. I well remember how, on my first day there, Carlino obeyed his instructions to 'Fit me Out'. Glancing at myself occasionally in the mirrors with which the place abounded, I saw what I took to be a veritable butterfly emerging bit by bit from the rather deplorable chrysalis that I had been. Even Henry's cap with the blue rings did not please Mr Carlino. He threw it into a waste-paper basket, with a frown of disgust on his powdered face. It was indeed a splendid fellow that emerged from the Gents' Clothing Department, new from shoes to hat, which, I remember, was a 'boater', encircled by a ribbon of white and green. Mr Carlino, I thought, was considering even a rather gaudy pin for my tie, which was new like the rest of me, but apparently decided against it. 'Perhaps in a few year-a,' he said. It was getting on for noon when he shoo'd me out of the shop, a different being from the one who had entered it. 'Good-a morning, Mr Marson,' he said. 'We will see you at nine-a to-morrow.' I replied to his bow by raising my boater. He was enchanted. 'Perhaps to-morrow a little-a hair-oil?' he said, and left me to make my way home.

You may be sure it was a dallying walk. At every shop window which boasted a mirror I paused to consider this apparition which I could hardly believe to be myself. I raised the boater to my own reflection again and again, and decided that I would do.

At The Grove, where I was not expected, I created a sensation. Aunt Jane, who was reading *Ouida* in the drawing-room, emerged at my mother's shrill cry. Both stood contemplating me, in the passage-way, as though I were some bird of strange plumage that had alighted before their unprepared scrutiny. Then Aunt Jane demanded, in a voice of outrage, 'Where is Henry's cap? It was lent to you to make an effect.'

I explained who Mr Carlino was and what he had done with the cap. 'After all these years!' said Aunt Jane. 'I could have kept it as a Relic.' She mourned for the cap more deeply than she had ever mourned for her husband, and it was only when Henry came in for his midday meal that her moaning ceased. He thought I was greatly improved, which it was not difficult for me to be.

His approval set me up, and I spent the afternoon walking our streets so that all might have the advantage of seeing me, and I gave that advantage to myself too, whenever a shop window had a mirror. I even raised my straw boater to one or two people I didn't know in order that I might have a little practice. But the time for straw boaters passed quickly enough. The winter was coming on and, still under the tutelage of Mr Carlino, I began to present myself at Chirk's wearing a bowler. Goodness only knows what I did there! I worked in several departments without much glory in any. It was known that I was under the guardianship of Mr Carlino and that I was a favourite of Mr Chirk. These two circumstances were fortunate for me; they earned me a certain amount of consideration, but it was not till winter was fairly upon us that I began to wake up to what it was all about. Mr Chirk sent for me.

I had seen little enough of him in the meantime. His son George, abandoning all thought of the stage, had gone to London where he was studying to be a barrister, in which profession, as I have already hinted, he found remunerative scope both as a lawyer and as an actor. He was at this time rather like Martin Harvey to look at. It was a dull jury which George could not shake to the roots. In these early days he occasionally came down from London to visit his father, and it was of one of these visits that old Chirk spoke to me that day when, under the guidance of Mr Carlino, I went to the attic that was his office. I was by now shooting up; I was well dressed in a shop-walkerish sort of way, and I wasn't bad to look at. Little though I saw of Mr Chirk, I was not surprised when he called me Mr Marson. He had old-fashioned habits and would have shied at the familiarity of calling me 'Guy'. What he would have made of our modern way when every Ronald is to everyone a Ron, and every John a Jack and even Cabinet ministers get very matey on television and address one another as Joe or Bill I don't know.

'I have come to the conclusion, Mr Marson,' he said, 'that you are wasting your time here.'

Well, that was forthright enough, and I should not have

been greatly surprised if the next thing was the sack. But then he said: 'When you left school at a rather earlier age than is usual, were you told by your headmaster that you need not consider your education to be complete?'

'No, sir,' I said. 'I was more or less thrown out.'

'That is as I thought,' Mr Chirk said. 'Well, let me take your headmaster's place, and direct your attention to this syllabus. You will see from it that there is such a thing as a technical college. Some of the teachers in it are very good men – professors, some of them, at the university, earning what they can in their spare time. Though, in my opinion, it is a disgrace to any university that their teachers are under such necessity.'

He uttered this rebuke, as he uttered all rebukes, very tenderly.

'Well,' he said, 'these classes begin in a few weeks' time. Take this syllabus home with you. Study it, and decide what classes you want to go in for. Let me know, and I will find the fees. They are very moderate.'

I told him how grateful I was and that I should be more than delighted to take advantage of his wonderful offer.

He handed me the syllabus. 'But what about the day-time, sir?' I asked. 'These are evening classes.'

'You will go on with your work here in the day-time,' he said, 'but' (with one of the rare smiles that he permitted himself), 'I don't think it will be long before you have had enough of us.'

He made a gesture of dismissal, and I was about to go when he said: 'My son George is coming down to visit me this week-end. I should be glad if you could find it convenient to dine with us on Saturday night. And will you ask that nice boy who lives with you, and who is with Mr Garrity, if he would care to come too. George will be pleased to see both of you.'

I promised to be there, to study the syllabus in the meantime, and to give his message to Henry. Then I went, feeling rather down in the mouth, as though I were an idle young rascal that Mr Chirk had no use for and that he had taken a kindly means of getting rid of me. It needed only a little reflection to convince me that he was right; that my heart was not, and never had been, in Chirk's, and that my ambition was not that I might be turned eventually into a shop-walker, even on such dizzy heights as Mr Carlino had reached. I wondered whether it was fair to be paid by Mr Chirk for doing next to nothing all day as well as attending classes at night; but I have always been a calculating sort of fellow, and decided that I would do him the favour of remaining in his shop until I had made myself ready to do something else.

That evening I mentioned Mr Chirk's invitation to Henry and he said he would be very glad to come. He was a far more industrious person than I was, and spent most of his spare time in our attic den. Much of my own time was spent there, too; but while Henry swotted at some abstruse subject, I sat on the floor and amused myself with a novel. He was anxious to see me occupied, as he was, with some definite course of study, but he made the best of things by recommending the books I should read, and often bringing these home, with Mr Garrity's permission, from the school's small library. So at least I made acquaintance with the works of Dickens and Scott and Trollope, which would never, if I had not met Henry, have come my way.

That evening I produced the syllabus that Mr Chirk had given me, and Henry and I went through it together. 'So,' he said, 'Mr Chirk has rumbled you at last. You're an idle young devil, you know. It's about time someone took you in hand.'

I felt rather ashamed that he, like Mr Chirk, had 'rumbled' me. He was himself, I knew, engaged in an effort, by correspondence, to fit himself for a London University degree. He had already sat for his intermediate examination and come through it successfully. There was one more examination before him, and when he had passed that, as he had no doubt he would, he could call himself a B.A. of London. And then, he confided to me, he hoped he would not only be giving a hand in general at Garrity's but find himself a member of the school staff. 'I think,' he said modestly, 'old Garrity's rather fond of me. He and I and Rosa could make the school rather better than it is now.'

This was the first time he had mentioned Rosa, Mr Garrity's daughter, and shied away quickly from the subject, as though he had said too much. 'Well,' he said, 'let's have a look at that syllabus.'

The subjects in which he himself had to pass, if he were to get his degree, were English, French, Latin, mathematics and history; and I knew that he was up to the eyes; so it was with some diffidence that I bothered him at all; but it was like Henry to do thoroughly anything he embarked on, and we spent a good hour discussing and rejecting this subject and that, until we finally decided that English, French and German would do to be going on with.

'Well,' he said at last, 'we'll call that settled; and now let's have a talk. It's a long time since we've had one.'

It was, indeed; and he had just joined me in my seat on a cushion with our backs to the wall, when we heard my Aunt Jane's voice coming stridently up the stairs. 'Henry! Henry! Come and meet Mr Mumbles.'

'Now who on earth is Mr Mumbles,' said Henry, none too pleased at the interruption. 'I've never heard of a Mr Mumbles. I suppose we'd better go down.'

18.

Like Henry, I had never heard of Mr Mumbles; and, when we got downstairs that night, I can't say that we saw any reason to regret that our acquaintance had not begun earlier. To make matters worse, Aunt Jane introduced him as Marmaduke Mumbles. It wasn't a bad night, warm enough; but Marmaduke Mumbles was wrapped up like a parcel addressed 'With Care'.

A woolly-looking overcoat was all round him; he wore a Scotch plaid muffler, and his hands were in woollen gloves. My first surprise on seeing him was that he had not kept his hat on, which he might have done with advantage, for he was as bald as a coot. A small silken black moustache stood out on either side of his nose which was blue and pointed.

However, what he seemed to us didn't appear to matter to Aunt Jane. She regarded the inconsiderable bulk of him – for in addition to his other disqualifications he was small and thin – with affection. 'This is Henry,' she said, ignoring me altogether. 'Henry, this is your new papa.'

She could say no more, being overcome by her good fortune in having landed so splendid a fish. Henry didn't know what to say. He was completely flummoxed, both by Mr Mumbles, who didn't rise from his chair, and by the circumstances in which he had met him. Henry had taken lately to smoking a cigarette or two, and in desperation he now produced a packet from his pocket. 'Will you have a cigarette, sir?' he asked.

Mr Mumbles spoke for the first time. His voice surprised us. It came like a lion's roar from a mouse. 'I neither smoke nor drink,' he said. 'Your dear mother has told me that you do not drink either. I was pleased to hear it. Wine is a mocker, strong drink is raging. I am sorry to know that you have taken to smoking.'

Aunt Jane looked glad that Mr Mumbles had so early and so forcibly expressed himself. 'Marmaduke is an undertaker,' she said, as though that explained everything.

Henry hovered uncertainly, clearly at a loss to know what was now expected of him. As for me, I had been ignored so far, and hovered on the fringes of what seemed like an episode in a mad-house. At last, merely for something to say, I asked: 'Where is Mother?'

Aunt Jane replied: 'She is gone out. I expect her back at any moment. Then we shall all be together to discuss Our Future.'

All this was happening in what she called the Drawing-Room, the very room in which long ago Uncle Shellabeer had instructed her to give me a shilling, no, sixpence – which I had never received – on my birthday. And at this moment my mother, who had been taking a walk about the streets, entered, saw me and Henry standing around, clearly 'flummoxed', and Mr Mumbles sitting bunched up in his chair. She pointed at him, asked 'Who's he?' and burst into laughter, which was anyone's response to a first sight of Mr Mumbles.

Aunt Jane flushed. Even her wattles, which always irreverently reminded me of a turkey's, went a horrid bluish red, and quivered. 'Emma,' she said, 'you forget yourself. I was about to introduce you. This is Marmaduke Mumbles, who is to be my husband. We are engaged.'

On the last word her outrage turned to pride. 'Mr Mumbles,' she said, 'is an undertaker.'

The words 'engaged' and 'undertaker' silenced even my mother. She gazed from one to another of them for a moment, and then said: 'Jane, you must be mad.'

Mr Mumbles' voice spoke to my mother for the first time. He roared in his mighty tones: 'She is a pearl of great price.'

My aunt was moved by this tribute. She looked as though in her opinion it was richly deserved. She bent and, to the horror of us all, kissed Mr Mumbles. Then she broke into tears and Mr Mumbles' overcoat-encumbered arm went round her. She sat beside him on the sofa and continued to weep. 'I was looking forward,' she said, between her tears, 'to such a happy night with Marmaduke meeting you all.'

'Well,' said Mother practically, 'you seem to have been mistaken. I can only repeat that you must be mad.'

She bustled off to the kitchen and at the same time Henry took my arm and whispered: 'Let's go for a walk.'

We sneaked out of the house, and when we returned an hour later Mr Mumbles was gone and Mother told us that Aunt Jane had gone to bed. She put a bit of food before us and said hopefully: 'Let her have her cry out. Perhaps she'll see sense by the morning.' But in this she was mistaken.

19.

The circumstances in which Aunt Jane met her mate were appropriately gruesome. Before her property was sold she had gone late one night to collect her rents in those slums where most of her victims were living. She reckoned to collect fifty per cent of her money on any one of her weekly visitations, and that night she had exceeded her average and was consequently in a good mood. But there was still one house at which she had not called. The occupier, Mrs Hill, had been in bed for some time, in the last stages of tuber-culosis, and the small nervous child who had answered the door always shut it quickly with the remark: 'Next week.' Buoyed up by the hope that Mrs Hill might be well enough to come to the door herself this week, and that she could utter her customary threat of 'putting in the bailiffs', Aunt Jane decided to try again. When she arrived she noticed that many blinds were down, including those of Mrs Hill's house. She knew well enough what lowered blinds meant, and was stricken to find that someone even more powerful than the bailiffs had got in before her. She hovered before the door for a moment. It had begun to rain, and she was on the point of turning away and hurrying home when the door opened and this small man who was Mr Mumbles came out. He looked up at the sky, saw that the rain was falling in earnest, and opened his umbrella. 'Allow me, madam,' he roared. 'I hope you haven't far to go on a night like this.' He offered Aunt Jane a share of his umbrella, and, thus escorted, she made her way home. They parted at the gate of The Grove, but there had been time enough for them to learn a great deal about one another.

Despite the gruesome circumstances in which they had met – for Mr Mumbles had been called in, as he put it, 'to superintend the last sad rites' – it was almost a gay procession. He was such a little man, and Aunt Jane was such a tall thin woman, that for him to keep the umbrella over her head required that he should almost walk on tiptoe, so that Aunt Jane suggested with a giggle that she should carry the umbrella and that he should 'well, I won't say cuddle up to me, Mr Mumbles, but keep a bit closer'.

So they proceeded, with him like one of a very small breed of dog being carried along on a lead. But he was aware none the less of the gravity and importance of his calling. 'You will understand, Mrs Shellabeer, being a relict yourself, that we have a part to play in the story of life, even though it is left to us to do no more than turn the last sad page.'

Aunt Jane thought that was beautifully put, thanked him for seeing her home through such dreadful weather, satisfied herself that he was not married – for she was, above all things, a most respectable woman – and arranged another meeting.

'I shall be delighted,' he roared. 'It's been so welcome a break in my lonely days.'

They were not lonely days that followed. Mrs Hill was efficiently put underground, and thereafter trade, as Mr Mumbles said, was slack. Whenever there was a funeral, which was not often, Aunt Jane attended it with no more emotion than if she had come to see her first husband run up a house; and between these mortuary occasions she and

Mr Mumbles saw much of one another. He was a member of some 'split that had splitted off the split', as he put it in describing the nature of the sect that had his adherence. Aunt Jane, after a time of probation, was admitted as a member of this split from a split, and had the joy of hearing Mr Mumbles from time to time roaring his joy in being different from other men. She was even induced by his example to tell how different she was from other women, and there she was not far wrong.

Well, I suppose all this was harmless enough and would have disturbed no one at The Grove if a ray of sunlight had not fallen on Aunt Jane while she was dutifully attending one of Mr Mumbles' funerals. To him, he confided to her later that day, she had seemed like an angel come to give a blessing to that sad occasion, and angels, except in marble, when they all had a striking family likeness, being rare in Mr Mumbles' experience, he proposed to her then and there. She bent down, a long way, and bestowed upon him a kiss, which he said fell upon the parched ground of his life like manna from heaven, and a few days later here was my mother telling her that she must be mad.

The next day Aunt Jane confided every minute particular of the romance to my mother, but Mother snorted and told her again that she must be mad.

20.

Aunt Jane and Marmaduke Mumbles were married about a month later. My mother was outraged and said darkly that she would take good care that a little mole like that never buried *her*.

It was altogether a restless and troubled month, but it was broken by our engagement to dine with Mr Chirk and his son George. Mr Garrity had also been invited to join the dinner-party and to bring his daughter Rosa with him. I had not met Mr Garrity's daughter, Rosa, till now, and George Chirk had changed almost beyond recognition. He was much taller than I remembered, and had the gravity of one who has found what he wants to do and is working hard at doing it. It didn't take me long to find that Mr Garrity had a high regard for Henry. 'Well, Mr Chirk,' he said, greeting George, 'I think you already have the pleasure of knowing Henry here. You will forgive my saying that he has turned out one of the best pupils I have ever had at the school, and I am looking forward to the time when he will take his degree and join my staff. I remember you, too. You were one of my earliest pupils, a great support,' he added with a smile, 'to our rather ramshackle school dramatic society.'

'Oh, that's all over now,' old Chirk said. 'George has forgotten all that dramatic nonsense, and hopes soon to be called to the bar. By the way,' he said to Mr Garrity, 'I must thank you for the loan of your daughter.'

He turned to me and Henry and said: 'I haven't told you how Miss Garrity has come to our rescue.'

A blow had befallen the old man. His housekeeper, who was also his cook, had left him at a moment's notice. She had a very ancient mother and a sister a little older than herself, which must have been pretty old, I calculated, re-calling the only occasion on which I had seen Mr Chirk's housekeeper. This sister had died in her sleep, and now Mr Chirk was without any assistance at all, for his helper had gone both to bury her sister and thenceforward to be the only companion to her aged mother.

This had happened just when he had arranged his little dinner-party. 'I was flummoxed,' he admitted, 'and went round to see Mr Garrity and call the whole thing off. Miss Rosa was present and volunteered to be cook for an evening.'

'You needn't worry about that,' Mr Garrity assured him. 'She's a very good one.'

'Well, here she's been since early afternoon,' said Mr Chirk, 'getting ready to feed this multitude.'

'I can hardly wait to see her,' said George. 'Father's been telling me endless stories of this paragon. I took lunch with him in town. Ah, here she is.'

We had been sprawling in armchairs in the rather dim little room that Mr Chirk called the drawing-room. We all instinctively got up on our feet when, with a knock at the door, Rosa Garrity entered. She was carrying a tray. 'Gentlemen,' she said, with a smile and a bow, 'your sherry.'

I remember her entrance now. She had put off the apron she had been using in the kitchen, and was wearing dusky red silk. She was altogether dusky: her eyes were of a dark blue and her hair was black. She was tall, much taller than her father, and the smile with which she made her little bow to us, lit up her face.

George Chirk and Henry hastened to take the tray from her, which was quite unnecessary seeing that a table was there to receive it. The honour fell to George, and he had no sooner taken the tray than she went, saying: 'I'll call you in a moment. Dinner is nearly ready.'

It was all over in a flash. Mr Garrity and Henry saw her every day and worked with her. Mr Chirk had seen her once or twice. George Chirk and I had not seen her at all. To me, she was a very pleasing girl, much more attractive than I had expected Mr Garrity's daughter to be; but to George it was a supreme moment. He rarely failed, when we met in after years, to recall it. 'Do you remember,' he would say, 'that little dinner my father gave – oh, years ago now – when Rosa came in with the sherry?'

Of course I remembered it. Who would forget so bright and ingenuous an apparition? But the effect on me was not what it had been on George. Do you believe in love at first sight? I have often doubted it, but there is always the case of George Chirk, and of Rosa, too, if it comes to that. The odd thing is that no one noticed it at the time – the way something flamed between them. No one, that is, except Henry Shellabeer.

Rosa called us in to dinner a few minutes later. Old Chirk sat at one end of the table, Rosa at the other, where it was convenient for her to be in and out of the kitchen between courses. Mr Garrity and I sat at one side of the table, George and Henry at the other. We had no sooner finished a course than George was on his feet offering to go into the kitchen in order that he might help Rosa in with the next. But she insisted on managing alone. 'Stay where you are, Mr Chirk,' she would say in that rich voice of hers that seemed part of her general duskiness and of the glowing dark clothes she was wearing. 'I may want you later to give a hand with the washing up.'

'Oh, we can all do that,' said poor Henry desperately. But as it happened, we didn't. 'I'll not have my guests put to such inconvenience,' old Chirk said when the meal was over. 'I still,' he added, looking fondly on his son, 'have some – though precious little – authority over this young man. Enough, anyway, to order him to roll up his sleeves and do his bit in the kitchen. The rest of us will now retire to my den and see if we can find a cigar. But before we do that, I shall ask you all to drink Miss Garrity's health. She has managed a rather tricky situation very well.'

So we all drank Rosa's health in a burgundy that seemed to me to be her colour, and then the old man shepherded me and Henry and Mr Garrity to his little room. He seemed to have no idea of what was happening under his nose. Nor had Mr Garrity. My own feelings about George and Rosa only clarified themselves much later. But Henry knew all the time, and there was nothing he could do. As we wandered home that night he hadn't a word to say either about the dinner or about anything else.

21.

What seemed to me a more immediate problem was that of my mother. The time for the marriage of Aunt Jane and Marmaduke Mumbles was drawing near; and my mother said: 'I can't abear seeing her making such a fool of herself. At her age she ought to know better. And what's Henry going to do, I'd like to know, when that ole churchyard mole comes in here and hangs up his hat.' She had solved the problem so far as she was herself concerned. She would walk out of the house and let them stew in their own juice. 'I come in here,' she said, 'to give her a hand when one husband died, and if she's going to be fool enough to take another that's her look out. Besides which,' she added with some insight into the real situation, 'I don't suppose she wants me, nor does he neither. So I'll go before I'm pushed. And another thing,' she said. 'If I die before him he won't have the burying of me. I wouldn't put a penny in his way not for nothing. I'll make that clear in my will.' It would be a strange will, if one was ever made, because I couldn't imagine there would be anything for Mother to leave save this decisive valediction to Mr Mumbles.

However, this was all to turn out differently from what we expected. I was still attending daily at Chirk's, but I hadn't seen the old man, save at the dinner-party, for a long time. I thought the moment had now come for me to tell him what I had decided to do about the syllabus of evening classes. He welcomed me in his room as cordially as if I had been one of the lights of his establishment, and approved of all the things which, with Henry's help, I had decided to do. He congratulated me, and handed over the necessary cash straight away. 'Now,' he said, 'I must settle my own problem.'

The problem for Mr Chirk arose from the departure of his housekeeper. He had heard from her that she would not be coming back, and he was very tired of dining out at a restaurant every evening, going home to a house that was lonely and was getting dustier day by day, smoking in solitude his cigar, and then, after making up, in a sort of way, his bed, getting into it and failing to sleep because it was unaccountably knobby.

'I've interviewed women, plenty of them,' he told me, 'but I haven't got one yet. I'm over-fastidious, I suppose, or I had got too used to the one I had.'

'Then you ought to try my mother,' I said brazenly.

I had been thinking a lot about my mother, and as much, I must confess, about myself. The coming of Marmaduke Mumbles had upset our lives. We had no home to go to. My quiet evenings, leaning against the wall of Henry's room, had become occasions I had looked forward to, and I had been especially looking forward to swotting there on all the subjects that Henry and I had chosen together. It was all ended now. Henry had taken to going out at night for solitary walks. My mother, too, was seeking 'places', and there was I left alone in Henry's little room, hearing from time to time the booming of Marmaduke Mumbles' voice and the cooing of my aunt's. It sounded like a lion having a heart to heart talk with a dove. I took care to leave them alone. My mother had warned me. 'You keep out of the way,' she said. 'I couldn't abear for you to see my own sister canoodling with that ole mole.'

I put none of these considerations to Mr Chirk. I thought myself wise as a serpent when I confined myself to his own problem. I pointed out that it would be a queer place for the entertainment of Mr George, knowing as I did that these visits from his son were among the few joys now left to the old man. As it happened, George had written to say that he would be coming during the week-end now approaching, which seemed to surprise Mr Chirk. 'He usually comes once a month,' he said, 'and now it's little more than a week since he was here before.'

I was not well enough up in the ways of the world to tell him that perhaps Miss Rosa Garrity had something to do with that. I could only stress that in a week or so my mother would be homeless and I would be homeless too.

'Bring her round to see me to-night,' he said.

<hr/>

22.

I did not see my Aunt Jane after she had married Marmaduke Mumbles. Nor did my mother, nor did Henry. He had lost Rosa Garrity and he could not now bring himself to enter The Grove. I was living with my mother at Mr Chirk's, who was well pleased with her, and Henry was living at Mr Garrity's. Mr Garrity and Mr Chirk were both surprised when, during that week-end of George's unexpected visit, the engagement was announced of him and Rosa. I have lived to be a pretty old man now, and I have never known a more impetuous engagement and marriage. Or a more successful one either. Mr Garrity had a widowed sister living at Wimbledon, and it was arranged that Rosa should go and live with this aunt until she was married. That left Mr Garrity in a hole, for Rosa, among much else, was a useful member of his school staff. But nothing would please her, or George Chirk either, but that they should be near one another till the marriage took place after George had been called to the bar.

Henry, during this time, was morose and unhappy. Once Rosa had packed herself off to Wimbledon, his mania for reading stopped, he took long walks by himself, and he would not on any account be in the house when Marmaduke

Mumbles was there. As Mumbles was there every evening, Henry became ostentatiously a stranger in his own home, and would not visit me in the room that was now mine at Mr Chirk's. Perhaps it was reasonable enough for him to say that he hated anything connected with the Chirk family. However, his mother's marriage, leaving him with no home to live in, was Mr Garrity's opportunity. Rosa's place on the staff had never been filled. Henry, who till then had been a minor teacher, was offered this place of second in command to Mr Garrity himself, provided he sat for and took his degree in reasonable time. The job involved living in the house. Henry took it, and settled down to work and forget, as young men do. Or at any rate he seemed to forget.

HAUNTED

If I could bend my sadness to abide
    In fealty to the gladdening rule of spring;
    If all the richnesses of June should swing
Across my heart, a deep, harmonious tide;
If Autumn all her silvern tenderness
    Should spin about me with like dewy threads
    To those that spiders throw from roses' heads
Athwart a morning lily's slenderness;
If winter's slow and ruminant content,
    In cold and numb Lethean wave on wave
    Should lap me round and bring me to the grave
Of all my troubled thought's experiment:
    How, even then, could I for long put by
    Dreams of the dead and those who yet must die?

Howard Spring